The Penhallow Train Incident

by

M. S. Spencer

This is a work of fiction. Names, characters, places, and incidents are either the product of the author's imagination or are used fictitiously, and any resemblance to actual persons living or dead, business establishments, events, or locales, is entirely coincidental.

The Penhallow Train Incident

COPYRIGHT © 2016 by M. S. Spencer

Cover Art by *Kim Mendoza*

The Wild Rose Press, Inc.
PO Box 708
Adams Basin, NY 14410-0708
Visit us at www.thewildrosepress.com

Publishing History
First Crimson Rose Edition, 2016
Print ISBN 978-1-5092-0660-5
Digital ISBN 978-1-5092-0661-2

Published in the United States of America

"Say, Rachel, weren't you taking tickets for the excursion on Saturday? You must have seen the victim. What did he look like?"

Before Rachel could answer, they heard an angry growl from the bar. "God damn it, can't a man eat his lunch in peace? God damn ghouls around here." Griffin scratched his stubbly chin and pointed a fretful finger at the women. "You'd think no one had ever been killed before, the way you people go on and on."

Rachel, enchanted by the way his eyes shimmered in the sunlight, didn't respond. Maude snapped, "Professor Tate, just because you're an old roué doesn't mean we can't enjoy a little mystery. Not much happens in Penhallow after all. We're entitled to some excitement."

Griffin bristled at her. "A man is dead, Maude. This isn't a movie."

"Well," she bristled back, "at least he was from away."

Griffin gave her a long, hard look and, before turning back to his plate, muttered, "Like me."

For some reason his words struck hard at Rachel's heart. She couldn't see his face, and knew it wouldn't show the hurt anyway, but she could feel it from across the room. To a Mainer, anyone who couldn't trace his Maine lineage back to at least the French and Indian War was considered "from away." Locals usually felt no more than amiable indulgence for the odd critters, but now and then the innate prejudice came out. "Maude—that wasn't nice. After all, I'm from away too."

Praise for M. S. Spencer

Dedication

To Dahlia George,
a born Mainah

Chapter One
The Incident

"Hey, look, Dad! It's a train!"

"A train, Joey? Where?"

A boy of perhaps eleven pointed down the steep hill to a group of low buildings, painted red and nestled next to the river. Flanked by a spider's web of railroad tracks, a bright green locomotive grunted and groaned at a side railing. Steam poured from its smokestack. Behind it, a long line of people waited before a ticket window. The little girl next to Joey jumped up and down, her braids bouncing in the sunlight. "Ooh, ooh, Daddy! Can we ride it?"

Their father nodded. "Yes, Janie. That's the train they told us would be making an excursion out to Brooks and back." He frowned but with a twinkle in his eye. "I don't know…it looks awfully big and scary. You sure you guys want to go on it?"

"Yes!"

"Oh yes, Daddy!"

"All right, if it's okay with your mother." He looked questioningly at his wife. "Jennifer?"

Jennifer threw him a joyous smile and began to skip down the hill. "Joey! Janie! Come on! Hurry!"

By the time the family reached the train, the line had disappeared and the ticket taker had begun to tack up a sign that read, "Window Closed."

"Oh no, are we too late?" Joey's lower lip trembled, and Janie burst into raucous tears.

The agent, a pretty woman of about forty, peered over her glasses at them. Her short blonde curls framed a heart-shaped face that seemed used more to laughter than to sorrow. Her hazel eyes crinkled. "I think we might just have four seats left. Let's see…" She made a show of checking her drawer and pulled off four tickets from a large roll. She handed them to Jim with a smile. "You're in luck!"

Jennifer turned to her husband. "How much is it, Jim?"

Her husband pulled his wallet out. "I picked up a coupon at the fairgrounds in City Park. They offered a special deal for Old Home Week—only five dollars per family." He gave the cashier the money, and the four of them sprinted toward the train.

Between the engine and the caboose, two passenger cars—one open car with benches and the other enclosed—waited patiently for the last passengers to board. Joey and Janie clambered into the open car, their parents puffing behind them. All but two of the seats were occupied—five by a bevy of old ladies dressed in frocks of a painful fuchsia hue with matching hats. A young couple with a baby, infant tackle stacked around them, took up three seats, while a large, swarthy gentleman sprawled on the single forward-facing bench. Joey turned pleading eyes on his mother. "Mom? There's only room for two. Is it all right if Janie and I stay out here?"

"Alone?" Their father scratched his chin.

Jennifer tugged at his sleeve. "They'll be fine out here, Jim. We can see them from there." She pointed.

Sure enough, the rows of seats in the closed carriage were visible through a rather grimy window inset in the door.

"Oh, all right. But you two—don't cause any trouble!"

Jim and Jennifer found two seats in the front of the second car next to the engine. Facing them sat an older man in a business suit and tie and a woman in a long granny skirt, who clutched a voluminous cloth bag. Neither of them acknowledged the newcomers. After a while, Jim and Jennifer gave up smiling at them and looked out the window.

The engine wheezed and the car heaved forward once, as though the train weren't quite used to moving and had to be kick-started. A young woman in a perky blazer entered from the cab. As the train jolted to life, she lurched down the aisle to the back of the car. Opening the door so both indoor and outdoor passengers could hear, she spoke into the microphone she carried. "Ladies and gentlemen, welcome to the Penhallow and Moosehead Lake Railroad. My name is Sarah and I'll be your excursion hostess today. Please feel free to ask any questions. Let—"

A chorus of "Hello Sarah!" interrupted her. She stopped, flustered, but managed to pull herself together.

"I'll start with a short description of the railroad line. During its heyday, a single track travelled the thirty-three miles between Penhallow and Burnham Junction, passing through the towns of Waldo, Brooks, Knox, Thorndike, and Unity to link up with the Maine Central Railroad. From its first run in 1870 until 1960, it carried passengers, mail, and freight to Burnham Junction. For the next twenty years, it only carried freight—mostly chickens from the processing plants that supported Penhallow's thriving economy. When the poultry industry collapsed in 1980, the P&ML turned to sightseeing trips like the one we're taking today."

She pointed toward the siding, where the ticket agent waved at them. The woman's cinnamon-colored shift fluttered in the breeze, setting off her slim legs. "Do you see Rachel, our volunteer? She's standing in front of the old freight house, which now doubles as a theatre. Most of the original buildings—the engine house, the offices, and the passenger station—are gone." Sarah riffled through her clipboard and held up a colorful brochure. "I do hope you all get a chance to take in a play while you're in town. The Water Street Maskers are a well-known summer stock group."

The young man, his baby stowed in a sling on his chest, called out, "What show they puttin' on now?"

Sarah consulted the brochure. "A rollicking version of *Seven Brides for Seven Brothers* will be playing through June 30. In the month of July they'll present the hilarious social satire, *You Can't Take It With You. Arsenic and Old Lace* is on the schedule for August."

The man's wife, who looked no more than eighteen and weighed more than all the other passengers combined, nudged him and said loudly, "Eric, you knows we cain't go to no theayter now we got the baby. You knows that."

Eric grimaced. "Lorelei, a'course I knows it. You don't haveta keep remindin' me." He dragged the sling over his head and handed it to her. "Your turn." He slumped down on the seat.

"Eric Andersen, you take that back."

"What, the baby?"

"No...I mean..." The girl looked confused.

Her husband grinned. "S'okay, honey. Just teasin'."

Lorelei gave him a rather damp smile and cradled the now-wailing baby in her lap.

The train acknowledged its duty at last and began to move, snuffling and clicking on the rails. It picked up speed as it followed tracks that paralleled a wide river. Sarah raised her voice. "Today we'll only go as far as the Brooks siding. The trip is about ten miles and will take an hour. Out the window on your right is the Passagassawaukeag River, which flows into Penobscot Bay."

A dark-skinned man sitting in the last seat next to Sarah raised his hand. In a heavy accent, he inquired, "What did you call the river, miss?"

"The Passagassawaukeag." She frowned at the ripple of giggles that swept through the carriage. "The word is from the Penobscot Indian language and means 'a place for sturgeon.'"

He raised thick, black eyebrows. "Sturgeon? What are...sturgeon?"

Sarah paused. As the pause lengthened, it became apparent that she had no answer to the question. Finally, the quiet man who sat across from Jennifer broke the silence. "A sturgeon is a very large, ancient fish."

The foreigner scratched his head. "Ancient? What do you mean?"

"Sturgeon have existed relatively unchanged for two hundred million years. That's why they're called 'living fossils.'"

Jim leaned forward eagerly. "Really? Prehistoric, huh? How big do they get?"

Reluctantly, the man replied, "The American breeds can grow up to fifteen feet long and weigh almost a ton. These waters used to teem with them. Until the turn of the twentieth century, smoked sturgeon meat was one of the United States' most important exports."

Jennifer, her eyes bright, cried, "Wait—doesn't caviar come from sturgeon? Did we produce that too?"

The man looked over his shoulder as though worried he'd be overheard, then spoke only a touch above a whisper. "Yes, caviar comes from sturgeon roe. In fact, the U. S. exported more caviar than anyone else until overfishing depleted the stocks around 1915. That's when the Russians took over the market."

The dark-skinned man tugged at Sarah's sleeve. "What did he say? What did the man say about caviar?"

Sarah repeated the explanation.

Jim whistled. "So people fished for these sturgeon right here in the Passa…Passagas…"

Over Jennifer's titters, Sarah pronounced, "Pass-a-gass-a-wau-keag."

"You don't say."

"Fancy that."

"Oh dear."

Silence fell as the train rumbled along beside the formerly sturgeon-infested river. Pine forests rose up a hill to their left and when the train veered away from the river, closed in on either side. After a few minutes, Jim rose. "I'm going to go check on the kids."

Jennifer laid a hand on his arm. "They'll be fine. How much trouble can they get into in that small a space?"

Meanwhile, outside, Joey and Janie were careening from one side of the car to the other, screaming at each other. "Look at that rock!"

"We're really hustling now!"

"Joey! Joey! See that boat out there! It's got sails!" Janie rushed headlong past the little family.

"Hey, kid, watch it! You stepped on my foot!" Eric bent down and rubbed his toe through the sock. His wife made anxious noises and continued to rock the baby. He grumbled, "Damned brats," and looked over his shoulder at the large man sitting behind him. "Where the hell are their parents, anyway?"

The fellow patted his implausibly black moustache and said in a pleasant, throaty tenor, "They're just children." He kept his eyes fastened on the window into the closed car.

Eric stared at him rudely. "Ain't you int'rested in the scenery?"

The other man's gaze swiveled to his neighbor's for an instant. "No."

Sarah emerged. "We're coming to the end of our journey." The train slowed as it neared a small, white shed and shunted onto a side rail. A sign nailed to the building said Brooks Station.

Joey, leaning over the side, cried out, "Hey, look Janie—cowboys!"

Sure enough, two rather scruffy-looking men with bandannas and three-day-old beards came riding up on ponies. They pulled out revolvers and shot a couple of rounds into the air.

"Oh my, it looks like those wicked outlaws are attacking the train!" Sarah cried, her mouth twitching.

Everyone tumbled out into the open car, jostling for the best view. The fat man remained seated, his gaze riveted on the window. Something caught his attention and he rose slightly, his mouth open. People swirled around him, but he paid them no mind.

Circling the locomotive, the would-be robbers shouted and waved their guns. Just then a man in chaps and a ten-gallon hat emerged from the little shed. He flashed his badge and a big grin and strode over to the cowboys. The riders pulled up short, their ponies pawing at the dirt. "What ch'all want, Marshal? We're jes' havin' some fun with these folks!"

"Git, or I'll shoot both yawl in the laigs!"

The two cowboys made a half-hearted attempt at bluster, shot into the air a couple more times, and rode off. The marshal ambled over to the train and winked at the children. "Howdy, folks, I'm Marshal Pettit, and that's what we do to crooks around heah in Maine."

Joey and Janie were—for once—too overcome to speak. The little old ladies, who had remained seated during the fracas, clapped their hands dutifully, then went back to whispering among themselves. The fat man took out a large, white handkerchief and wiped his brow.

The marshal jumped down and uncoupled the engine from the carriages. Sarah said, "Time we headed back. Marshal Pettit? You'll keep us safe on the homeward journey, won't you?"

He tipped his hat. "Sure will, ma'am." He shouted to the engineer. "Take her away!" The locomotive chugged forward a few yards, then backed up onto a stub siding before pulling onto the main track heading in the opposite direction. Pettit switched the tracks, and the locomotive backed up again, neatly reconnecting with the cars. A small cheer went up from the passengers, and the engineer waved and tooted his horn.

The businessman and his companion had come out at the beginning of the reenactment, but quickly reclaimed their seats without so much as a word to anyone. Jim and Jennifer made their way back inside, while the rest of the passengers remained in the open car for the return trip.

When the train arrived at the Penhallow station, Joey and Janie came running down the aisle to their parents. "Wow, Mom, Dad, that was cool! Wasn't it cool? That was the coolest."

Their parents stood up and shooed the children out. The silent couple remained seated until the car had emptied. Then, without looking at each other, they stepped down the aisle. The woman went on through the door, but the man hesitated at the last row and looked down. He stooped, put a hand out, and shook the seatback. At that moment Sarah appeared from the cab. The man held up a hand. "Miss, you might want to take a look."

Sarah peered over his shoulder, blinked, and fainted dead away.

****

"Another Geary's, Rachel?"

"What? Yeah, I guess so. Just to keep you company, Maude."

"Thanks." Her companion, a woman of about sixty with close-cropped, iron-gray hair and the beginnings of jowls, gave the word all the sarcasm she had available. The bright brown eyes that reminded Rachel of an intelligent squirrel sought out the waitress. "Hey,

Katie, can you bring us a couple more?"

The waitress, a compact brunette with a wide grin, brought two bottles over. As she uncapped them, she nodded at the window behind the two women. "Looks like we're in for a blow." Rachel and Maude followed her gaze to Penhallow Harbor. The sky to the north held piles of white cloud, cascading down the cliff to hover over the mouth of the river as it flowed into Penobscot Bay.

Rachel stared at them dubiously. "They don't look all that threatening to me."

Katie shrugged. "Ask Griffin. He considers himself our resident weather expert." All three shifted to stare at the tall man seated at the bar, his back to them. The cap, flannel shirt, and worn trousers with suspenders should have signaled an old salt, grizzled and wrinkled, but they knew better. Griffin was only about fifty, but he liked to pretend he was time-worn and crusty. It rarely worked. Any vulnerable woman who took note of his strong chin, deep blue eyes, and thickly curling, salt-and-pepper hair would immediately recognize a sexy man with depths of feeling only a special strategy could penetrate. Add to that a barrel chest, long-fingered hands, and shapely legs, and you had what Maude described as a latter-day Prince Valiant—"Only without that stupid hairdo."

Griffin twisted on his stool. "Cumulus. Five thousand feet. They'll pass out to the bay."

Katie shook her head, but Rachel noticed a gleam in her eye. "No sirree, those are storm clouds. You folks from away can't read 'em like we do. See that gray mass over there by Young's?"

"Huh." He peered at it, his eyebrows wiggling.

"Most likely smog."

"Smog! That's ridiculous. How could we have smog in Maine?"

"Wood fires." The man turned back to the bar.

Maude rolled her eyes. "Griffin gets less verbose every day."

Rachel demurred. "To be fair, he's never been much for words."

"True. Hardly said two or three since he arrived in Penhallow...how long ago? Two years? Wait, wasn't that just about the time you moved here?" She winked. "You sure there was nothing going on between you two down at Queenstown University?"

Her companion glared at her. "I told you before. I didn't know him then. He was a professor of Middle Eastern history at the Institute, and I was a lowly instructor in Anthropology in the college. Paths like ours never crossed."

"Institute?"

"Institute of Higher Learning." She raised her voice. "It's a glorified think tank for the most eminent scientists and academicians. Gives 'em an excuse to laze around dreaming up inoperable systems and unworkable theories to gum up our lives."

"Whoa, somebody has a chip on her shoulder."

"I can't help it." Rachel pondered her former colleague, his head bent over his plate, and whispered, "Griffin was a prick then and he's a prick now. Too bad he's so handsome."

Maude sniggered. "Yeah, too bad."

The subject of their abuse did not react, and after a moment the women returned to their beers. When Katie arrived with two plates piled with lobster rolls, French fries, and coleslaw, Rachel asked her, "So, have they identified the corpse yet?"

The waitress nodded, her eyes alight. "Yeah—Sheriff Quimby was in this morning. He says the guy was a foreigner—Omar something. I couldn't possibly pronounce his name. Some kinda Middle Eastern type."

Maude glanced toward Griffin. "Middle Eastern, huh? *Hmm.* And he was shot, you say?"

"That's what the sheriff says. Shot with a .45 caliber—just like the ammunition in Elmer's and Hank's guns. Only theirs were blanks. Somebody used real live deadly bullets."

"Gracious me." Maude dunked a French fry in ketchup and splashed Tabasco sauce on it. "So how come no one heard the shot?"

Rachel snorted. "Maude, *hello*? Elmer and Hank were banging away at the same time. Come to think of it, the murderer must have planned it that way."

"Oh, really. Now you're Miss Marple. What makes you think it was murder?"

"Well, what else could it be?"

"Suicide? Accident?"

Rachel showed these suggestions the disdain she was sure they deserved.

Katie had remained standing by their booth, ignoring the increasingly desperate signals from the two tourists at the next table. "Say, Rachel, weren't you taking tickets for the excursion on Saturday? You must have seen the victim. What did he look like?"

Before Rachel could answer, they heard an angry growl from the bar. "God damn it, can't a man eat his lunch in peace? God damn ghouls around here." Griffin scratched his stubbly chin and pointed a fretful finger at the women. "You'd think no one had ever been killed before, the way you people go on and on."

Rachel, enchanted by the way his eyes shimmered in the sunlight, didn't respond. Maude snapped, "Professor Tate, just because you're an old roué doesn't mean we can't enjoy a little mystery. Not much happens in Penhallow after all. We're entitled to some excitement."

Griffin bristled at her. "A man is dead, Maude. This isn't a movie."

"Well," she bristled back, "at least he was from away."

Griffin gave her a long, hard look and, before turning back to his plate, muttered, "Like me."

For some reason his words struck hard at Rachel's heart. She couldn't see his face, and knew it wouldn't show the hurt anyway, but she could feel it from across the room. To a Mainer, anyone who couldn't trace his Maine lineage back to at least the French and Indian War was considered "from away." Locals usually felt no more than amiable indulgence for the odd critters, but now and then the innate prejudice came out. "Maude—that wasn't nice. After all, I'm from away too."

Maude tossed her head. "Yeah, well. You're different." She finished off her beer. "Gotta go. I'm filling in for LuAnne at Hannah Sundstrom's place over on Bridge Street this month."

"The Trinket Shoppe?"

"Yup. Before Hannah died she asked LuAnne to keep it open until her estate was settled." She stood. "You want to keep me company?"

Rachel checked out Griffin's rigid torso and

sighed. "Okay."

Later that evening, she drove the two miles home to Amity Landing, a tiny village on the bay made up of Victorian cottages, most of which were only used in the summer. Founded as a religious retreat camp, pocket-sized houses had replaced the original tents set up by Methodists from all over Maine. Some still bore the names of the visiting campers' home towns—Rockport, South Thomaston, Orono. And most had, for better or worse, preserved the original plumbing.

Not Rachel's house, however. Perched halfway up the hill, it had a beautiful view of the little harbor and the bay. She had snapped it up when Audrey Carver, her real estate agent, let slip that it had a disposal and a dishwasher. She loved Amity, but after a lifetime as an itinerant academic, she treasured modern conveniences.

As she turned the key in the lock, a nerve-wracking yowl came from the other side of the door. "Shut up, Spot. I don't want Old Man Clemson to call the cops again." A tortoiseshell cat met her on the threshold with a snarl. After emptying a can of food in his bowl, she poured herself a drink and went to sit on the deck. Her large front yard—a rarity in Amity—opened to the sky, allowing a breathtaking view of the Milky Way. At the bottom of the hill, the water glistened under the floating moon.

She sipped her drink and thought about the retired professor and professional grump who had moved to Penhallow the same year she did. She'd been drawn to him then and tried to make friends. "Just friends," she'd told herself. It had only been three years since Michael's death after all. *I wasn't ready for a relationship.* She figured they could reminisce about

Queenstown University and share a beer or something. He'd dismissed her with a brusque "I don't talk about Queenstown, and I try not to talk to women."

Offended, she'd kept her distance since then. *Still...there's got to be more to him.* And she didn't mean the swimmer's build, or the way his faded jeans hugged his butt, or his constant expression of distaste. Nor the way his azure eyes sparkled at Tommy the bartender's jokes, or his booming laugh. *Nope. It's that air of mystery—even tragedy—around him. I wonder why he left Queenstown so abruptly?* She thought of his remark about not talking to women. *Could he be suffering from a broken heart?* The thought always cheered her.

Still, as she lay awake in bed, she thought of him.

****

"I couldn't eat another bite, Cary."

"Ah, come on, Rachel. Look at that lobster—there's got to be a ton of meat left in it."

Rachel pushed her plate toward her companion. "Go for it."

Cary took the lobster, picked up a spindly leg, and deftly twisted it off. His eyes on Rachel, he slowly sucked a sliver of white meat out.

She laughed. "Oh please, Cary. Come on, finish up. I want to walk down to the water while it's still low tide."

"All right, all right." He wiped his mouth with a napkin and stood. A man in a butler's apron stepped forward and slid the plates silently from the table, disappearing into the kitchen. Cary called out, "Thanks, Helmut. We'll be outside." He whistled to an enormous Great Dane, who lumbered upright, reminding Rachel

15

of a troll rousted from his sleep. "Come on, Romeo!" Taking Rachel's hand, he led her through the glass door to a long greensward that sloped down to the bay. Now, in the languid gray light of a late afternoon, the tide had receded, leaving a swath of rocky shore exposed. Hungry gulls hovered high in the air and dropped periwinkles onto the boulders scattered on the ground like great boils on a giant's face. Far out in the channel a loon moaned. Cary shrugged off his jacket and laid it on a chaise. "Pretty balmy for June, isn't it?"

Rachel nodded. "I guess the storm moved out to sea. There were some dark clouds over the harbor yesterday."

"Weather bureau didn't predict any rain. More likely what you saw was smog."

"That's what Griffin claims. It's ridiculous. Maybe Connecticut, Massachusetts, and New Jersey are awash in particulates, but that doesn't mean the pristine coast of Maine is."

Cary held up his hands in horror. "Are you saying the eminent professor Tate and I agree on something?"

"Look, just because you two got off on the wrong foot—"

"You mean, because I brought jobs and investment, not to mention a fucking playground to Penhallow—all of which he protested—that's no reason to dislike each other? Tate wants to keep this town a backwater for aging hippies like himself. Come on, Rachel, you know he's a prick."

Rachel combed her fingers through her blonde curls. She might have recently used the same term to describe her neighbor and former colleague, but her natural tendency to defend the underdog kicked in.

Wait—underdog? Griffin Tate? I don't think so. She surveyed her host. Short, with thinning hair that had clearly suffered the ministrations of a gradual dye, he walked leaning slightly forward as though itching for a fight. He and Griffin couldn't have been more unalike. Cary Marx—successful businessman, entrepreneur, marketing whiz, possessor of an on-line degree, and millionaire at the age of thirty-five—versus Griffin Tate, grizzled before his time, retired early from a faculty position at Queenstown under mysterious circumstances, sailor, and part-time fisherman. One loved dogs; one ate nothing but beef. One played squash, tennis, and bridge; the other kept a snake. *Granted, Phoebe is a beautiful and rather sweet king snake, but still...*

Cary bent down and picked up a pebble. He leaned sideways and, with a flip of his hand, tried to skip it across the cove. Instead, it sank into the water about two feet from the shore. He tried another one. It slipped off his palm before he could toss it. After taking out his frustration on some nearby rocks with limited success, he remarked, "Hey, did I mention that Sheriff Quimby has asked for my help with this murder?"

Rachel doubted the statement was entirely accurate. Ever since Cary moved to Penhallow and built the huge mansion at Kelly's Cove, he seemed to feel he had the right to run the town. Being Mainers, they let him maintain the delusion so long as he didn't actually do anything. "Really? I didn't know you had a background in forensics."

"What? No. But Sloane and Marx has an office in Kuwait. You heard the victim was a Middle Easterner, right? So I know something about Arabs and that

17

crowd." He tried and failed to skip a third stone.

Despite herself, Rachel was intrigued. "Does Toby think it was murder?" *Take that, Maude!* "What did he tell you?"

Cary took a step backward, and his foot sloshed in the mud. "Damn. My new Ferragamos." He pulled a monogrammed handkerchief from his pocket and wiped ineffectually at his heel. "About the dead man? Lessee. He's from Egypt—some kind of academic or scientist at Cairo University. The state police have asked for information from his institution, but I doubt whether they'll get much. I told Quimby I'd have some of my people get in touch with our contacts in Cairo and check it out."

Rachel could just see the expression on the sheriff's face. Toby was from Machias, the last scion of an old Downeast logging family. He didn't suffer fools gladly. "Well, I'm sure the police will be most appreciative of your input."

Cary gave her a quick look, then took her hand. "Come on, Rachel, you know I'm trying to fit in here. Since Sloane and Marx relocated from Boston to Penhallow, we've done everything we could to be a good corporate citizen."

She had to agree, albeit reluctantly. "Yes, you have, Cary. But I'm sure the police are fully capable of handling a murder."

Cary started to retort, but stopped. After a second he said airily, "Fine. You'll sing a different tune when I hand them the fellow's dossier." Left unspoken were the words, *and the mayor gives me the key to the city and the police eat crow.*

Rachel checked her watch. "Oh, dear, it's late. I

promised Maude I'd go to the gym with her. I'd better be toddling. Thanks for the lunch." She evaded his clinging fingers and walked up the beach to his driveway and her car.

He whistled. She almost turned around, but just in time heard him shout, "Romeo, heel!"

Times like these, a pet snake has a certain appeal.

Chapter Two
The Photograph

The air was cool and a thick fog blanketed the roads when Rachel drove to her office at the Penhallow Historical Society the next morning. As she walked in, the telephone rang. "Rachel! It's Maude. Guess what! They've arrested someone in the Arab's murder!"

"What? So soon? Who is it?"

"Dunno—but I just saw Toby and he's going to call you. Since you took tickets that day they want to see if you can identify the suspects."

"Why do they need me if they've already made an arrest?"

"Um. Er. No idea. Wait—maybe they didn't actually arrest them—they're holding them for questioning. Or maybe they just found them. Whatever. You'd better get over to the station."

At that moment Rachel's cell phone went off.

"Rachel? This is Toby…I mean Sheriff Quimby. Can you drop by the station? We want to ask you a few more questions."

"More? I already told you everything I saw the day of the murder."

"Murder? Who said anything about murder?"

"Well, Cary Marx said—"

A sound came through the receiver that clearly indicated what Toby thought of meddling outsiders.

"We haven't made a definitive call on the cause of death."

"What do you mean? Wasn't he shot?"

She could almost hear him counting to ten. "Yes, but without a suspect or a motive we're not yet ruling out accidental death." Rachel had a feeling he'd consider it badgering if she pointed out that Elmer and Hank had used blanks. To also mention that the incident occurred in the middle of nowhere would only make it worse, so she kept mum. After a slight pause, Toby went on. "Actually, I've…uh…got a detective from Augusta here. He wants to hear your story."

Rachel looked at the stack of papers on her desk. "I can't come now. How about this afternoon?"

She heard whispered voices. "The lieutenant has several meetings today. Can you come by about three?"

"Three thirty it is."

At precisely three twenty-five Rachel walked the three blocks to the police station. The sheriff, a rotund little fellow with a bad comb-over and a smile that lit up the universe, ushered her into his office. From behind the desk rose a lanky, sandy-haired man. He gestured to a chair. As Rachel sat down, Toby took a step toward his desk, then an awkward step back to lean casually against the credenza. "This is Lieutenant Blanchard of the Maine State Police. He'd like to ask you a few questions."

"Sure."

The man shuffled some papers and regarded her with undisguised suspicion. "State your name please."

"Rachel Tinker."

"Your full name."

Rachel cast a glance in Toby's direction. He

21

nodded. "Annabelle Rachel Tinker."

Blanchard jotted it down. "According to the file, you sold tickets for the train excursion on June 15."

"Yes."

"Can you describe the passengers?"

Luckily, she'd had to do this only four days before, so the list still lay on top of her memory pile. "Of course. There was a family of four, two adults and two little kids. And another family—I remember they had a stroller and no one could figure out how to fold it up so they left it with me. I think this was their first baby because they really didn't seem to—"

The detective hastily interrupted. "Yes, yes, I understand." Rachel knew he was thinking, *Why do I always get the cases with these small town hicks who ramble on and on without getting to the point?* "That's seven. I understand a total of twenty persons were on board. Who else?"

"Let's see. A couple—he was much older than she—and the victim of course—"

"Of course," he seconded, his tone dry.

She pretended not to hear. "The Red Hat society ladies—"

"The what?"

"Red Hat. When I'm old I'll wear red...you know." In the face of the man's continued silence she stammered, "It's a...er...social club. For women over fifty. They wear purple dresses and...and red hats." Blanchard still said nothing, so she stumbled on. "There were maybe five of them. Let's see...Edna Mae Quimby"—she bowed at Toby—"Deirdre McGilvery, Eunice Merithew..." She counted on her fingers. "Oh yes, and Audrey, and LuAnne."

Blanchard turned to the sheriff. "We have their names and addresses, correct?"

"Correct."

He turned back to Rachel. "And that's it?"

"I think so. Wait—there was another single gentleman."

Toby jerked. "Another man? You didn't mention…" He stopped when Blanchard held up a finger.

"Yes?"

"I forgot all about him until now. Sorry, Toby. See, he arrived an hour early. We were still waiting for Richard to get there, so I let him buy an advance ticket. He said he'd come back at boarding time. I don't recall seeing him again."

"Could he have boarded the train without your noticing him?"

Rachel considered. "Maybe. People usually line up at the locomotive and go from there to the back. He could have climbed onto the open car from the other side. "

Blanchard wrote something down. "And what did he look like?"

"Um, a bit…heavy."

"You mean fat. White?"

"Sort of light brown. And he spoke with a slight accent—it could have been French. I'm not sure. He had rather greasy black hair and stooped slightly, but I think he was, in fact, quite tall."

"How tall?"

"I'd say six feet or so. Oh, and he had a nice moustache. Flowing."

"Eyes?"

"I don't recall."

A look of irritation passed over the detective's face. He turned a page. "Anyone else?"

"I don't…think so."

Toby said, "Sarah was on board, wasn't she?"

"Well, naturally." Rachel felt the blush before it reached her face. *Why should I feel guilty?* "I thought you were only interested in the passengers. In that case, you should include Pete—Pete Pettit. He played the marshal this time. And the engineer, Richard Daly."

The sheriff's forehead wrinkled. "Where was Stan?"

"He was…uh…indisposed." Bad enough the detective thought she was a country bumpkin without gossiping in front of him. Blanchard didn't have to know that Stan Holiday hadn't made it back from his date in Searsport in time to drive the train. This new romance of his had everyone in Penhallow jabbering. Rumors were flying that the woman in question possessed a bit of a shady past. *Just gossip.*

Blanchard interrupted her ruminations. "That makes nineteen. Who was the twentieth passenger?"

Rachel drew a blank. "Twentieth?"

He said patiently, "Seventeen tickets were sold. Add in the three crew members and it comes to twenty. So who bought the seventeenth ticket?"

Silence settled softly on the room. Finally, Rachel stammered, "I…don't know."

"All right, we'll leave that for now." The detective rose. "We've interviewed the crew, one of the families, and four of the…red hatters, but so far we haven't been able to locate the other passengers. Any idea where they came from?"

Rachel thought it over. "I had the impression the families and the older couple were tourists—in town for Old Home Week. They may be long gone. I have no clue why the two single men were there."

He opened a file and picked up a sheet of paper. "Would you recognize them if we brought them in?"

"Maybe."

He shoved a picture at her. "How about these people? Do they look familiar?"

The faded black and white photograph showed a young girl and a middle-aged man. Neither one smiled. The girl clutched a flowered purse and seemed to be leaning away from the man. "No. I've never seen them before."

"Look closely."

She did, but the faces didn't ring a bell. "Sorry."

"Okay, thanks for your help. We'll be in touch." He started shuffling papers, and Toby walked Rachel out of the office.

Instead of going back to the historical society, though, she hit the gym for a little exercise, then took a walk along Church Street. The gracious white Victorian mansions, built during Penhallow's heyday as a shipbuilding center, soothed her. Giant oak trees shaded the sidewalk, and early summer flowers—bright daisies, nodding campanula, and spiky salvia—spilled out of their beds. An old man paused in his gardening to doff his cap. How she loved this town! Since they built the Route One bypass around it, tourists rarely stopped, heading north instead to Acadia and Bar Harbor. Penhallow had enjoyed a long, pleasant descent into obscurity, and now only former flower children and old seafaring families called it home. *Cary was right about one thing at least.* Instead of the expensive galleries and high-end restaurants of Camden, Penhallow had a grocery co-op and a shoe store that had been family-run since the 19th century. And, of course, Durkee's—where the lobster rolls came uncorrupted with mayonnaise or celery and the Penhallow Bay ale only came in bottles.

She stepped off the curb to allow a couple to pass. The woman caught her eye. *Now, where?* She stared after them. A tall man in a rather shabby suit and a shorter woman in a long rayon challis skirt. *That's right—they were on the train.* At that moment, the woman adjusted the strap on her flowered purse and looked back over her shoulder. A shiver went up Rachel's spine. *Oh my God, it's the woman in Blanchard's photo.* She opened her mouth to call, but the two made a quick right and disappeared down an alley.

Rachel stood on the sidewalk, unsure of her next move. *Back to Toby? Follow the couple?* Blanchard hadn't explained why he was interested in them. The photo had been of a much younger couple—a man in his forties and a mere slip of a girl, maybe seventeen. This woman had to be in her late twenties. *That flowered purse, though—I'm sure it's the same one I saw in the picture. How weird is that?*

Rachel abruptly spun around and loped down the alley. The couple was nowhere to be seen. She checked her watch. Five-thirty. She had time to close up the office, go home, shower, and find Maude. *I need some advice.*

She was locking the building door when an ancient Jeep roared past going at least twenty miles an hour above the speed limit. Griffin gripped the wheel, and from the look on his face, something had infuriated him. She watched the car head down Main Street. *He's going to Durkee's.* She followed him.

When she arrived at the restaurant he was at the bar, slugging down a whiskey. "Griffin? What's wrong?"

"You."

"Me?"

He pushed the shot glass across the bar to Tommy. "Hit me." When Rachel continued to stand next to him, he barked, "It's that boyfriend of yours—the blockhead from Boston."

"Cary? What's he done now?"

"Ah, so he *is* your boyfriend."

"I didn't say that."

"Well, is he?"

Rachel didn't like the direction of the conversation and changed the subject. "What did Cary Marx do to you?"

He stared at her a long minute before answering. "He's stuck his nose into that train incident out in Brooks last week. Claims it wasn't an accident, but murder, and now he's hounding *me*."

"You? What for?"

"Evidently this fellow—the *victim,* was an Egyptian archaeologist." He rolled his eyes. " So Marx is asserting to anyone who'll listen that I knew him and probably murdered the chap for some artifact or other."

"Really?" Rachel almost giggled but thought better of it. "You're not an archaeologist, though."

"I know that and you know that, but tell Mister correspondence-school-MBA-with-a-Porsche, that. He just lumps all us academics in together. He'll probably finger you to the cops next."

This time she did laugh. "Griffin, you are too funny. Tommy—can I have a whiskey too, please? JD if you've got it." She took a sip. "I can see why Cary would be confused. After all, you *are* a professor of Middle East history. So there is a connection, however slight."

"Yeah, but I don't know the guy from Adam. What'd they say his name was? Omar something? I heard he was on the faculty of Cairo University. So where and how would I be acquainted with him?"

Rachel said mildly, "You were in Cairo in February, were you not?"

Griffin slammed down the glass. "Not you too! For the last time, I went to Cairo to give a lecture at the American University on the distribution of food recipes beyond the boundaries of the Ottoman Empire." He paused and his eyes grew distant. "See, my theory is that some basic dishes like yogurt cucumber dip and bulgur and tomato salad—dishes that you find from Somalia to Kazakhstan—were not spread by the Turks as is commonly assumed, but much earlier, by Ethiopian and South Arabian traders. The recipes moved east and north, *not* west and south. Take the Biblical story of the queen of Sheba. She brought spices and other foodstuffs *north* to Jerusalem in the tenth century BC—long before the hordes came out of the steppes of Central Asia. Why, I could—"

"I know about your hypothesis, Griffin. I read your book. It was...er...gripping. But about the dead man— you can see why people might wonder. After all, this fellow was probably in Cairo when you were there.

Maybe he came to Maine to see you."

Griffin, who had obviously forgotten all about the offending Cary in his enthusiasm for his pet theory, abruptly stood. "Hogwash. I can see why Marx is infatuated with you. Birds of a feather." He stomped out the door.

A voice at her elbow made Rachel jump. "Aha, so the curmudgeon is jealous."

"Maude!" Rachel wanted to remonstrate, but first she wanted to savor the idea. *If only those blue, blue eyes would look at me with affection instead of irritation. Just once.* "I truly doubt he's jealous. I don't think he's capable of any emotion other than outrage."

"Ha. So tell me, what are you doing in Durkee's this time of day?" Maude returned to her booth, and Rachel followed.

"Griffin almost mowed me down in the street, and I wanted to break his skull in a sympathetic environment."

"I see. By the way, what did Toby want?"

"Oh my God, I forgot all about that. Maude, he had some state police detective with him. He asked me about the passengers on the train. There's one missing."

"Missing?"

"I mean, seventeen tickets were sold, but I could only remember sixteen people."

"What about Sarah and Pete?"

"They wouldn't need tickets."

"True. Stan?"

"Stan wasn't there. Richard substituted at the last minute."

"Didn't make it back from Searsport again?" Maude snickered.

"No. You know, I hope he isn't in over his head. I hear Noreen Fowler's history with men is a bit dubious."

"Noreen Fowler?"

"She's the girlfriend. Moved to Searsport maybe two, three years ago. Edna Mae told me she married one of the Ely boys—you know, the one who died in that horrible accident with a wood chipper."

"Oh, yes. I remember hearing about her now. Claimed her first husband abandoned her, didn't she? No way of knowing what happened before she got to Maine. But Bigger Ely's death, now, that happened right in Unity. Lotta unanswered questions around that so-called accident. *Hmm*." Maude pushed her plate away.

"I don't know. All I know is, she's supposed to be a bit shifty."

"Well, anyone who can go through two husbands before supper is bound to incur at least some distrust." Maude sipped her iced tea.

Rachel mulled the idea over. "If she did bump them off, it's a sure bet it wasn't for their money. Edna Mae says she drives an old Buick with more than a hundred thousand miles on it."

Maude perked up. "Maybe she's on the lam."

"Ha, ha. Anyway…" Rachel felt around for the original thread of the conversation. "Anyway, what if that seventeenth person is the killer?"

"Or maybe there wasn't a seventeenth person at all. Someone probably tore the ticket off by accident and threw it away. Remember, Sylvia worked the window last time. She's always tearing them in half by mistake. I'll bet that's what happened."

It seemed reasonable. "Well, it's not my problem." Rachel stood. "I've got to get home."

"How come?"

"For starters, I never got a shower after the gym."

Maude sniffed. "I thought I smelled something rank."

"Hey! It's not that bad."

Katie came over and dropped the check. "You heading home for a shower?"

Rachel made a face. "Who needs enemies…"

It wasn't until she reached her house that she remembered about the couple.

Should I call Toby? Sudden fatigue smothered her brain, and she flopped on the couch. Whenever she spent time with Griffin—fleeting though it usually was—she came out of it emotionally drained. He seemed to tease out the meaner side of her nature—and left her regretting most of what she said to him. *Why does he have to be so grouchy all the time? Or is it just with me? Does he just not like me?* Her lips quivered. *All right, that's enough for one day.*

She got up and went to the back door. "Spot! Spot! Come on in, it's suppertime." The little cat slipped between her legs and headed toward the kitchen. Rachel filled a small bowl with dry food and went off to take a shower.

She'd eaten a hot dog wrapped in a lettuce leaf, downed a couple of glasses of Pinot Grigio, and settled down with a good book when the phone rang.

"Rachel? Did I wake you?"

She waited for the large lump in her throat to dissolve while she tried to come up with a clever retort. "No." *Oh boy, that should set him back on his heels.*

"What do you want, Griffin?"

"I...uh...wanted to apologize. I was a bit out of line back there."

"..."

"Did you say something?"

"I...er...it's okay."

A snuffling sound came through the receiver. "That Marx—he just gets my goat. I don't know what you see in him."

Was Maude right? Rachel sat up and smoothed her hair. "Everyone gets your goat, Griffin. You need to lighten up a bit."

"I know. I thought once I got away from academia my stress levels would lower, but there always seems to be something going on here." He paused. "Well, anyway, I thought I'd better call and take my lumps."

A blubbering mass oozed and churned in the cavity where Rachel's heart used to be. "I said it was okay."

There was silence at the other end for a minute. "Look, do you want to have lunch tomorrow?"

Bam bam bam. Rachel held a hand to her chest to stop the pounding. "Uh, sure. Durkee's?"

"Nah." His voice held a hint of humor. "They know me there. How about Ripley's?"

The restaurant across the street from Durkee's was a dark, sticky, sports bar with the best hamburgers in midcoast Maine. "Okay."

"All right, I'll meet you there at one." He rang off.

By her reckoning, Rachel slept a total of ten minutes that night.

****

The next morning she was greeted by a tottering pile of unanswered mail on her desk. It took her four hours to slog through it and when she finally looked up, the wall clock said 12:45. "Uh oh." She ran into the bathroom, fluffed up her hair, as usual thanking the good spirits for her mass of still-golden curls, ran lip balm over the rosebud mouth Michael had loved to paint, and changed her underwear in memory of her mother's constant reminder to "Keep fresh, dear."

As she waited at the light to cross High Street, a pair of pedestrians caught her eye. *It's them!* She started to follow, but they turned down Beaver Street. Torn, Rachel paused. *The police have probably already questioned them. It's none of my business. Besides…Griffin.* Even if she weren't dying to have lunch alone with him for the first time, she knew he'd blow up if she were late. She stepped off the curb.

Griffin waited in a back booth. "You're late. Want to play Buzzword? I've got the clicker."

Romance right out of the box. "No, thanks."

The waitress came over with two pilsner glasses. Griffin clinked her glass. "Took the liberty of ordering for you. Since you were *late*." Rachel chose to ignore the jibe. After a while, he asked, "So, how's the history racket? Any visitors?"

She knew he knew damn well that was a sore subject. *Is he being deliberately spiteful?* "Look, if you just invited me to lunch to pick on me, I have my cat for that."

"A cat! I didn't know you were a cat lady."

Rachel got up. "I'll see you later."

"No, wait. Sit down." He held out his hand and gave her arm a diffident pat. "I'm…not used to company. Especially female company. I'm sorry."

She sat down, but kept a watchful eye on him while

she drank her beer. After a few minutes of silence, she felt the need to fill the void. Pointing at a long white scar that cut across the back of his right hand, she asked, "How did you get that?"

His jaw tightened. "None of your business."

Well, this is going well. "Sorry. Do you want me to move?"

"No, no of course not. I'm the one who should apologize." He took a huge gulp of beer. "I seem to spend an awful lot of time apologizing to you. It's just…it's just, you bring out the worst in me."

Whew, and I thought he didn't like me.

"I…I like you, Rachel." He swallowed the rest of the beer.

Oh great—there goes the heart again. "You have a funny way of showing it."

"I know. Look," he crumpled up a napkin, "I'd better tell you why I left Queenstown. Or at least one of the reasons."

Rachel assumed the position. "I'm listening."

"Hang on. Hey, Wanda, can I get another beer?" He held up the empty mug. Rachel waited him out. "See, in the immortal words of Ronald Reagan, 'I didn't leave the Democratic Party. The Democratic party left me.' "

"What the hell does that mean?"

"I'm getting to it, woman. Honestly, you have no patience."

"Takes one to know one."

He almost laughed. "Touché. What I mean is, over the last couple of years I became disillusioned with Queenstown University and the academic community in general. It's not that obvious in an esoteric field like mine, but the whole atmosphere has changed. Intellectual debate and diversity have all but disappeared there."

Rachel nodded. She too had seen her beloved Queenstown—a place where, in her youth, students and professors went head to head on the great issues— degenerate into a bland, tasteless stew of politically correct liberal talking points.

Griffin took the glass from Wanda and continued. "Three years ago, I had a call from an old friend—a law professor who specializes in the Constitution. A few weeks earlier he'd written an op-ed concurring with some comments an originalist made pertaining to a case before the Supreme Court." He broke off. "You do know what an originalist is?" Without waiting for an answer, he continued. "It's a jurist who believes the Constitution should be read literally and in accordance with the writings of the founding fathers. Anathema to the activists infesting our law schools who like to call the Constitution a 'living document' subject to modern interpretation. Well, within hours of publication my friend became persona non grata in academic circles— branded a conservative buffoon and then all the usual labels—racist, sexist, etc." He flicked at the glass pensively.

Rachel finished her beer. "And?"

Griffin started. "What? Oh, anyway, he told me he'd been invited to give the keynote speech at a conference in the Taft Center for Politics, but now some of the younger, more radical members of the faculty were agitating to withdraw the invitation. He wanted to know whether he should cancel or stick it out. And like the naïve person I am, I told him by all means to come, that a great university is the place for vibrant discussion, yada yada yada."

"Let me guess—he accepted and was treated to disruptions, jeers, and insults."

"And that was just the professors. The students ultimately shouted him down." He grimaced. "I was appalled and embarrassed, not to mention mortified, that I'd talked him into it."

"What did you do?"

"I wrote a letter to the Queenstonian blasting the school. Then I went on television and radio berating the Ivy League for becoming a cesspool of stunted, close-minded, ignorant, petty, prejudiced dinosaurs."

"So you didn't mince words."

"Well, you know me." He picked up a peanut and broke it apart with two fingers. "Long story short, they fired me."

"I thought you had tenure!"

"No, the Institute is separate from the university and has a different type of organization. They don't have tenure. It didn't matter, though—I was ready to leave. I'd had it with those folks. So...I picked up my toys and sailed up to Penhallow."

Rachel studied him. Beyond the indigo eyes and dappled gray hair that usually absorbed her attention, she detected lines of pain etched in the corners of his mouth. She ached for him and almost reached out to touch his hand but drew it back before he saw the movement. *He'd only misinterpret it.* "Well, you don't seem to have cheered up much."

He grinned. "This *is* cheerful, Rachel. You should see my disgruntled face."

"Hey, you two, cut out the lovey dovey stuff. You

ready to order?"

Rachel picked up the menu. "I'm starved."

Griffin sized her up. "You mean you're not a delicate little flower with a sparrow-like appetite? Just my luck."

For answer, Rachel announced loudly, "I'll have the stuffed blue cheese double burger with fries and slaw, Wanda. And another beer."

As they came out of Ripley's an hour later, Rachel almost ran into a teenager dragging a flower-print backpack behind her. It reminded her of the couple in the photograph. "I just remembered. I have to run over to the police station. Thanks for lunch, Griffin." She gave him a peck on the cheek and left him standing, with his mouth open, on the sidewalk.

She found Sheriff Quimby filling out a form. He put the pen down and waved her to a seat. "Just responding to a survey on police brutality. Not having witnessed any here on the mean streets of Penhallow, it didn't take long. What is it?"

"I think I have something for you."

"On the incident? Fabulous. Detective Blanchard has been on my ass to get results. Between you and me, I don't like him very much."

Coming from Toby, that statement was the equivalent of dispatching the detective to the deepest level of hell. She said mildly, "He does seem a trifle...pushy."

"You betcha. So what ya got?"

"When I was in here last, he showed me a photo of two people, a young girl and a man."

Toby opened his desk drawer and pulled it out. "This one?"

"Yes." Rachel took it. "I think I know who they are. Or rather, where they are."

"And?"

"I'm pretty sure this is a younger version of the quiet couple on the train." She pointed at the picture. "The woman I saw on the street was carrying the same handbag as the one here."

Toby pursed his lips. "Are you sure? There are all kinds of these here pocketbooks. Edna Mae must have fifty of 'em."

"Yes, I'm sure. I know it's odd for a woman to keep one that long—"

"Not at all. Edna Mae has some from way back in high school. She says you never know when you'll need that particular color or size. And since she's always gallivanting around, she changes her damned handbags every day." Toby grumbled, but the hint of a fond smile scampered across his lips.

"She *is* busy, isn't she? She and the other red hatters were on the train the day of the murder. Did she see anything?"

"Nah. Too busy yakking. I interviewed her of course—"

Rachel could just see the diminutive, pot-bellied sheriff trying to interrogate his own wife, a formidable woman twice his size.

"—but it was a waste of time. The only thing any of them noticed besides themselves was the little baby. Gawd, Edna Mae went on and on about that baby and how Cindy had better get her act together soon and get hitched and…well, you know the drill."

"Yes, Toby. Now about the two people. Do you need a description?"

"Yeah, to corroborate." Quimby pulled out a sheet of paper. "Here's the statement from the couple who sat across from them on the train. 'Man—fifties, medium height, slightly balding, bland face. Woman—close to thirty, sallow, mousy. Wore a granny skirt and carried a big flower-print bag. Both very quiet.' He was the one who discovered the body."

Rachel dropped the pen she'd been playing with. "He was? How come that wasn't in the newspaper?"

"This is a police investigation, Rachel. Some facts are better left classified until we know more."

"Well, what did he say? How did he find him? Where was he?"

Toby stood up and paced. "All right, I'll tell you but you have to promise to keep it to yourself for now. According to Sarah, he was exiting the train and noticed the victim had fallen off the seat. When he touched him, he saw blood. He brought it to Sarah's attention, and she called 9-1-1."

"That's it? That's your precious secret stuff? You don't even know the man's name?" Rachel stood, hands on hips. "Wait, if he found the body, why didn't you question him?"

Quimby's chagrin was palpable. "Because Sarah let him go before we arrived. He claimed he had an urgent appointment and couldn't wait." He shook his head. "I can't believe she didn't have the presence of mind to keep him there."

Rachel thought of the petite nineteen-year-old. "You're being a little unfair. I doubt whether Sarah has had to deal with a situation like this before." She thought a minute. "Is he a suspect?"

"Everyone's a suspect, Rachel. We have no idea

where the bullet came from. We haven't found a gun."

"So, it's not suicide."

"We're not ruling anything out. Now, if you'll excuse me." He opened his office door and bundled her out.

She turned and stuck a foot between the door and the jamb. "What if I see those people again? What do you want me to do?"

"Call me." He knocked her foot away and gently closed the door.

Feeling restless, Rachel decided to go back to work. She let herself into the historical society, turned the sign over to OPEN, and went to her office. Immersed in a treatise on the Scottish roots of Penhallow, she didn't hear the entrance bell ring below. She looked up from her desk to find the woman from the photo standing in her door, her purse clutched to her bosom, staring at her. "Are you Rachel Tinker?"

"Yes. Can I help you?" Rachel thought frantically. *How do I call Toby without spooking her?*

"You're the town historian?"

"Yes."

The front door dinged again. The woman glanced over her shoulder. Then, eyes wide with fear, she tossed the purse at Rachel and ran. Rachel picked it up and, without hesitating, hid it in the file cabinet. Then she went out to the hallway and walked down the spiral iron stairs to the ground floor. The woman stood near the door pretending to examine an exhibit on Main Street businesses. Beside her, the man from the photo whispered rapidly in her ear, his hands balled into fists at his side. She cringed a bit but stood her ground.

Something told Rachel not to mention the purse.

"Hello there—can I help you two?"

The man turned. His face was no longer bland. In fact, the rage sluicing from him forced Rachel to take a step backward. He spat out, "Who are you?"

Excuse me? "I am the director of the Penhallow Historical Society. Who are you?"

This seemed to throw him. The woman touched his arm. "Dad, this lady simply showed me where the restroom is. There's no need to be rude."

Rachel made a quick calculation. "That's right. No trouble finding it, I hope?"

"None at all. Thank you." She took her father's arm. "This looks like a very interesting museum. It's too bad we don't have time to look around right now. Thanks for your help." She walked out, accompanied by a now rather subdued parent.

Rachel stood in the middle of the hall. *What the hell was that all about?* Finally she flipped the sign to CLOSED, locked the front door, and stumped back up the stairs to her office. She moved deliberately to the cabinet and pulled the purse out. For a short minute she considered taking it straight to Toby. Then she opened it.

In the main compartment, she found a packet of tissues, a pen, a ten-dollar bill, a comb, and a piece of yellowed paper, folded in half. She unfolded it. It was a deposit slip from the Penhallow Bank and Trust made out for $233.68, dated August 2, 2005.

Chapter Three
The Bank

"So, what do you make of it?"

The sheriff shook the purse. "You say she just tossed it at you?"

"And ran. She told her father she was looking for the bathroom."

"And you didn't contradict her?"

"No."

That seemed to suffice, for Toby merely said, "I see." He smoothed out the piece of paper. "This deposit slip appears to be the only significant item in the purse." He peered at Rachel. "You do know Penhallow Bank and Trust went out of business a decade ago?"

"No, I didn't. It must have been open when she made the deposit in 2005, though, right?"

The sheriff picked up Blanchard's photo of the couple. "And you're sure these are the same people?"

Rachel pointed. "It's the same purse."

"Indeed." He tapped his fingers on the desk. "Okay, I think this bears investigating. I'll send a message to Blanchard, then give Claire, over at the City Clerk's office, a call. She handles the records of financial institutions for the city. I'll see what she can dig up on the Penhallow Bank and Trust."

Rachel stood up. "I'll check the town archives. See if anything significant happened on..." She glanced at the slip. "August 2, 2005."

"Righto. Let me know what you find out."

She left the station and walked back to the historical society. An hour later found her cursing loudly. *Wasn't cleaning up the archive files my first priority when I took this job? What the hell have I been doing?* The cabinets—stuffed with letters, newspaper clippings, and mementos in no particular order—would take weeks to sort out.

As she sat on the floor, a pile of newspaper advertisements from the 1930s in her lap, she had an inspiration. "The Republican!" The local newspaper had been in existence for a century. *They'll have news items on business closings, I'm sure.*

She marched the few blocks to the Penhallow Public Library and climbed the stairs to the circulation desk. "Hi, Wendy."

The dark-haired girl in hand-strung beads and a long jersey dress looked up from her computer screen. "Oh, hi, Rachel. What can I do for you?"

"I want to check past issues of the Republican. Do you have them online?"

Wendy ran her fingers over the keyboard, forcing the dragon tattoo on her forearm to dance and jump. "No. Sorry. We had them on microfiche, but when Fred came on as librarian he had them burned. Said it embarrassed him to work in a library that still uses nineteenth-century technology."

"So the records are lost?"

"Yup."

"Too bad we can't lose Fred."

She shrugged. "He's okay. He lets me leave early on Wednesdays for my lute lesson." She held up a

43

beringed finger. "You might try the newspaper offices. They probably keep their own issues on file."

"Good idea."

Rachel walked up to the strip mall that housed the offices of the Penhallow Republican Observer. As she pushed open the door, a hand landed heavily on her shoulder. "I hope you're not posting a personal ad for a new boyfriend." Beneath Cary's playful words squirmed just a tinge of uncertainty.

She shook his hand off as firmly as she dared. "Hi, Cary. No, I'm here to look something up. What are you doing?"

"Delivering an op-ed. Harrison likes to get my perspective on things. We're thinking of making it a regular feature at the paper."

Oh, God.

He tried to pinch her cheek and missed. "So, what have you been up to?"

"Oh, this and that. Look, I'm in the middle of a project—I'll see you later."

Cary's eyebrows went up. "I see. I'll—"

"Are you going to move out of the way or do I have to use the back door?" The gruff voice held no hint of either playfulness or uncertainty.

Rachel backed into the office and Cary moved with her. Behind him towered Griffin, clearly in a very bad mood. He elbowed Cary aside, brushed past Rachel, and went to the clerk. "I want to place a notice in the paper, Monica."

"Sure, Griffin. We've got three forms. What kind of notice is it?"

"I want to tell whoever's letting their Great Dane dump in my front yard that I have now acquired a shotgun and I'm not afraid to use it."

"Hey," squeaked Cary. "Where do you get off blaming a Great Dane? I don't walk Romeo anywhere near your house." He puffed out his chest, looking for all the world like a bombastic rooster. "I don't usually frequent *that* side of town."

Griffin spun around, his face purple with rage. "So it *is* you. I knew it. No one else around here needs a hulking animal like that to prove his manhood. Keep that hound off my property or I'll fill your ass with buckshot. You hear me?"

Monica and Rachel grinned at each other. Nothing like a little testosterone to enliven a dull morning. They waited, looking forward to the show.

"Well...yeah." Cary seemed at a loss for words, greatly disappointing the two women. He circled around Griffin, dropped a piece of paper on the counter, and trotted out.

Griffin continued to glare at the door, then swung around. "What are you two giggling about? Gawd, *women.*" He grabbed the form and went over to a table and began to write furiously.

Rachel turned to Monica. "Wendy, over at the library, thought you might have back issues of the Republican in your archives."

"Of course. How far back do you need?"

"Ten years?"

Monica pushed her chair away from the desk. "Oh dear. I think so, but they may be only the paper copies. Jerry has been downloading back issues for a couple of months, but I'm not sure he's gotten that far. What are you looking for?"

"Any articles on the Penhallow Bank and Trust."

"I don't remember that one."

"It closed its doors a long time ago. I want to find out when and why."

Rachel knew Griffin stood behind her by his scent—a mixture of allspice and lemon balm. The co-op sold the hand-made soap he used and she had often stopped to sniff the spicy but sharp aroma. He said, "What's this all about?"

She toyed with the idea of not telling him, but if he was willing to help…"An interesting piece of paper came into my hands today."

"Uh huh."

"Well, if you're not interested…"

"No, I am. Tell me."

Monica interrupted. "Look, guys, I've got to lay out tomorrow's paper by three. Let me get you settled." She led them to a dusty back room furnished floor to ceiling with cabinets holding wide, thin drawers. "What dates do you want to check?"

"Um, I guess ten—no, twelve—years ago. That would be 2003. Then we can work our way to the present."

Griffin pulled a drawer out and laid it on the work table. "So, we're looking for anything to do with Penhallow Bank and Trust?"

"Yes."

"Is this part of your research?"

Rachel hesitated. "No. It may have something to do with the murder."

He slammed his hand down on the table. "Damn it, Rachel! Why are you sticking your nose into this? It's bad enough that that asshole Marx is sniffing around."

"There's no need to shout, Griffin. I didn't get

involved on purpose. It fell into my lap. Literally." She told him about Blanchard's photo and how the woman had given her the purse. "I can't help but think the deposit slip has some meaning. She was terrified of something."

"From what you said, it wasn't an 'it' but a 'who.' Her companion."

"N...no, I don't think so. He was near apoplectic at first, but she didn't seem all that afraid of *him*. It's not like she was trying to run away or anything."

"True. You say she called him 'Dad'?"

"Yes. So at least we know they're related."

Griffin picked at the stubble on his chin. "The obvious question is, why you?"

"Me? I don't...well, maybe she was interested in the historical society."

"And would have given the purse to anyone there?"

"Maybe she figured only an archivist would look at that deposit slip and think it might be important."

"And try to track down more about it. Did you happen to check your own files?"

Rachel rolled her eyes. "Why, how clever of you! That never occurred to me."

Griffin pursed his lips. "Some crack investigator you are. Why don't you head back to your office and do some real research for once?"

"Of *course* I checked them. Duh."

"And? What did you find?"

"Er..." *No way on earth am I going to tell him what an unholy mess my files are in.* "Nothing." *Short and sweet. And vague.*

He shot her a look. "Seems odd, and you such a

brilliant historian. So I guess you can help me here then. You take 2004."

She wasn't about to let him order her around, especially since this mystery belonged to her. "I'll choose my own year, thank you very much." She yanked out the drawer closest to her, realizing too late it was labeled 2002. *Wouldn't hurt to start earlier. Just in case.*

After a minute, Griffin said, "So, what else was in the purse? A wallet? Any form of identification?"

"No. Just what I told you."

"So she must have been intending to dump the purse on someone. It wasn't spur of the moment."

"How do you know?"

"She would have had more stuff in her purse—you know women."

Rachel had had about enough of his snide sexist comments. "Look, cut out the swipes at females, will you? I'm tired of it. Some woman must have really laid one on you to inspire that much hostility."

Griffin's face drained of color, and his mouth opened and closed.

"What is it? You look like a dying mackerel."

"Um. Nothing. Sorry. Won't do it again."

Did I hit a nerve? I wonder... He looked so stricken that she took pity. "At any rate, you're right—the purse had clearly been cleaned out. And she lied to her father—she said she'd come looking for a bathroom."

"Did you go along with it?"

"Yes." When his hands shot up in the air she said hastily, "Wait! If you'd seen the frightened look on her face you would have lied too."

Griffin took a deep breath. "Okay. We might as

well get started."

Two hours later they had reached the end of 2004. Griffin stretched. "Let's recap. We found two articles on PB&T and two hundred fifty-three advertisements or notices. Nothing of interest. The bank was established in 1949 and seems to have been a solid institution."

"Okay, so now we get to the important years, 2005 and 2006. The deposit slip was dated August 2, 2005."

Griffin returned the older trays to the cabinet and checked the labels on the other drawers. "I don't see…looks like those years are missing. Damn."

Rachel went to find Monica. "What gives? Our target years are gone."

Monica looked up from her computer. "Oh, yeah, I forgot. Some guy came in the other day and asked to borrow a couple of trays."

"Why didn't he just look at them here?"

Griffin appeared at the door. "Does she know what happened to the drawers?"

"Gone," Rachel nearly wailed. "Some stranger took them."

Monica's eyes widened in alarm. "Hey, it wasn't like that. He said there were several items about his grandmother that he wanted to scan into his computer. He promised to bring them back today or tomorrow." At Rachel's expression she added, "Jerry has let people do that before. I didn't think it would be a problem."

Griffin sucked in his breath. "What did the guy look like?"

"I don't remember exactly. Sort of nondescript. Brown hair. Older. He left his card."

"He did? Why didn't you say so!"

"Sheesh, Rachel, what's all the fuss about?"

Griffin interrupted. "Where is it?"

Monica scrabbled around on her desk while the other two seethed. "Here it is." She handed it to Rachel.

Griffin read over her shoulder. "John Green, Financial Consultant. New York, New York." He looked at Monica. "No number."

Rachel turned it over. "No wait, there's one scribbled on the back. 555-0123. Sounds fishy."

Griffin pulled his cell phone out. "One way to find out." He dialed the number. "It's ringing. *Whup*—went to voice mail."

"What's the message?"

" 'You have reached 555-0123. Please leave a message.' "

"Phooey."

"I guess there's nothing to do but hope this guy brings the trays back."

Rachel picked up her purse. "I can do something. I'm going back to the police station."

She had reached the sidewalk when Griffin tapped her shoulder. "Coming with."

Rachel remembered her promise to Toby not to divulge Green's possible role in the murder. "*Urp*...um...Actually, you'd better not. I'm not supposed to talk about it."

Griffin drew back. "Rachel Tinker, there's a word for women like you."

"Hey, I'm sorry. I forgot that Toby didn't want me to talk about the murder. Anyway, this John Green may have nothing to do with it."

"Well, what are you going to see our esteemed sheriff *about* then?"

"He was going to check the bank's incorporation

records at the City Hall. If you come with me, he'll guess that I've taken you into my confidence."

"So what?"

"Maybe he'll stop telling me what's going on." She gave him a sidelong glance. "You wouldn't want that to happen, would you?"

He shrugged. "Doesn't matter one way or the other to me. I'm just helping you out. Couldn't care less."

"Right, then. I'll just head over to Church Street. See you later."

As she stepped off the curb he grabbed her arm. "All right, I admit I'm a little intrigued. Meet me at Durkee's when you're done." He turned on his heel and walked down the street before she could refuse.

She found the sheriff on the phone. "Yes, Detective. I understand, Detective. I'll wait till you get here to do any more investigating…all right. Tomorrow when?…Eleven? Okay." He hung up and wiped his forehead. "God, I hate these big city policemen. Always getting their britches in a knot over every little thing."

He gestured Rachel to a chair. "So, any luck? You were going to check your archives, weren't you?"

"Yes. No joy." *I've got to get to work on those files.*

"How about the library?"

"I tried there, but when Fred was hired he had all the old microfiches burned."

"God, I hate these big city librarians. You came up empty, then?"

She shrugged, frustrated. "I went to the offices of the Republican to go through their back issues for any mention of the bank. Toby, two years' worth of newspapers is missing—2005 and 2006."

"So?"

"The deposit slip was dated 2005."

"Oh, yeah, right. When you say 'missing,' exactly what do you mean?"

"Monica says a man fitting the description of the older gentleman in Blanchard's photo borrowed them."

"*Hmm*. Suspicious."

"Yes. Somehow I doubt he'll bring them back. Something must have happened in that time frame he wants to hide."

"Maybe. Wish I knew why Blanchard is interested in him."

Rachel pulled out the business card. "I almost forgot. He left this with Monica. Gives his name as John Green."

"Green, eh?" Toby checked his notes. "That's the name Blanchard gave me for the two folks he's been trailing. One minuscule iota of information he let slip." His brow furrowed. "If he'd only tell me what he's got on them."

"Could it have something to do with the bank?"

"I doubt it. Claire went through the records at the courthouse for me. PB&T filed for bankruptcy in September, 2005."

"That's a month after the deposit slip was filled out…Did she specify the reason for Chapter Eleven?"

He shook his head. "She only gave me the docket number."

"There must be a record of the case."

"I know. I was about to get Mikey on it when Blanchard called. That was him. I told him about your sighting and the deposit slip, and he ordered me to cease and desist till he got here."

"He's coming tomorrow morning?"

"Yes."

"Why is he so riled up about this? Does he think those two are involved in the murder?"

The sheriff tossed a wry smile her way. "As I said, the good detective has not seen fit to include me in his deliberations."

"What about me? Can I go check the court records?"

"You'd need authorization, and if I gave it to you he'd have my badge. Sorry." He rose. "Thanks for the help, Rachel. We are making progress."

"At least on something."

She started to head toward Durkee's, but the stress of the day chose that moment to settle like a bag full of bricks on her shoulders and she found herself yawning. *Screw him. I'm going home.*

The cat greeted her with a howl.

"I don't need any crap from you, Spot. I've had it with males." She plopped half a can of wet food in his bowl and left him grudgingly gobbling it up. A handful of almonds in one hand and a whiskey in the other, she propped her feet on the coffee table and switched on the Bangor news.

"…found in the water under the fishing bridge in Penhallow. Have they identified the body yet, Lou?"

"No. The police are circulating this photo of a woman."

A grainy picture loomed onto the screen. It appeared to be an image from a surveillance camera. Rachel put down her glass and leaned toward the television. The sightless eyes of the woman who'd given her the purse stared back at her. "Oh. My. God."

Her cell phone rang. "Rachel? Where are you?"

"Griffin! Are you watching the news?"

His voice rose from fretful to strident. "I *said*, where are you?"

"I'm at home." She snipped the words off. "The news. Are you watching the news?"

"Why would I be doing that? The Sox are playing."

"Where are you?"

"I believe I asked you first." He sighed loudly. "I'm at Durkee's waiting for you. Like I said I would be."

Rachel tried not to scream. She took a big gulp of air and let the words rush out on the exhale. "It's the woman. The woman with the deposit slip. She's dead."

"I'm coming over." She heard a click and a buzz.

Fifteen minutes later the screen door slammed, and Griffin stalked in without bothering to knock. He went straight to the kitchen, filled two glasses with ice, and poured whiskey into both. Carrying them to the living room, he handed one to Rachel without a word. Without a word, she took the remnants of her old drink and poured them into the new one. She set it down. For a second she stared at it, then reached out to pick it up again, but Griffin gently moved the glass away and took her in his arms.

She'd thought she was fine until then.

The tears flowed, and she hiccupped and gurgled about life and death while he muttered unintelligible words into her hair. When what had been a mild need for a tissue grew too urgent to ignore, she left his shoulder. A couple of wipes and a swig of bourbon and she could look Griffin in the eye. He dabbed ineffectually at his soaked shirt with a dirty handkerchief. "Better?"

"Yes, thanks. It's just…I feel so *responsible.*"

His eyebrows rose. "Responsible? Why?"

"She came to me. She gave the purse to me. She wanted me to help her. And for that she was murdered."

"We don't know anything of the sort. What did they say on the news?"

"Only that her body was found in the Passagassawaukeag."

"She could have fallen in. She could have committed suicide. From what you told me she was very upset."

Rachel recalled the young woman's face. "Not upset. Frightened."

"But not of the man she was with?"

"N…no. I don't know how to describe it. She seemed…hunted. But determined." She took another sip of bourbon and settled back on the cushion. *So what if Griffin's arm happens to be resting on the back?* "Griffin, we've got to find out who she—they—were." She turned to find his face inches from hers. "And what she was afraid of."

He gazed into her eyes, his own inscrutable, then faced the television. "No. You have to let the police handle it."

Rachel, who had forgotten what they were talking about in the overwhelming desire to kiss the man next to her, couldn't think of anything to say.

Finally, he mumbled, "Turn it up—it looks like they're talking about her."

She did as she was told.

A bold headline announcing Breaking News filled the screen before Sheriff Quimby's face appeared.

Someone pressed a microphone under his chin. "…found about five-thirty by Kenny Cross. He was fishing off the bridge and snagged a white object floating by."

A reporter asked, "How long had she been dead?"

"The coroner is examining her now. We won't have any answers until tomorrow." He started to leave, trailed by shouted questions.

"Did she drown?"

"Was it suicide?"

"Who is she?"

He shook his head and waved before ducking into a squad car.

The camera trained on a reporter. Short and stumpy, he tugged at his wrinkled polo before attempting to smooth his waning hair. "That was Sheriff Quimby of the Penhallow police, Andrew. It looks like we won't get any more information tonight, but he's scheduled a press conference for tomorrow at noon."

"Is he going to discuss the first murder—the train incident, Lou?"

"Hopefully, although he didn't mention it tonight."

"Did anyone ask if the two deaths are related?"

"The sheriff only said that, so far, there's no indication of either foul play, or of a connection between the two deaths."

The anchor turned to his partner. "So, Bambi—"

Griffin jerked upright. "*Bambi?*"

"—are we looking at a rash of thrill crimes down there in the hitherto bucolic town of Penhallow?"

Bambi shook out her hair and touched her ruby lips before facing the camera. "I certainly hope not,

Andrew. My grammy lives in Penhallow."

Andrew stared at her for a long moment before turning to the camera. "Thank you, Lou. Keep us posted."

Rachel muted the volume. "What should I do?"

Griffin patted her shoulder. "There's nothing we can do tonight. Toby knows about your encounter with the woman, right?"

"Yes."

"So he'll probably want to see you tomorrow."

"Yes, I suppose so." She put a hand to her mouth. "I forgot—Lieutenant Blanchard will be there."

"Who?"

"The state police detective. He's the one who showed me the photo."

"Why?"

"Why what?"

"Why will he be there?"

"Toby told him about me and the deposit slip. He said he was coming out from Augusta tomorrow."

"So he doesn't know his quarry is kaput yet?"

Rachel shook her head. "This is no time to be facetious. I'm sure it's been reported by now. And Toby surely would have called him."

Griffin sipped his drink. "Why did this Blanchard bloke go back to Augusta? Isn't he investigating the corpse on the train?"

"I don't know. I assumed he was, but now I think of it, except for his questions about the passengers, he didn't seem all that interested in it."

Griffin shrugged. "Who knows? Maybe he isn't. Maybe he's pursuing a cold case and this was just a fishing expedition."

"Maybe. I wish we could have found something on the bank. It's very frustrating."

Her companion bent forward and pinched her chin between his thumb and forefinger. "There's...nothing...we...can...do...tonight."

"Nothing?"

For answer he let go of her face, drew her into his arms and kissed her. The kiss was tentative. She kissed him back, tentatively. "I..."

"Shut up." This time they didn't come up for air for a while. When they did, they stared at each other as if seeing one another for the first time. He said, "I...uh...didn't mean to do that. I..."

She rose. "Oh, I see." She picked up Spot and nuzzled him, hoping Griffin couldn't see her tears well up. "I guess you'd better go then."

He stood. "Okay. But...um, actually...what I meant to say is...I've been meaning to do that for a while. But I wasn't sure...I didn't know...I didn't think..." He trailed off.

The bewildered look in his cerulean eyes as he shifted his weight from foot to foot reminded her of a kindly giant bobbling a baby bunny. She went up on tiptoe and touched her lips to his cheek.

The response was immediate. Griffin swept her up off the floor and charged through the kitchen door. Confronted with the refrigerator, he stopped, turned, and plunged in the opposite direction. Ending up where they'd started, he bellowed, "Where the hell's your bedroom?"

She pointed at the ceiling. "Upstairs."

Without another word he leapt up the steps, only banging her head once on the banisters, and dropped her on the bed. Then he stood, legs set wide like a latter-day Paul Bunyan, and folded his arms.

She lay where he'd dropped her, panting. "Now what?"

"You tell me."

Oh, for heaven's sake. "Come here, you great gob of indecision."

Those seemed to be the words he was looking for, since for the rest of the evening he proved to her just how decisive he could be.

Chapter Four
The Robbery

Rachel woke up alone, except for a cat angrily swishing his tail back and forth over her face. "Get off me, Spot!" She rolled off the bed and landed in a large pile of clothes. The activities of the night before roared back in vivid sound and color. "Griffin?" No answer. An unexpected rush of despair flooded over her. "Griffin?" Still nothing. She found a bathrobe, tossed cold water on her face, combed a few of the many knots out of her hair, and went down to the kitchen. A note lay on the table.

Went home to recuperate. Talk later. G.

A slight smile lit her face as she conjured up an image of sapphirine eyes boring into hers while their bodies rose and fell in perfect harmony. Parts of her she hadn't thought of in ages made their presence felt, and she knew she could hardly wait to have them paid attention to again. She collected juice, a bowl of raspberries, and English muffins, then set about making breakfast. Spot deigned to join her, and she gave him a treat.

The telephone rang as she was finishing her coffee. "Rachel? Sheriff Quimby here. Lieutenant Blanchard is with me and would like to hear your story. How fast can you get here?"

Rachel calculated swiftly—shower, dress...*I'll*

*clean up the mess later...*plus the twenty-minute drive from Amity Landing to Church Street. "About forty minutes."

"Well, haul ass, young'un. The representative of the state police here is an impatient man."

Thirty minutes later Rachel walked into the sheriff's office. Blanchard stood, arms folded, leaning against Toby's desk. Toby huddled in his chair. She announced, "Well, I'm here."

The tall, gaunt detective looked her up and down. "My years of training and extraordinary powers of observation have made it possible to see that already. Sit down, Ms. Tinker."

Either he actually has a sense of humor or he's a poster child for the lumpenbureaucracy.

"I understand you recognized Mary Green."

"Who? Oh, the woman in the photograph. So that's who she is."

"Her real name is Mary Pinkney. Green is the alias they're using now that they're back in the States. Tell me, in your own words, what happened yesterday."

Rachel repeated what she'd told Toby about both her first encounter with the Pinkneys and then the episode at the historical society. "Now, you tell *me* why you're interested in these people."

Blanchard pursed his lips. "All right, but this is strictly confidential. Ten years ago, she and her father, John Pinkney, robbed the bank he worked for."

"Wait a minute. If he worked there, don't you mean he embezzled money?"

"Embezzlement is usually accomplished over time, removing small amounts of money through accounting gimmicks. It's done stealthily and without violence.

John Pinkney overpowered a security guard, broke open the vault, and removed an extremely large amount of cash in the space of half an hour. In my business we call that grand larceny."

Rachel's eyes widened. "Oh my…Wait a minute. And you're saying Mary Green—I mean, Pinkney—helped her father steal the money?"

"Yes." Blanchard hesitated. "I guess there's no reason not to give you a little background. This case has been sitting on my desk for nine and a half years. I'm so close…" For a minute the light of battle shone in his eyes.

"So…" prompted Toby. "How did he do it?'

"You mean the robbery? Let's see—it was in the summer of 2005. John had been working as a teller at Penhallow Bank and Trust for two years—"

"Penhallow Bank and Trust!" Rachel and Toby gaped at each other.

Toby was the first to register outrage. "How come the Penhallow police weren't informed?"

Blanchard's eyes flickered and his earlier confidence wavered. Finally he grunted, "Need to know basis. State business. Besides, it was before your time."

He ignored the unintelligible sounds emanating from the sheriff and went on. "Pinkney must have been planning the heist for a while. He chose a day when the entire staff left the bank for a birthday lunch. Citing a headache, he stayed behind. Mary entered the bank by the front door and, while she distracted the guard, John knocked him out. Together they emptied the vault."

"And they got away?"

"Yes. John had the keys to the vault, so he locked it up after they'd taken the money. No one at the bank knew it was missing for another sixteen hours."

"What about the guard?"

"He was a retired janitor and, according to his co-workers, given to drink. Claimed he'd tripped and fallen—he probably would have said anything to save his job."

Toby tapped a pencil. "I'm surprised they weren't caught quickly. They don't sound like very slick operators."

"John was slick enough. He knew Belize doesn't have an extradition treaty with the United States and had already bought tickets. Took off from the Manchester airport while the police were still checking Logan and Kennedy. As far as we know, they stayed in Belize for nine years. We finally picked up a fresh lead about three months ago."

"And you've been tracking them?"

"Yes. They entered at Miami and worked their way up the coast taking buses and commuter trains. They did a lot of backtracking and side trips, leaving a very crooked trail. Brilliant, really." He shook his head in admiration. "I couldn't believe my luck when I heard about the train murder."

Rachel's jaw dropped. "Excuse me?"

He didn't appear to notice her disapproval. "I've been on the alert for any word of them in Maine. Then, when Quimby filed a report that a man fitting John Pinkney's description had witnessed a murder, I knew I had him."

"Had him for what?"

"The robbery, of course." He produced the semblance of a satisfied smirk. "And maybe a murder as well. Who knows?"

A short silence ensued. Finally, Toby mused, "Statute of limitations on Class A felonies is six years—"

"Unless they leave the state. That tacks on another five years."

"So…" Toby seemed to be counting on his fingers. "Statute has another year to run. Why do you suppose they came back now?"

"Not sure. They may have hidden some of the cash up here and needed it. Also, John's wife just died."

"John's wife! Did she live around here?"

"Yes. She went by the name of Hannah Sundstrom."

Toby sat up. "Hannah Sundstrom owns—or rather, owned, a little store on the corner of Washington and Bridge Streets. She died in May."

Rachel added wonderingly, "Hannah Sundstrom…Amazing. I went to her funeral." She gazed at Blanchard. "Was she involved?"

He shook his head. "We couldn't pin anything on her. She had an ironclad alibi from her sister Ingrid."

"You know," Rachel said slowly, "I'm not sure the daughter—Mary?—was involved either."

Blanchard snorted. "Again, years of training, etc., etc., tell me that when a family member is present while a crime is being committed, distracts the one person who could stop it, follows the other family member out of the country, and *doesn't come back for ten years,* that family member is guilty as sin."

"Why was she killed then?"

"Killed?"

"She washed up by the pier last night."

Blanchard glared at Quimby. "You didn't tell me

that."

The sheriff stuttered, "You haven't given me a chance."

Rachel continued to muse. "I think she was forced to help her father. I think he killed her because she wanted to confess."

"I beg your pardon?"

"It's the deposit slip. It had the name of the bank and the date on it. She knew I'm the Penhallow historian. She assumed—or rather hoped—I'd be curious about the bank. A long shot, yes, but perhaps it was the only means she had to communicate. What other reason could there be for her to give me the purse?"

"So let me get this straight. Your theory is she was trying to give you a clue as to her identity?"

"Of course! Why else would she lie to her father?"

"Why else indeed?" He made a half-hearted attempt at a chuckle. "Maybe she was tired of life in Belize and longed for a cushy jail cell in Maine. Just because she got cold feet and wanted to turn herself in doesn't mean she didn't voluntarily participate in the crime."

"What? No! I'm positive Mary was never an accomplice."

Blanchard snapped his fingers. "With all due respect, Ms. Tinker, you know nothing of the sort. This is my case. It has been since 2005. I know everything there is to know about it. And Mary Pinkney helped her father rob a bank. Trust me."

He opened a file and started riffling through the pages. Rachel understood she was dismissed, but couldn't resist a parting shot. "So, tell me why, the day after she slipped me the purse, her father killed her?"

He looked up. "I'll get back to you on that. Right after the sheriff here briefs me on it. Oh, and by the way, don't even consider telling anyone what I just told you. If anyone mentions the murder witness, his name's John Green. That's all you know. Capisce?"

Rachel didn't respond. Until then it hadn't occurred to her to broadcast her hard-won information, but she now felt the gossip seed sprout and flower.

Toby escorted her to the door. "Sorry, Rachel, we have to prepare for the press conference. Thanks for your help." He winked and mouthed, "I'll be in touch."

At loose ends, Rachel decided to walk down Main Street to the waterfront. She took a left on Front Street and strolled down to the old railroad station, which also housed the Water Street Maskers, a summer repertory theatre. Maude sat on the bench in front of the shabby red building.

"Maude! I'm glad you're here."

"Of course I'm here. You know I'm in charge of the box office on Saturdays."

"What are the Maskers putting on next month?"

"*You Can't Take It With You*." She grinned. "We tried to get Griffin Tate to play the cantankerous old patriarch, but he spat on us."

Rachel was not tempted to commiserate. Nor to tell Maude about the evening spent with said Tate. "Did you hear about the murder?"

"What are you talking about? Of course I have."

"I mean the second one."

"What?"

"You remember when they found the dead man on the train last Saturday? Well, this man named John

Pi...I mean, Green, discovered the body. Last night Kenny Cross found Green's daughter floating in the river."

"Really?" Maude rested her chin in her hand. "So they're figuring this John guy killed both of them?"

"No idea. But Toby's holding a press conference at twelve. I'm going to go."

Maude checked her watch. "I'm off at noon. I'll try to find you there."

****

The crowd in front of the courthouse nearly rivaled that at a Penhallow High School basketball game. Rachel skirted the edge and managed to slide into a space between the owner of Jolson's Shoe Store and a van marked Channel 8. A few minutes later, Blanchard and Toby came out of the building. Toby introduced Blanchard, who blew into the microphone.

"Afternoon. The purpose of this press conference is to update the public on the progress of the investigation into the murder of Omar Masri."

The crowd remained expectant although one voice in the back observed loudly, "Who the hell cares about that guy? What about the girl?"

Blanchard gazed over the assemblage. "We'll get to that. Now, Masri was from Egypt, here in the States on a tourist visa. We have contacted the authorities in Cairo. They...uh...haven't gotten back to us yet."

Rachel wondered just how high tech the Egyptian police department was.

Blanchard continued. "We've learned that he was a professor at Cairo University, specializing in Middle Eastern archaeology. We have yet to find anyone in the United States who knows him or knows why he ended up on the Penhallow and Moosehead Lake Railroad last Saturday."

The same voice from the back yelled, "Forget about him—what about the dead girl? Who is she?"

Others in the audience began to clamor for answers.

Blanchard raised his voice. "The man who found Masri's body was accompanied by a young woman. That woman was found dead last night."

One of the gaggle of reporters shouted, "You think this guy knocked 'em both off?"

"We're not sure...we're—"

"So are we talking about a serial killer?"

"No, no!" Blanchard tapped on his mike, vainly trying to regain control. "The investigation is in its preliminary stages. We're trying to establish the identities of the dead woman and of the man who discovered Dr. Masri."

Rachel stared at him. *What the—? It's not like he doesn't know who they are.*

"I have here copies of a photo of the two people in question."

Toby interrupted. "Delbert, could you please circulate this?" He handed a sheaf of papers to a young man, who proceeded, with a determined, if rather scared, expression, to pass them out.

"The police have declared this man to be a person of interest. If anyone knows him or has seen him in the vicinity of Penhallow, please report it to us immediately."

One reporter handed his copy to Mr. Jolson, who looked at it, shook his head, and passed it on. At that moment Maude came up beside Rachel. "What'd I miss?"

"Not much. Blanchard's passing around an old photo of the Greens."

Maude snatched a copy as it went by. Her eyes widened and she tapped the paper. "Hey, I know them—that's Hannah Sundstrom's husband John Pinkney and their daughter Mary. John abandoned Hannah and disappeared years ago. That's when she went back to her maiden name."

Rachel took hold of her friend's arms. "Why? Do you know why they left?"

"Sure, everybody knows. They were having an incestuous affair and ran off to some island in the Caribbean."

"What about the Penhallow Bank and Trust?"

"What about it?"

"Didn't he rob the bank?"

Maude's eyes grew round. "Rob the bank?"

Rachel said impatiently, "Blanchard says John and Mary Pinkney robbed the Penhallow Bank and Trust in 2005."

"Couldn't have been John." She squeezed her eyes shut. "If I recall correctly, the two of them disappeared a month before the bank went bust. They were long gone when Edward Crocker—he was the bank president—announced the loss of a good chunk of the bank's capital. He filed for bankruptcy right after that. We always figured old Crocker just mismanaged the place into a hole. He wasn't prosecuted for anything."

"Was the money ever recovered?"

"No, and poor old Mrs. Weems had her life savings in there. You remember her, don't you? She was the cook over at Edna Drinkwater Elementary." Maude squeezed her eyes shut. "I think Mary Pinkney went there. I know I had her for math at Penhallow High."

"The bank…" prompted Rachel.

"What? Oh, yeah. Of course, there weren't many other accounts besides Betty's by that time. They'd all moved to the new First Fourth Bank because it didn't have a minimum and gave away a free toaster with a new account."

"Then it couldn't have been much—the missing money, I mean."

"I really don't remember. We could ask Bert Weems—Betty's son. Maybe he knows something."

At that point the crowd began to seethe around them, and Rachel realized the press conference was over. She beckoned to Toby, but he just waved and followed Blanchard. Turning to Maude, she said, "Doesn't Bert Weems eat lunch at Ripley's on Saturdays?"

"He eats there every day. Bachelor farmer."

"Let's go." When they entered the restaurant, Maude pointed out a big, burly man in overalls hunched over a bowl of chili at the bar. She sat down on the stool next to him. Rachel chose a seat on his other side. "Hey Bert—have you met Rachel Tinker?"

He didn't look up. "Nah. Whatcha want, Maude?"

"Mind if we join you?"

He waved a languid hand and kept eating. Maude ordered a burger and Rachel asked for iced tea. "Nothing to eat for you, hon?"

"Um, I guess I'll have a salad, Wanda."

"Waalll, either you're on a diet or in love." The waitress didn't wait for a response and went off, leaving Rachel's blush unremarked.

Maude nudged her behind Bert's back. "So...which is it?" She sniggered.

Rachel thought fast. "Oh, it's just that pretty green dress I bought up in Bangor at the convention last month. It...uh...shrank, and you know how it goes so well with my eyes. I can't bear to give it up so...I..."

Maude winked. "Okay, you can tell me when you're ready. I know it can't be that old reprobate Griffin, so you must have met someone in Bangor, eh?"

Luckily Wanda brought their meals at that moment, and Rachel could legitimately avoid the question. After Maude had swallowed a large bite of hamburger, she turned to Bert. "Rachel here was asking about Penhallow Bank and Trust. Remember it? Your ma had an account there."

Bert let out a vicious epithet. "Lost everything she had. Everythin' I would have inherited too. Lost the house in town. That motherfu—I mean, Crocker, stole it."

"That's not how I heard it, Bert," said Maude mildly. "Crocker was just a bad businessman. Your mother's account was one of the last there before he went bankrupt."

"Bankrupt, yeah. So why didn't he give her back her money? Answer me that?"

"I guess he didn't have it."

"What do you mean? There was over two million dollars in that vault."

Rachel put her fork down. "Really? Who did it belong to?"

"Some guy from Chicago placed it in escrow with PB&T while he negotiated this big contract. It was supposed to be wired to him when he was ready, but then Crocker suddenly closed the bank. When he reopened it a month later, he filed for bankruptcy."

"The man never got his money?"

"Nope."

"Then why didn't the police arrest Crocker?"

"'Cause they're fools." Bert's voice rose in frustration. Wanda came over and set another mug of beer down in front of him.

Maude touched his elbow lightly. "I'm sure they didn't have enough evidence of wrongdoing, Bert. These things happen with banks. It probably has something to do with financial regulations. Who knows? I don't remember the bankruptcy at all. We were all preoccupied with John and Mary Pinkney's affair."

Bert spilled his beer. "Mary Pinkney? Why are you bringing that up again?"

"I guess she's on my mind. Didn't you hear? She and John came back to Penhallow. They were on the train when that guy was killed."

Bert stopped chewing. "Mary's here? In town?"

Maude took a forkful of coleslaw. "She was. She fetched up by the fishing pier last night."

"Dead?"

"Well, duh."

Bert rubbed his chin. "Damn."

"What is it?"

"Nothin'."

Maude paused and put a hand to her mouth. "Oh my gosh, I forgot! You were sweet on her, weren't you? I remember you making googly eyes at her in my class." She leveled a severe look at him. "Joey Petelin told me you asked her to the prom, but she turned you down because…because…"

He slammed a callused palm on the bar. "Maude Jewett, you know damn well those stories weren't true. Her dad was a bully, yeah, but he didn't…he didn't…" He picked up the mug and gulped down the beer. Wiping his mouth, he spat out, "And she didn't turn me down. Mr. Pinkney refused to let her go with me. Said he'd heard bad things about me. And that damned cow of a wife of his—she didn't have the guts to intervene. Mary liked me. She told me so."

Rachel could tell Maude didn't believe him, but fortunately he was too overwrought to see the look of incredulity on her face. She almost put a hand on Bert's arm but thought better of it. "I'm so sorry, Bert."

He didn't look at her. "Water under the bridge. Er…" He reddened. "So, was it suicide?"

"They don't know yet—or they aren't telling us."

He slid off the stool. "I'm off."

"So soon?" Maude nodded meaningfully at his glass, still half full.

"Yup. Gotta go castrate a sheep."

Neither woman could think of a retort in time.

Maude finished her burger and asked Wanda for the check. "I'm scheduled to watch Hannah's store again this afternoon. "

"Oh? Any rumors on what's going to happen to that space when Hannah's estate is settled?"

"LuAnne doesn't know. She died intestate—that's without a will—"

"I know."

"—so the bank has to wait some period of time—a year I think—for creditors to come forward and all her bills to come due. LuAnne's been keeping the store open because she promised Hannah she would."

"Then it could go on the auction block." Rachel thought about the little place on Bridge Street. "She had some nice things."

Maude clucked her tongue. "A lotta junk. She'd pick up souvenirs on all her trips and then sell 'em here as artifacts. Used to go on those Smithsonian tours with her sister Ingrid."

"You mean after her husband and daughter disappeared?"

"Yeah. We all wondered where she got the money to go gadding around the globe, but LuAnne says they inherited a chunk of change from their grandmother."

"I don't think I ever met Ingrid. Did she come to the funeral?"

Maude signed her name on the receipt and handed it to Wanda. "Sure did. She was the one in the blonde wig—remember? Big hawk nose and a bosom you could land a plane on. Does nails for a living—calls it fingertip illustration."

Rachel tried to recall the faces of the people who came to Hannah's funeral. She drew a blank. "Is she still around?"

"I think so. Haven't seen much of her since her sister died. I heard she was going to move into Hannah's house up on Bluff Road."

"Does Ingrid inherit the store?"

Maude shrugged. "I doubt if she'd want it. Never showed much interest." She chuckled. "Maybe John Pinkney will get it."

Rachel stood up. "I think I'll go with you. Last time I was in the shop she had a lovely little music box on display."

"You want to buy something? Come along then. The more stuff you take off my hands the better—I swear there's more junk every time I go."

"Maybe it spontaneously reproduces." Rachel left a tip on the bar and followed Maude out.

They walked down Washington to Bridge. The store occupied the ground level of a free-standing brownstone, the date 1910 carved into the scalloped and embellished lintel. A sign painted in florid letters on the window read—

THE TRINKET SHOPPE
EXOTIC KNICK-KNACKS ~ NO JUNQUE ~
CONSIGNMENTS

Maude unlocked the door and let Rachel in. "I'm going in the back to get the register and cabinet keys."

Rachel wandered around the room. Victorian shoes and hats were piled willy-nilly on one counter. A glass case displayed pieces of estate jewelry as well as some old coins and political pins. In one corner, a life-sized mummy case leaned against the wall. Near the front window she found her music box in a tall, glass-fronted cabinet. When she tried the door, it wouldn't budge. "Maude, can you open this cabinet?"

The older woman scrabbled through a drawer. "I don't see a key for that one, but I have a hair pin. Maybe that'll do." She fiddled with the lock until the door sprang open.

Rachel gently picked up the box. The tiny figures of a man and a woman danced on it, he in white tie and tails and she in a sequin-studded, feathery evening dress. It reminded her of Fred Astaire and Ginger Rogers in *Top Hat*. She looked for a knob or key to wind. "How do I make it play, Maude?"

The older woman took it from her. "I guess that key's lost as well. *Hmm.* Hannah sure didn't keep this place up. No wonder she never had any business."

"Would the hairpin work on the box as well?"

"Let's try it." She wiggled the pin in the tiny hole, twisting it back and forth. "Got it!" The figurines began to twirl, and the tune to "Diamonds Are a Girl's Best Friend" tinkled cheerfully.

Rachel laughed.

"What are you giggling about?"

"It's the song—it always amuses me."

Maude touched the female figurine's white dress. "Never thought you were into bling, Rachel."

"No, I'm not really." Griffin's face rose before her and she smiled a secret smile. "The riff on female independence appeals to me, that's all." She held the box up. "How much is it?"

Maude took it from her and turned it over. "Fifteen dollars."

"Whew."

"Ten dollars? I'll throw in the hairpin."

"Done." Rachel pulled a bill out of her wallet. "By the way, what did Hannah do when John and Mary left?"

"It's funny you should ask. She didn't speak to anyone for months, but if you saw her in the co-op or around town she didn't seem sad or depressed."

"Well, if you're right and the two were engaged in...er...improprieties, she'd hardly be upset they were gone."

Maude huffed. "I didn't say I believed the rumors. It's just that no one offered a better reason for why they ran off. Mary was in her senior year at Penhallow High, and they didn't seem particularly hard up."

I wonder how far her memory goes back? As though making idle conversation, she asked, "So, what did John do for a living?"

"*Hmm.* I don't remember…something dull." Maude raised her eyes to the ceiling. "Accountant or…Something to do with money."

Rachel grinned. "Yes, you might say that."

"I beg your pardon?"

"What? Oh…um…nothing. Never mind." *I've already spilled the beans to Griffin. I don't need to broadcast it to the entire midcoast region via Maude.* "I'll get out of your hair then."

Maude pursed her lips. "Okay…for now. But you owe me an explanation, missy."

As Rachel left, the sun dropped down behind the hill to the west of the town. She considered going back to her office, but her thoughts were too jumbled to get any work done. *I'm going home.*

She got her car from behind the historical society and drove back along High Street to Amity Avenue. When she reached the village, she took the left fork that passed through the park above the marina. She paused a minute to watch the sailboats coming in from the bay, then drove up her street and pulled into the garage.

As she trudged up the cellar steps to her kitchen, she noticed light coming from under the cellar door and smelled something alien—cigar smoke? When the cat wasn't at his usual post by the Friskies, Rachel felt a frisson of fear run up her spine. *Too many deaths, too many conspiracies floating around.* She didn't need any more mystery. Her throat constricted, she croaked, "Who's there?"

From the living room came a deep voice. "It's me, Rachel. Didn't you see my car?"

"Griffin!" She went in. "I came in the back way and—"

Sitting on the couch was her erstwhile lover, in a beautifully tailored navy suit that rendered her breathless. Next to him sat an enormously fat man, his olive brown face concealed by a magnificent moustache, his small, black eyes both cold and anxious. A large cheroot smoldered in a saucer on the coffee table.

One man jumped to his feet. The other, with much groaning and wheezing, pushed himself off the couch and extended a mammoth paw. Griffin said, "I'd like you to meet George Hamdani, of the Institut français d'archéologie. He'd like asylum."

Chapter Five
The Fugitive

"Pardon me?"

Hamdani looked from Rachel to Griffin, confusion writ large on his face. Griffin coughed in vexation. "You heard me, Rachel. You do know what asylum means, don't you? If not, may I direct you to the dictionary?"

Rachel kept her own irritation on a tight leash. "Griffin Tate, I do not appreciate your tone. Nor do I appreciate being treated like some sort of...of church."

"Church? What are you talking about?"

"You know, sanctuary."

"Sanctuary is different from asylum."

"In what way?"

"Well, for one thing...wait a minute. You're just trying to distract me from the issue at hand. Are you or are you not going to take George here in?"

Rachel surveyed the mountain that was George Hamdani. Perspiration beaded his forehead, and he seemed to be having trouble catching his breath. "No."

Hamdani latched a pleading hand on Griffin's arm and spoke with an unfamiliar accent. "My dear professor, cannot you be more agreeable? I am in great need of this beautiful lady's help."

"I'll try." Griffin made a herculean effort and produced something approaching cordiality. "Forgive me…Miss Tinker. I guess I wasn't making myself very clear. I meant only that George here needs a place to stay for a bit. Until we sort things out."

His forced smile did not fool Rachel. "Things?"

"Before we get into that, he hasn't eaten in two days." Griffin nodded toward the kitchen. "As you may have surmised, he's not equipped to fast for very long."

Really? I'll bet he could go a year. "Certainly. Can I get you something to eat, *Mister* Hamdani?" With any luck the sarcasm dripping from her lips would puddle under Griffin's feet and he'd slip in it.

Griffin deftly avoided the trap. "Thanks. I'll have a sandwich. George? What can Rachel get you?"

Hamdani nodded enthusiastically. "You are very kind, Miss Tinker. I am devastated to be coming to you in this precipitate manner. When my circumstances improve, it will be my very great pleasure to make it up to you in any way you desire."

Well, when you put it that way… "I may have some chicken salad. I'll go check." She opened the refrigerator and took out a Tupperware container, lettuce, and bread. Griffin came in and retrieved two plates from the dish rack. As he carried napkins and glasses from the cupboard, he whispered to Rachel, "Thanks for doing this. You'll understand why it's important in a minute."

She punched him to hide the mushy smile that crowded out her aggravated scowl. "Beer?"

"Perfect."

Rachel opened three bottles while Griffin took the sandwiches to the dining room table. One glance at the delicate Duncan Phyfe straight chair and another at Hamdani's humongous behind and she pushed the ottoman toward him. "You'll be safer on that."

Hamdani nodded gravely and sat down.

She waited while the men wolfed down their food. "Okay, spill."

Griffin wiped his mouth with a napkin. "George is from the Institut—"

"You told me that. He's not French though, is he?"

The big man beamed. "No, no. Although French is my second language. English, alas, is only my third. No, I'm from the most beautiful country in the world, the land of the spreading cedar, of blue Mediterranean waters, of snow-frosted mountains."

"And that would be…"

"Lebanon, of course."

Not one to let a paean throw her, Rachel addressed Griffin. "And?"

"Oh right." Griffin gulped down his sandwich. "I'll cut to the chase. He witnessed the murder and is afraid if he comes forward he'll be considered the prime suspect."

"Which murder?"

His eyes popped. "Which…Oh right, I forgot about the woman. No, I mean Omar Masri. George saw him shot."

"Does he know who did it?"

"No. He was watching Masri through the window and saw him fall."

"The window—of the railroad car?"

"Yes."

"Why?"

"Why what?"

Rachel counted to ten. "Why wasn't he watching the staged attack on the train like everyone else?"

"Ah, that brings us to the reason he doesn't want to go to the police."

"I have an idea. How about you let Mr. Hamdani explain?" She turned to the subject of the discussion, who reluctantly pushed his empty plate aside. "Why are you here and why did you go on the train excursion?"

Griffin harrumphed. "George's English is fine for academics, but it would be better if I tell the story."

"Did he tell it to you?"

"Yes, but in Arabic."

"I forgot you knew the language, Griffin."

Griffin made a wry face. "As much as anyone can—the most damnably difficult tongue on the planet."

George—caught with the bottle at his lips—swallowed loudly. "No, *mon ami.* I cannot agree. English—it is English that is the most impossible to learn."

Griffin opened his mouth to argue the point when Rachel pinched him. "Will *someone* please tell me what's going on?"

He sighed. "Yes, well, when I got home this morning George was waiting on the porch."

"You two know each other?"

"Only by reputation. And"—Griffin flashed a happy smile—"he read my treatise on recipe migration!"

George said, "Yes, it was quite interesting. Completely, utterly wrong, however."

"Oh, yeah? My thesis is backed up by thousands of documents and it makes perfect—"

One, two, three. "Griffin?"

He heaved another sigh. "Okay. George is an

expert on ancient South Arabian culture, as well as a noted authority on early written languages of the Middle East. Omar Masri focused on archaeology of the civilizations along the upper Nile."

"And those are?"

"Nubia, down through Sudan to Ethiopia—the Red Sea region." Hamdani finished off his beer with a satisfied burp.

Frowning at him, Griffin resumed. "George and Masri had collaborated on a couple of papers linking early Nubian culture—in Upper Egypt—to the cities of South Arabia. Something about architectural similarities—"

George leaned forward and interjected helpfully, "To be precise, we studied similarities in their methods of calculating the calendar. Certain architectural features were used by both to determine solstices, et cetera. Features found nowhere else in the Middle East."

Griffin nodded. "Anyhoo, George had been working on a book about the identity of the queen of Sheba for five years. You know, the queen who came bearing gifts to King Solomon? The location of her kingdom has never been definitively established, although if the Biblical account is correct, it must have flourished in the tenth century BC."

Rachel interrupted. "I just read an article that said they haven't yet found conclusive evidence of *Solomon's* existence, let alone the queen of Sheba."

The Lebanese professor made a sound better suited to an aroused field mouse. "Ah, but I—George Hamdani—found proof...potential proof..." His eyes grew shifty. "Er...proof that there is evidence...quite good evidence…that she did exist."

Sorely tempted to applaud his prize-winning display of academic fudging, Rachel refrained. *They'll never get to it if I interrupt them again.*

Griffin had moved on. "George wrote a book outlining his theory and six months ago gave the draft to Omar for review. Masri promptly plagiarized whole sections of it. Worse still, he co-opted George's thesis and published an article taking full credit for it!"

Coming as she did from the academic world, Rachel knew a high crime and misdemeanor when she met one. "Oh my God. What did you do?"

George shook his head, his jowls wobbling. "What could I do? I hadn't published the book yet—it was only in the second draft. And then Omar left the country immediately after his article came out. He was beyond my grasp."

Griffin spoke. "A footnote in George's draft about the queen of Sheba's tomb had caught Masri's attention, and he became obsessed with finding it."

The Lebanese added, "It's never been located."

"Wait a minute, I'm confused." Rachel scratched her chin. "You just said no one knows where her kingdom was, so how do you expect to find her grave?"

Griffin glared at her. "If you'll let me finish…Masri went to Cairo. He must have come across some kind of reference to it in the Egyptian Museum that mentioned Axum…What, George?"

The Lebanese shut his mouth with a snap. "Nothing. Go on."

"Armed with that information, plus whatever clue he'd gleaned from George's work, he went haring off to Ethiopia."

Rachel puttered around in the morass of unfamiliar words and picked out the least recognizable one. "Axum?"

"An ancient kingdom in northern Ethiopia. Dominated the Red Sea trade for several centuries in the early Christian era. Some think Sheba's realm preceded Axum, and was perhaps subjugated by them."

Rachel took a minute to absorb this. "So Masri went to Axum after publishing his paper. What did George do?"

"All he *could* do—write a scathing letter to Cairo University and proclaim Masri's perfidy in every peer-reviewed journal that would let him."

"And wait for my revenge." George picked up his plate and looked wistfully toward the kitchen."

"Another sandwich?"

His eyes lit up under the heavy lids. "You are too kind."

Rachel came back with a second, slightly smaller, sandwich. The big man picked it up and hefted it with a meaningful glance at his hostess, who merely blinked at him. Griffin took up the story again. "We don't know what Omar found in Ethiopia, since instead of coming back to the States, he hopped a flight to France. George followed him there."

She looked at Hamdani. "Followed him? How?"

The fat man quickly took a large bite so he wouldn't have to reply. Rachel waited patiently, and for once Griffin kept quiet. Finally, he said, "I…er…consulted with…er…colleagues in Cairo, who told me he'd gone to Axum. I just missed him there, but saw him boarding a flight to Paris at the airport in Asmara. I was most discreet, like a James Bond. He never knew I was present." He seemed quite proud of himself.

Rachel reflected that George resembled the master spy about as much as he resembled Mikhail Baryshnikov, but kept it to herself. "You stayed on his trail in France?"

"Yes. He spent his time snooping in antique shops around Saint-Germain-des-Prés. From there he flew to Vienna and did the same thing."

"What was he looking for?"

George drew a long face. "I wish I knew. Whatever it was, it had to do with the queen's tomb."

Griffin put in, "He's guessing Masri found a reference in Ethiopia or Cairo to an artifact indicating where she was buried. He was using George's research to zero in on whatever it was."

She cocked a head at the Lebanese. "And George continued to track him?"

"Yes, back to the United States."

George finished his beer with a sigh. "I caught up with him in Boston. It was there it transpired…there occurred…we had…an…er…unfortunate altercation."

"An altercation?"

Griffin grimaced. "They got into a fight in a restaurant."

"Ah."

"A mere exchange of fisticuffs. I would have bested him forthwith had the authorities not interfered."

Griffin rolled his eyes. "The police broke up the scuffle and hauled them down to the station. They were lucky they weren't both immediately deported."

Hamdani stopped chewing long enough to whine, "I tried to explain what Omar had done, but they wouldn't listen to me—only to him." He picked up the sandwich again and grumbled, "The man is a consummate liar."

"He concocted some fable that George was consumed by jealousy of Masri's preeminence in Middle Eastern archaeology—"

George made a rude noise.

"—and had stalked him across the globe. Oh, and he threw in that George tried to seduce his wife as well. Suffice it to say, the police bought the line and were about to pop George on a plane—"

"And have a parade for Omar."

"—but at the last minute Harvard intervened."

"Harvard?"

"Yes. George held a visiting professorship there last year and they've been trying to lure him back. The Dean of Faculty offered to vouch for him to the police if George would promise a return engagement. He's a very popular lecturer."

"So all's well that ends well."

"Not really."

It was beginning to look like they'd never leave. Rachel got herself another beer from the refrigerator. "What happened then?"

"Well, the police let him go with a warning not to contact Masri, but when the sergeant returned their possessions, George happened to notice a plane ticket among Omar's papers. A ticket to Bangor."

Rachel pointed an admonishing finger at George. "So you shrugged off the police warning and tailed Masri to Maine."

Hamdani hung his head, revealing the beginnings of a bald spot. "And from Bangor to Penhallow."

87

"And you followed him onto the train."

He sighed. "Where I saw him struck dead."

"I see. And now you think if you go to the police they'll arrest you."

"Yes."

She looked at Griffin. "Where do I come into this?"

The room had darkened while the men shared their tale, and she could just make out two sparkling blue eyes in the shadow of Griffin's face. "I'd like you to put George up for a while, until we decide what to do."

"Why can't *you* put him up?"

"Because of your boyfriend."

She asked brightly, "Cary?" and was rewarded with a snarl.

"Yes. I told you he's got this bee in his bonnet that I had something to do with Masri's death. It's true that before George caught up with him, Masri had called me."

"He did! What did he want?"

"He knew of me and my work and that I'd retired here. He wanted to know if I had ever collected any artifacts in my travels—specifically, Nubian ones. I told him no. I fear my response was less than civil."

Rachel chuckled. "Really? You?"

Griffin brushed off the dig. "At any rate, Marx has decided that this was enough for me to want to murder the man. He's been hanging around my house, asking my neighbors questions. You can imagine what he'd make of the good professor Hamdani."

Rachel saw the writing on the wall, and it said, *Better get the guest towels out. And buy some more beer*. "Do you have any luggage?"

Griffin didn't wait to answer, but ran out with a cheery, "I'll get them."

Them?

A minute later he puffed up the deck stairs with two suitcases the size of steamer trunks. "Where do they go?"

Rachel toyed with the idea of making the man sleep in the living room, but he'd probably break the sofa frame. "In the middle room upstairs. There's a powder room between it and my study he can use."

Griffin pushed the suitcases up the narrow wooden stairs one at a time. Hamdani followed him, with Rachel bringing up the rear. She showed him where everything was, then left him unpacking. Griffin followed her. "You're an angel to do this."

"Do I have a choice?"

He touched her nose with his finger. "Yes. You always have a choice."

She gazed into his eyes, wishing she were faced with a different dilemma, like where to kiss him first. Instead, she opened the door.

"Rachel, I—"

"It's okay. I don't mind."

"It's not that. I…uh…" He mumbled something. She caught the tail end of the sentence. "Wish it were me staying here."

A round little ball of happiness bobbed up and down in her chest. "Me too."

His eyebrows went up. "Oh? Oh! Oh, that's…great. That's won—"

She pulled his head down, blew the hair off his forehead, and kissed him full on the mouth. His lips held on to hers for a long moment. As his arms went round her waist, she pushed him away. "Not now."

He grinned. "As long as it's not 'not ever,' I can wait." He walked out whistling.

Rachel leaned her back against the door. *Maybe you can wait, but I don't know how long I can.*

From above came a loud crash and an oath in a guttural language.

Rachel decided it was a good time for a walk.

****

When she returned all seemed quiet. She climbed the stairs and knocked on the guest room door. Hamdani opened it, wearing a sleeveless undershirt and voluminous boxer shorts. "Oh my, oh my...er...if you'll excuse me a moment." He slammed the door. A minute later he opened it again. This time he wore the long white robe known as a *jellabah*. "I do most sincerely apologize for my *déshabille*. It is rather warm up here."

"Yes, the air's a little stuffy, isn't it? You can open the windows if you like, and there's a fan on the bureau." She hesitated. "You don't have to stay up here, you know. You're welcome to come down."

"Thank you. I do have some work to do at present, but I would be most gratified to keep you company later." He nodded at the darkened window. "Tate felt it would be better that I not be seen much in daylight."

Rachel considered the advice sensible—a man of Hamdani's bulk would be hard to miss. "All right. I'll be in the living room if you need me."

She got herself a drink and turned on Channel 8. A flashing graphic trumpeted "Happening Now" and a well-coiffed and made-up Bambi appeared, her cherry-tinged mouth an O of excitement. "Thrilling developments concerning the recent events in what used to be the languid little town of Penhallow. A man has just been arrested, charged with the murder of his daughter! He has also been implicated in the first death that took place on the Penhallow and Moosehead railroad excursion on June fifteenth. For more information, we go to Lou Albert at the Penhallow police station. Lou?"

The camera caught Lou spitting his gum into a tissue. "Oh, hey…Bambi. We've learned that the accused is named John Pinkney, formerly of Penhallow. He returned from abroad recently with his daughter Mary, the victim. We haven't heard of any motive for the killing so far, but there are rumors circulating of a rather ugly nature. I can't go into it now—we're still checking our sources."

"How did the young woman die, Lou?"

"Drowned. She was found floating in the Passagassawaukeag River by the old chicken processing plant. Coroner says her lungs were filled with fluid."

Bambi's co-anchor chimed in. "What makes them think it was murder and not suicide? Or an accident?"

"Harold? Is that you?" The camera went to split screen, revealing a neat little man in a bow tie and seersucker suit. Lou grimaced, his eyes narrowed and his nose pinched, leading Rachel to wonder if the two had issues. "The *experts* say there were signs of trauma to her head, and scratches on her face and arms consistent with defensive wounds. She probably fought an attacker off."

"Wait—didn't you report that a fishermen found the corpse floating under the walking bridge? The riverbank there is piled high with riprap. Couldn't the injuries have been sustained when she fell onto the rocks?" Harold's voice held just a hint of condescension.

The question seemed to fluster Lou. "Look, I'll get back to you when we have more to report, okay?"

His response drew a snippy, "Well, keep us posted."

Bambi jumped in, her tone soothing. "Lou, is the suspect in jail?"

"Yes. He's being held until he can be arraigned."

The sound of an elephant negotiating the turns of a winding staircase came from above. George appeared in the front hall. He saw Rachel and took a step into the living room, knocking the table lamp from the side table. As he fumbled with it, Rachel muted the volume. "George, there may be some good news for you."

He plopped down in the massage chair, which groaned in unenthusiastic welcome. "Oh?"

"They arrested a man for the second murder and they're making noises about his being implicated in Masri's death. You may be off the hook."

The telephone rang. "Rachel? Griffin here. I've some news."

"They caught John Pinkney."

"What? Oh, you know. So our work there is done."

"They might also charge him with Masri's death."

"Really? That would be swell."

Swell?

"Tell George I'll come over tomorrow and we can regroup. Hopefully the police will get off their asses and make a good case. We need this thing wrapped up."

"You make it sound like they're accountable solely

to you."

"I'm a citizen, aren't I? They're called public servants for a reason."

"That reason being to please you?"

"Yes." He paused. "And to see that justice is done, of course."

Rachel yawned. "Whatever. I'm going to bed. And I'm going to work tomorrow. I've got a ton of stuff to go through. You can let yourself into the house."

"Thanks for the permission."

Was that sarcasm in his voice? Rachel was too exhausted to care. "Good night, Griffin." She put the receiver down only to have the telephone ring again. "Hello?"

"Rachel! Glad you're up. I'm coming over."

"Cary? What are you talking about?"

"There's news breaking out all over. The sheriff finally took my advice and put out an APB for the guy who discovered the body on the train and they caught him. I just came from the station, but that dolt Quimby wouldn't give me any information. Says I have to wait till tomorrow like the rest of the town." She heard teeth grinding. "Who the hell does he think he is?"

I think the same sentence I used with Griffin is appropriate here. "You make it sound as though the police are accountable only to you."

"Hey, who underwrote that new fingerprint scanner for them? Who subsidizes the police bowling team? I've done a lot for this town. Yeah, I think I'm owed a little deference."

And this is where the roads diverge. "Cary?"

"Yes?"

"Don't come over."

"What? I want to talk to you."

"I'm going to bed. I'm tired. I don't want to see you tonight."

Dead silence, except for heavy breathing, came through the phone. Finally he ground out. "Fine. I'll see you tomorrow then."

With a supreme effort, Rachel chirped, "Thanks ever so much for understanding," before slamming the receiver down. She looked up to find George grinning at her.

"I perceive that you have an active social life."

"Tell me about it." She stood. "I hope you don't mind, but I really do think I'll head upstairs. You know where the kitchen is."

To her surprise he didn't take the bait. "If I might make a cup of coffee, that would be lovely."

Hiding her chagrin, Rachel made it for him, then trudged up to her room. The last thing she heard before turning out the light was a crash and a groan.

Chapter Six
The Detective

"The sheriff will see you now."

"Thanks, Ginger." Rachel followed the sergeant to Quimby's office.

Blanchard leaned against the wall, arms crossed. Toby beckoned Rachel inside. "Morning, Ms. Tinker. Thanks for coming in on a Sunday. No rest for the weary, eh?" He shot a mutinous look at Blanchard. Turning back to Rachel, he pulled out a rickety wooden chair. "Won't you sit down?" Rachel sat.

In a feeble stab at sincerity, Blanchard muttered, "First, we'd like to thank you for all your help, Ms. Tinker. If you hadn't recognized Mary we would never have managed to collar John Pinkney."

"You're welcome."

"Now, once Sheriff Quimby has finished up the paperwork, I'll be taking him back to Augusta to face robbery charges."

"Robbery charges! What about the murder?"

"Murder?" He raised his eyebrows. "First of all, the medical examiner has not yet determined that Mary Pinkney was murdered. Even so, I'm less concerned about her than about bringing her father to justice for grand larceny."

"What? But that's crazy, why—"

Toby fidgeted. "Rachel, the lieutenant here is

correct. There is some question about whether Mary's death was a suicide and not murder. That's why we've postponed the arraignment until Wednesday."

Rachel pursed her lips. "That's not how they reported it on the news."

Blanchard sniffed. "And your point?"

"Well...um."

The detective continued. "I think the most rational explanation is that the two of them came back here—whether to collect more of their loot or for some other reason—and Mary was overwhelmed with guilt."

"Doesn't that cast doubt on your theory that she was an accomplice?"

"Not at all. This was her first visit back to Penhallow—"

"That you know of."

"Forgive me, Ms. Tinker, but I've been working this case a long time. I would know if they came back before this. My point is, she comes home for the first time in ten years. Surely she would have mixed feelings—confusion, grief, guilt, homesickness. It would not be unreasonable that she decides to end it all."

Rachel had to acknowledge the soundness of the argument, although not aloud. Toby said something under his breath.

Blanchard steepled his fingers. "If you insist on further evidence, how about this? If John Pinkney had killed his daughter, you'd think he'd be long gone. You know where we picked him up?"

"No. Where?"

"At the scene of the crime. He was wandering around the fishing bridge. Why would he do that?"

"Maybe he was wiping out evidence."

Blanchard hesitated, then rallied. "Look, Ms. Tinker, I don't have the time or the inclination to debate this with you. This is police business. I intend to take my prisoner back to Augusta."

"Er, Lieutenant?" Toby's voice cracked on the question mark. "You may have overlooked one detail." Blanchard spun around and goggled at the sheriff, who gamely stood his ground. "Mr. Pinkney is in my custody and, while the cause of death for Mary Pinkney is still pending, I intend to charge him with the murder of Omar Masri. I'm afraid I must insist on my prerogative. I cannot allow you to remove my prisoner until that investigation is complete."

The goggle turned into bluster, transmuting gradually into fury. Finally, Blanchard pivoted on his heel and stormed out. "This isn't the last you'll hear of this, Sheriff."

At that moment, Cary Marx appeared in the doorway, blocking his exit. Blanchard shoved him aside. Cary stumbled, but with a supreme effort, turned it into a swagger as he entered Quimby's office. "I'm here," he announced.

Rachel so wanted to say, "So what?" but left it to Toby. The latter surprised her by raising a hand. "Thanks for dropping by, Mr. Marx. Your help and advice have been invaluable."

About to deliver herself of a satisfyingly snide remark, Rachel noted Toby's slightly upturned lips and shut her mouth. *He's smarter than I thought.*

Cary's shoulders relaxed. "Yes, well, any time, Quimby. So what's with the murder charges?"

"We're working on them. I need positive

affirmation from the coroner that Mary Pinkney was murdered before we can charge John Pinkney with that crime. Meanwhile, we're holding him on suspicion of the murder of Omar Masri."

"The Egyptian? Why?"

"Masri was killed by a bullet that passed through the back of his head. John and Mary Pinkney sat five seats behind him. At the time he was shot they were the only other passengers in the compartment. Short of some fancy sniping or accidental ricochets, no one else could have done it."

"Interesting." Cary headed to the door. "I want to interrogate him. Take me to him."

Toby injected just the right dose of regret into his words. "Oh golly, I wish I could let you, Mr. Marx. I'm sure with your experience in the Middle East you could tease out a motive just like that." He snapped his fingers. "But I'm afraid we have to wait a bit. Tell you what, you stay near a telephone, and I'll call you when the time is right."

For an instant, Rachel thought Cary would fly off the handle, but he merely shrugged and, with a resigned smirk, said, "Okay."

"That's wonderful. I can't tell you how much we appreciate your input." Toby showed him out, giving him a delicate push as they reached the threshold. He closed the door just as Cary turned around, his mouth open.

Flattery really does get you somewhere. Rachel grinned. "Well played, monsieur."

Toby cocked his head. "I don't know what you're talking about, Rachel."

"Very smooth." She stood. "Can I ask you a

question? Why don't you want Blanchard to take Pinkney?"

He tapped a pencil on the desk. "There's something that puzzles me about our good detective. He turns up after the Masri murder, claiming to have been sent by Augusta to investigate, but he only seems interested in John Pinkney and this purported bank theft. "

Rachel was intrigued. "You think he's not a policeman at all?"

"Oh no. I checked with Augusta. He's the real deal. And they did send him to look into the murder. He just doesn't seem to want to. Since he got here, he's only been asking questions about the couple."

"He may be one of those cops who just can't let a particular case go."

"Looks that way. I'm beginning to wonder if there's more to this than a simple robbery." He rose. "I've got to go check on the ME's progress. Thanks again for your help."

When Rachel reached her office, Griffin lounged on a bench by the front door. "Historical Society's hours are clearly marked on the plaque over there. That makes the second time you've been late. This lack of punctuality is a cause for concern."

"Nice to see you too." Rachel unlocked the door.

Griffin followed her in. "Aren't you supposed to be watching Baby Huey?"

"I thought you were scheduled for the wellness check this morning."

"I did go over for a minute. We had a pleasant chat about murder. He seemed hungry."

"That's because he finished off my last haunch of venison last night."

"Hey, he's a fine specimen of a Lebanese man. It's in their genes."

"Or maybe it's all those beans they eat."

"*Foule?*"

"I beg your pardon. It's a little early to be calling me names, don't you think?"

"Huh? Oh, I meant *foule mudammes*—that's the Arabic name for stewed fava beans. Delicious. If you like that sort of thing." He touched her hand lightly. "How did you make out last night? George didn't mash you, did he?"

"If you mean flirt, no, he was a perfect gentleman. He did, however, mash several fragile antiques passed down through generations of Tinkers. He's not particularly nimble."

"Ha, ha. Listen"—his hand went up to her cheek—"I…er…thought we could catch a bite of lunch?"

Where's that pitty-pat noise coming from? Oh. Me. "Okay."

"You can tell me all about what Toby had to say."

Pitty pat. "Where to?"

"How about we head up to Searsport—there's a new bistro that just opened up. Probably has lobster rolls. I know you like that touristy crap."

"You'd do well to cultivate a taste for it, Griffin. It would make you more popular in town." When his fit of giggles had subsided, she hitched her purse over her shoulder. "Let's roll."

"You're such a card, Rachel."

As they drove up Route One, she told Griffin what had transpired at the station. He whistled. "Curious. The plot thickens. Methinks the case is becoming rather convoluted."

"Maybe they're not the same case."

"'They?' You mean, the two deaths? Gotta be—too many coincidences. This Pinkney fellow is sitting right behind a guy who gets shot in the back of the head. The daughter comes to you for help and is found floating face down the next day. Pinkney's totally guilty, which lets Baby Huey off the hook."

"That's what I told him."

"Me too. And yet—he still feels vulnerable. Either that or he likes the comforts of your home."

"He'd better not get used to it."

Griffin leaned over and nuzzled her ear. "Agreed."

Pitty pat.

He sat back. "Okay, turn left here. Now right on Union Street. There it is—Salmonello's." He chuckled. "Not what you'd call a felicitous choice for a restaurant name."

They walked into what a native Mainer might envision a traditional Italian trattoria to be. That is, if a traditional trattoria consisted of a room filled with Formica tables and farm implements, a salad bar, and a wall of pinball machines. "Doesn't look like lobster roll is on the menu. Too bad," Griffin said jocularly.

The place was empty except for a group of women at the bar talking in loud voices. A girl of about sixteen with a long braid and braces skipped over to them. "Anywhere."

Rachel knew that Griffin was biting his tongue to keep the retort at bay and loved him for it. "Thanks."

They found a table as far away from the din as possible, which wasn't. Griffin ordered a carafe of their house wine—"Please, God, at least make it Italian"—and they perused the menu. Without looking up, Griffin asked, "So, how did George strike you?"

"He only hit the furniture."

"No, I mean, do you think he's telling the truth?"

"About what?"

"Really, Rachel, I'd hate to think you're being deliberately obtuse. His story of Masri's perfidy."

"I don't have any idea. You're the Middle East expert. Does it make sense?"

"There are lots of stories out there of fanatical academics pursuing the elusive tomb or artifact. It's not impossible. I have a call in to a friend at Harvard."

"Harvard? Oh, right, about George."

"And one to a friend at Cairo University about Masri."

The waitress plunked a basket of bread and a glass carafe on the table. Drawing two plastic wine glasses from her pockets, she inserted the bowls into the bases and set them down. And left. Griffin poured a smidgen of wine into his glass. With an affected simper, he rotated it, then sipped, holding the wine on the tip of his tongue before swallowing it. His eyes opened wide. "Whaddya know? It's excellent. How refreshing."

Rachel sipped hers. "You're right. Go figure."

He called the waitress over. "My dear child, can you tell me the name of this delightful beverage?"

"Huh? Oh, the wine? I'll go ask Dad." She shuffled back a minute later and read from the back of her hand. "Tig…Tin…Tignanello, he says." She read further. "Two thousand nine vintage. Dad gets it from his cousin in Tuscany. He says it's ready to drink now." She smiled perkily, the fluorescent light pinging off her braces.

"Tell Dad he's right. Thanks…"

"Sally. You want some more time?"

"No, we're ready. Rachel?"

"I'll have the tagliatelle al ragu Bolognese."

"The spaghetti in meat sauce. Gotcha. You?"

"How's the veal?"

"My brother just brought it in from Kenworthy Farm. You know, the place that raises all those weird breeds? Calf got its leg caught in a fence and they had to put her down. Butchered her yesterday. That's why it's on special."

With a slightly green face, Griffin handed her the menu. "I'll have that."

Rachel laughed. "For a tough guy you can be pretty squeamish."

He produced a rueful grin. "I suppose if I'm going to eat it I should be able to hear how it made its way to my plate."

Sally returned and slid tiny simulated wood bowls of wilted lettuce drenched in what looked like tomato soup under their noses. "Your salads."

Rachel took a gulp of wine to fortify herself and said with determination, "I'm going in."

Griffin watched her take a forkful, chew slowly, and push the bowl away. "I hope the wine and not the salad is a portent of things to come."

They took a moment to gaze into each other's eyes before waking up to the fact that they were gazing into each other's eyes. In the lull, while both desperately sought something to say, a raspy female voice rang out.

"I tell you, Jackie, that sheriff was way outta line. He as much as told me I'm a liar!" They both turned to see a woman of about fifty with a staggering cascade of pumpkin-colored hair. Her red lipstick was a little smeared, and her lashes, thick with mascara, blinked rapidly.

Rachel nudged Griffin. "I think that's Noreen Fowler, Stan Holiday's girlfriend," she whispered. "At least she looks like the woman Edna Mae Quimby described."

Confirming Rachel's guess, a tiny woman with a nose that could follow a cold scent twittered, "Well, Noreen, you gotta admit your story sounded pretty flimsy. I mean, there were witnesses who saw John on the train."

"Witnesses? A buncha tourists who were busy watching that moronic cowboy show. Probably didn't give him a second glance. John's not exactly a standout in the looks department. I love him for his personality."

"Personality? Or money?" The klatch broke out in snickers.

"Laugh all you want, Ellen. I'll swear he was with me that day."

Someone in the back of the pack cried out, "And what day was that, Noreen?"

She hesitated. "Last week. I forget the day exactly."

Jackie piped up. "It was last Saturday."

"Wait a minute." A tall, gaunt woman in jeans spoke slowly. "Wasn't Stan Holiday up here with you last Saturday? I thought I saw you two on the sidewalk by the cafe."

Noreen gulped down her beer. "That was earlier, Betty Jo. John came by later."

Betty Jo seemed to mull this over, then stubbed out her cigarette. "But I ran into Maude Jewett in the Penhallow co-op last week, and she told me Stan was supposed to drive the train." She wagged her chin. "That he missed it because he was with you, *Noreen*."

The voices rose and intertwined in a cacophony of anger and insults, and the women spilled out the door. Before Rachel could comment, Sally brought their meals. She laid a huge bowl mounded high with pasta redolent of tomato, pork, and basil before Rachel. The veal arrived as a paper-thin scallop, sautéed and simply dressed with lemon slices and capers. A half-moon of perfectly carved roasted vegetables snuggled next to it.

Rachel dug into the tagliatelle. Meanwhile Griffin cut off a small piece of veal. He touched it to his lips, then breathed, "Oh my God," before swallowing it. He cut another piece and placed it in Rachel's mouth. It melted on her tongue. After sharing hers, they fell to and finished off the dishes, Rachel fighting the urge to lick the plate.

"Ah."

"Ah."

"I wonder why the salads were so awful?"

"That's all you can say?" Griffin sat back and closed his eyes. "Sally probably made them."

After two fine cups of espresso, they drove back to Penhallow. When they reached the historic society building, Griffin jumped out of the car and unlocked his Jeep. "I'll see you later. I need a few hours to savor the memory of Sally's father's cooking."

Rachel stuck her head through the car window. "When are you going to take the full-figured archaeologist off my hands?"

Keys halfway to the ignition, he slapped his forehead with his free hand. "Oops—I forgot all about said esteemed colleague. Let me first go home and see if Harvard and Cairo have returned my calls."

"If his story proves out, does that exonerate him?"

"Probably makes him look more guilty. I mean, he's admitted to stalking Masri."

"Is plagiarism enough of a motive for murder?"

"As the man said, 'Where do I go to get my reputation back?' Masri stole his ideas and his text. What do you think?"

Rachel foresaw a long, dreary period of evening tête-à-têtes with someone other than Griffin. "If they charge Pinkney with the murder…"

"We're a ways from that."

"Griffin, I…"

He kissed her nose. "Me too. We'll find a way to get the little tyke out of the house. You could come visit me. You know, to bring a peace offering. Or soup."

"Right. If anyone saw me waltz up to your house on Bridge Street, they'd probably send out the cadaver sniffing dogs."

"Why?"

"Because they'd figure I'd killed you and was going back to clean the blood off the floor."

He kissed her again. "You probably will some day. I'm not an easy fellow to get along with." His eyes suddenly clouded. "Or so I've been told."

Rachel brushed a tendril away from his temple. "What happened to you?"

He fiddled with his keys, then turned on the engine without looking at her. "I'll let you know when I hear anything. Give my love to George."

Rachel stared after his car as it roared off. *Just what I need, another mystery.* Something told her she'd better solve this one—her happiness might depend on it.

****

It would take two more days to roust Hamdani from his nest. He evidently liked her cooking—*he probably likes anybody's cooking*—and, fortunately, had become slightly less accident-prone as he moved about the house. As for Rachel, she seriously considered taking Griffin up on his suggestion of a soup offering, but knew the good citizens of Penhallow—mainly Maude, if not the perennially inquisitive Edna Mae Quimby—would have palpitations if they thought she and Griffin were…well, anything but enemies. After that one wonderful night, she found herself thinking of him constantly, and not just with her head. *I hope these affairs resolve themselves soon. I want to get back to mooning over him.*

Griffin came by the house when he'd heard from his friends. He found Rachel and George in the kitchen, George, as usual, eating. "Okay, your story checks out. Seems most people in the field were aware of Masri's tendency to steal other people's opuses—or is it opi? Anyway, that's why he never rose above an assistant professor at Cairo. Rumor is they kept him on because his family is extremely wealthy and powerful."

George gave a delighted cluck. "Such marvelous news! It is a great joy to know one's reputation is secure. I am exceedingly grateful to you."

Griffin remained grave. "So I think it's time we went to the sheriff and you told your story."

The fat man drew back, eyes wide. "But as you say, that would make it even more likely he will consider me a suspect."

"They've already charged Pinkney with the crime.

Your information might help them to trace Masri's movements. There must have been contact between the two before the day of the murder."

"Er. I'm not sure I want them to do that."

"Do what?"

"Trace his movements. At least not yet."

Rachel eyed him. "Do you perhaps have something else to share, George?"

"No! Well, nothing of importance to the police. I…uh." He stopped, both chins quivering.

"We can't help you if you don't come clean."

He looked from one to the other and heaved a deep sigh. "All right, but you must promise to breathe not a single word to anyone about this. Swear you won't reveal my secret or go chasing after it?"

"We swear."

Rachel wondered if Griffin were maybe a little too quick to give his word, but said nothing.

"All right." After a hopeful flick at his empty plate was met with a blank stare, he went into the living room. Draping his gargantuan body across the couch, he left Rachel the massage chair and Griffin to stand. When they were settled, he began. "I told you Masri was searching for the queen of Sheba's tomb. Well, he didn't actually *glean* a clue from my research about the queen's gravesite. It was the central thesis of my paper. In the course of my research at the Egyptian Museum I came across a…a reference."

"A reference? To what?"

George's eyelids lowered, obscuring the sudden furtive look in his black eyes. "That's not important. At any rate, it mentioned the existence of a map that would lead to her burial site."

"A map! What kind of map?"

"I don't know. That's all I could discover." He closed his lips tightly. Rachel had the impression he was choosing his words very carefully.

What is he hiding?

He continued. "I thought my research had reached a dead end and had returned to Paris, but Masri—with the aid of my work—managed to find the...item to which the note referred. It led him first to Ethiopia and then to Europe. I decided to follow him, hoping to get a hint as to what he was looking for."

Griffin mused, "You said he was checking out antique shops in Vienna and Paris. He must have asked for something specific. Did you question the shopkeepers?"

"In Paris, yes. Most of them described him as very evasive. First, he would ask whether they had any Middle Eastern artifacts, then he would poke around the store, and soon after, he would leave without further comment. Unfortunately, I lost track of him in Vienna."

Rachel sat up. "Could he have been looking for the actual map?"

"Or for whoever knew the location of the map." Griffin pursed his lips. "Why else would he end up in Maine? It's not exactly a prime spot for antiquities."

"Indeed."

Griffin gazed at him speculatively. "That's why you don't want to leave, isn't it? And why you don't want to be detained by the police. You think there's a clue somewhere here, and you want to find it."

"Yes. You are correct, at least in part, Tate. My theory is that he was not searching for the map at all, but for a person—someone who knew where it is."

"Or could help him."

Hamdani pointed a stout finger. "You."

The accused jerked upright. "Me?"

"He called you, did he not?"

"Yes, but he didn't ask for help. He just inquired about my collections. Of which I have none."

"Still, it's all very odd." Rachel stood up and said firmly, "George, much as I love your company, you're eating me out of house and home. If you're going to stay in town, I think it's time you found a hotel."

The big man cast a pleading eye in Griffin's direction, but the latter shook his head. "No way."

A wan smile plastered on his face, George sighed. "All right. I shall go and pack my portmanteaux." He lumbered up the stairs. They listened fondly to the thuds and clatters coming from his room. Rachel called up. "Do you want me to make a reservation? The Comfort Inn is very nice."

"Do they have a restaurant?"

I might actually miss the old guy. "Yes."

"Very well then."

Rachel made the call, and Griffin carried the trunks downstairs. As he lugged them out to his car, he gave Rachel a kiss. "Call you later."

Rachel had finished a refreshingly quiet meal of crackers and peanut butter when the telephone rang. "Uh, Rachel?"

"Hey, Griffin. That was quick." Her heart warmed at his voice. *I wonder if it's not too late for him to come back?*

"I'm home. Rachel? I found something interesting in my mailbox. It must have been pushed way to the back since it was postmarked ten days ago."

A gnarly thumb poked at her chest. "What is it?"

"A letter. From Omar Masri."

Chapter Seven
The Letter

"He must have sent it the day he died."

"Or the day before. You know how slow Murray is."

The old mailman happened to be very dear to Rachel, but she didn't have time to take up the cudgel for him. "What does it say?"

Griffin didn't immediately reply. He finally mumbled, "I think it's better if you look at it. Is it too late for me to come over?"

"I guess not." *Oh God, why am I squeaking?*

"Okay." She heard a click.

The sun had descended behind the mountain when Griffin pulled into the carport. He walked up the back steps to find Rachel on the deck, drink in hand. "Did you make one for me?"

"No. What would you like?" She continued to gaze out at Penobscot Bay. It probably looked like indifference to Griffin, but it was really an attempt to veil the euphoric expression on her face, not to mention the vein that throbbed on the right side of her neck.

He gave his customary huff, then said, "I'll just go get a beer then, shall I?"

"Make yourself at home."

He huffed again and went inside, reappearing a minute later with a bottle in one hand and an envelope in the other. "Come inside where the light's better."

Rachel obliged.

He pulled a sheet of paper from the envelope, unfolded it, and laid it on the dining table. "All right, if you'll kindly focus your attention, perhaps you can make out this execrable writing."

Rachel took a look, then bent closer. "I can tell English is not his native language. Let's see...It says, 'Dear Monsieur Tate...'"

"Yeah, I got that far." Griffin's tone bordered on derisive.

"Okay, smarty pants, what's that word there?" She pointed.

" 'Need.' "

"Oh." She bent down again. " 'I need your ass...' "

" 'Assistance.' Unless you were talking to me?"

"Stop it, Griffin." She kept reading. " 'Assistance in a small matter of great importance.' "

"Rather poetic."

"*Shh.* 'I have found the key to an ancient mystery, the location of the...the—' "

" 'Queen of Sheba's tomb.' "

"Cool. So George is right."

Griffin pulled the paper toward him, holding a finger under each word as he read. "It's a bit clearer here. He says, 'This key could change the entire theory of the direction of the march of civilization, much like your seminal work on the migration of recipes across the Middle East—a book which I read with enormous interest.' "

A snuffle came from Rachel's vicinity. Griffin ignored the interruption. " 'Professor, you are held in very high regard in the academic community—' " He raised his voice to drown out the second, more audible snuffle. " 'On the other hand, my reputation has endured malicious attacks by jealous rivals—' "

"Boy, you can say that again."

" '…my reputation has endured malicious attacks by jealous rivals. If I retrieve the object, will you do me the honor of authenticating it? Together we can bring it not just to the attention of the academic world, but of the cattle!' Here he's written four exclamation points."

" 'Cattle?' "

Griffin's brow furrowed. "I think he's literally translating the Arabic term for the masses—in other words, the people. He wants to publicize the map to the world. But why me? Why come to me?"

"I'm not sure we'll ever know."

Griffin continued to speculate. "Did he come here specifically to meet me? Or did I just happen to be situated conveniently on his trail of clues?"

Rachel sipped her drink. "Remember, George thought he might have been looking for a person rather than the artifact itself. He could be right, that that person was you."

"Possibly."

"He called you, didn't he?"

"Yes, but he didn't mention any of this. He only asked about artifacts."

"Maybe he was feeling you out—trying to get a sense of whether you could be trusted or not."

"Trusted?"

"With his secret. Or whether you were just another crackpot academic who would steal someone else's discoveries without a qualm."

"Like him."

"Like him." She put the glass down. "For once, maybe your irascibility helped. When you shot him down, he figured you weren't interested in horning in. That's when he wrote the letter." She raised her eyes to the ceiling. "That bit about your 'seminal work' sounds more like opportunistic sycophancy than true admiration."

"My, aren't we free with the multisyllabic words tonight? Mean ones at that."

"Whatever."

Griffin rubbed his forehead. "Which still begs the question, why me? Why come here to Maine?"

"You were in Cairo giving a lecture last February. He could have heard of you, or gone to the lecture, and realized that your expertise could be an asset to him. Then, when he came to Maine and heard you were here in Penhallow…"

"Or he came to Maine *because* I'm here."

"No…" Rachel shook her head. "Read the letter. He came for the object of his search. He wanted you to authenticate it."

He took the paper back and read. "He says he's already found the key." He looked up. "It could have been anywhere along his route."

"Well, *something* brought him to Penhallow. My guess is a clue—or maybe even the map itself—is here. We need to retrace his steps and find it."

"Why us?"

"Because"—she picked up the letter—"we want to 'change the theory of the direction of the march of civilization.' Plus I want to get it before George does."

"You despicable little creature, you. I seem to recall we swore not to jump his claim."

"Oh, we'll share it with him, but don't you relish the adventure?" She looked at him from under her eyelashes.

He put the beer down, circled the table, and drew her up into his arms. "Something tells me every day is an adventure with you."

"I'll take that as a romantic gesture."

"You ain't seen nothin' yet."

****

"Wake up, sleepyhead."

Rachel sat up and banged her head on Griffin's chin. "Ouch."

"Sheesh. Your reflexes are on autopilot, aren't they?"

"Well, of course they are—that's why they call them reflexes, dummy. Are you okay?"

Griffin touched the affected area gingerly. "I suppose. Look, it's almost eleven o'clock. Channel 8 just announced that John Pinkney will be arraigned today. I think we should get down there."

"Why?"

"To tell Toby about the letter. Plus, I want to see how they plan to successfully charge Pinkney for the murder of someone he's never met."

"If you know the means and opportunity, you don't necessarily need motive—at least not at this stage."

"You've been watching Perry Mason again, haven't you?"

Rachel rolled out of bed. Only then did she discover that she was naked. She looked back at the rumpled sheets, the blanket on the floor, and the pillows distributed evenly over the entire room. "What did we do last night?"

"You don't remember? You were an animal."

The blush raced across her cheeks. "Really?" It came out in a very small voice.

Griffin reached out and flicked her nipple. "A warm, cuddly, pussycat kind of animal. Would you like to see the claw marks?"

She ran into the bathroom and slammed the door. Putting the lid down on the toilet, she sat down to review her state of mind. Crowding out any sort of practical question was how much she wanted another round of lovemaking. *Right now.* Her nipples tingled at the prospect. She stood up and stared at herself in the mirror. *Get hold of yourself, Rachel.* Two deep breaths later, she felt calmer. Until she stepped into the shower and the warm water hit her, reminding her of Griffin's fingers heating her body to heights of passion she'd only read about in books.

Somehow she managed to get through the shower and came downstairs to find a sumptuous breakfast laid out. Griffin sat reading a newspaper, coffee mug at his elbow. He looked up. "What? You told me to make myself at home."

She surveyed the eggs, sausage, and toast, and tucked a napkin under her chin. "Well, this once. I'm not used to having someone underfoot."

"That's why I had George soften you up. I take up a lot less room."

"True. I hope you're a little more graceful as well."

He stood and did a little pirouette. "Now hurry up."

An hour later, they parked in front of the police station. Griffin let out an oath. "We forgot George."

"I suppose it would be helpful to have him tell his story at the same time you show Toby the letter."

"Tell you what. I'll head over to his hotel and roust him out. You go in and stall Toby. Maybe he can put off the hearing."

He roared off and Rachel entered the building. She knocked on the sheriff's door and stuck her head in.

"Not now, Rachel. I've got to get this paperwork done before the hearing."

"But Toby, I have news."

He straightened. "To do with the murder?"

"Yes."

"Well?"

"I…uh…can't tell you yet. I'm waiting for Griffin. He has the letter. And George has a story to tell you."

"George?"

"George Hamdani. He was on the train that day. He's an archaeologist. Like the deceased."

Toby made a note, then looked up again. "Letter?"

"Griffin found a letter that Omar Masri mailed to him before his death. Masri was not just an idle tourist, Toby. He came to Penhallow with a purpose."

"And you think this purpose relates somehow to his murder?"

Toby is so much more perceptive than we ever give him credit for. "The coincidence is just too great."

Toby pushed his glasses up onto his forehead. "Are you saying you know why John Pinkney murdered Masri?"

"No! I mean…" Suddenly all the little threads to the plot canvas went spiraling off in all directions. Nothing made much sense. *If it wasn't Pinkney, then it has to be George.* "I don't know." *Really lame, Rachel.* "We…uh…think maybe there's someone else out there with a motive, that's all." *Sorry, George.*

Toby stood. "Well, I can't keep holding Pinkney on suspicion. If you've got concrete evidence of another person's guilt, I'll let him go. Otherwise, I'm moving ahead—he's still the only person who could have shot Masri."

"What about Mary? Couldn't she have shot him?"

The sheriff snapped his head up. "What?"

Rachel felt a surge of relief. "Mary was in the train car next to her father. She could just as easily have shot Masri. Maybe that's what she wanted to confess."

He sat back. "That wouldn't explain why she gave you the purse. Plus, in light of her recent demise, I'm guessing she was more victim than perpetrator."

Worth a try. Again, sorry George. She tried a different tack. "Did you find the gun?"

He shook his head. "Not yet."

"Well, how can you assume Pinkney shot someone when there's no evidence of a connection and no gun?"

Toby was spared an answer by the arrival of Griffin and George. Griffin pushed past the big Lebanese and threw Masri's letter down on Toby's desk. "What do you think of that?"

Rachel had a feeling that Toby would not be inclined to stop everything and read, so she pulled Griffin aside. "Let's let George tell his story first, shall we? For the timeline."

Griffin waggled his eyebrows at her and opened his mouth, but shut it again. "All right."

Toby folded his arms. "I'm listening."

So Hamdani told his story to an increasingly bemused sheriff, leaving out the part where he meant to find the artifact himself. He also downplayed rather successfully the importance of the find, making it sound more like an academic parlor game than a deadly contest of murder and obsession. Unfortunately, all his hard work came to naught when Griffin read Masri's letter out loud, emphasizing the flowery phrases about the march of civilization, as well as the reference to malicious rivals. When they were done, Toby tapped his pen on the desk. "Thanks for the information. Now if you'll excuse me, the hearing's about to start."

"What? You mean, you're going ahead with it?"

"Of course. Nothing you told me has changed my mind about Pinkney. You haven't given me a motive—unless it could be ascribed to you." He regarded Hamdani. "You say you were in the open carriage looking forward into the first car where Masri sat. At that point most of the other passengers were outside as well. I think at least someone would have noticed you raising a gun and shooting through the window. We would also have found shards of glass. Which we didn't." His lips turned up. "So for now, well, my money's on Pinkney."

Rachel had a flash of intuition. "You found no shards of glass anywhere? Not even outside?"

"No." He walked out the door before anyone could catch him.

They followed him down to the courthouse. A policeman let him in the back door, leaving the trio to find their way to the main entrance. There, a mass of people milled around, whispering excitedly. When the doors opened, the crowd poured through. George, Rachel, and Griffin were carried along with it and managed to slip out of the stream and find a space on the back wall. Griffin, who towered over the audience, relayed what was happening. "Two cops just brought

Pinkney in. He sure doesn't look like a killer. What an innocuous looking bugger."

Rachel remembered Mary's terror and Pinkney's furious face that day at the historical society and begged to differ.

"Okay, the judge has arrived. He's reading some papers. He's beckoning to Toby. Toby's speaking—"

"What's he saying?"

"Shush, I can't hear. He must be explaining the charges to the judge."

"What—" Rachel's question was lost as someone jostled her elbow.

A high nasal voice screeched, "Lemme through. Lemme through. I wanna talk to the judge!" Rachel pressed into Griffin's side to let the woman pass, and her heart skipped a beat. *The woman at Salmonello's. Noreen.* "Griffin! Did you see who that was?"

He looked down his nose. "Isn't she the harridan who kept interfering with my enjoyment of that magnificent meal the other day? Noreen something."

"Noreen Fowler. Stan's girlfriend."

She watched the orange beehive hairdo bob along toward the front. Griffin continued his commentary. "Pinkney just blanched. Toby's turned to Noreen. Now the judge is asking her a question. She's answering."

"Griffin!"

"I can't help it. You keep poking me and yammering in my ear. Wait. The judge is about to make a pronouncement."

A deep bass voice rang out. "Are you saying, ma'am, that John Pinkney could not have committed the murder because he was with you?"

"Yes."

121

Griffin whispered, "The bailiff just nudged her."

The woman raised her voice. "Yes, Your Honor."

"And do you have any proof?"

"First, I wanna ask a question."

"Go ahead."

"A family member can't be forced to testify against another family member, right?"

"Only very close members. A husband and wife are usually not required to testify against each other."

Her reedy voice shrieked in glee. "There you are. Since I'm his wife, and I say he was with me, you gotta believe me, right?"

An expectant silence filled the room.

After a lengthy pause, the judge said quietly, "Sheriff Quimby, I think perhaps your case is not as cut and dried as advertised. I have no choice but to release Mr. Pinkney on bond pending further investigation. Bail is set at..."

"Your Honor!"

"Yes, Sheriff?" The judge held the gavel up.

"I would submit that the defendant is a flight risk. We are still investigating the second death as well—that of his daughter Mary Pinkney."

"I'm aware of that. That is why I'm setting his bail at one hundred thousand dollars." He banged the gavel and went out through a curtain behind his desk. Toby gestured to two policemen who led Pinkney out a side door.

As the spectators filed out, Rachel watched Noreen. She stood stock still in the rapidly emptying courtroom. Then, with a face that would frighten a Gorgon, she chugged down the aisle and outside. Another woman stood up, pushed her way into the aisle, and followed her out. Her blonde hair and large nose struck Rachel as vaguely familiar. *She looks a lot like Noreen. Or is it someone else...*

Griffin pinched Rachel. "I'm guessing the wicked witch Noreen doesn't have that kind of cash on her."

"What do you suppose she expected to happen?"

"I don't know, but this case—"

"Or cases."

"—is deteriorating into a Shakespearian comedy plot. I suggest brain food."

"You mean red meat? Oh goody."

George perked up. "My treat!"

Nobody argued with him.

They settled in a booth at Darwin's Pub and ordered. George, to the slack-jawed surprise of his companions, chose a large salad, dressing on the side. Noting their reaction, he patted his stomach. "I'm reducing."

Rachel clucked encouragingly, and Griffin pressed his lips together in a tight line.

When the waitress had gone, George leaned over the table, his beefy elbows taking up most of the surface. "So, who was the female Medusa in the courtroom?"

"Don't know much about her. I'd only seen her once before." Griffin sipped his beer.

Rachel put in, "She lives in Searsport. Moved there about three years ago. Lots of gossip swirling around her. Mainly about men."

Griffin closed his eyes. "She was at the center of that swarm of female insects at Salmonello's, wasn't she? As I recall, they were talking about Pinkney then. She was claiming he'd been with her 'that day.' "

"Meaning the day of the murder. That's what she swore to the judge too."

"So?"

"So, I was on duty at the ticket office that morning, and Stan called me to say he'd been held up in Searsport and couldn't make it down to drive the train. We all assumed he was with Noreen since he'd been bragging about it."

"Stan Holiday, the train engineer?"

"Yes."

Their meals came. George eyed Rachel's cheeseburger with envy but said nothing. She tried to refrain from smacking her lips as she ate, but Griffin had no such compunction. When he'd swallowed a large bite, he wiped his mouth and patted his stomach. "This burger's almost as good as the ones at Ripley's. Yum."

George took a deep breath and spoke to the wall over Griffin's shoulder. "The woman's story sounded pretty far-fetched, I thought."

"What! You don't believe a buxom, butt-wagging bimbo could be married to that pallid weasel? Agreed." Griffin wiped a speck of ketchup off Rachel's chin with a napkin.

She pushed his hand away. "It's easy enough to find out. Toby just has to demand to see a marriage certificate." She finished her burger, to George's obvious disappointment. Dunking a French fry in the juices, she raised it to her lips and sniffed appreciatively. The poor man, his eyes moist, sighed and pushed his salad around on the plate.

"Either way, she must have a reason for her claim. Why else would she come out of the woodwork like that?"

Rachel picked up another French fry. "Gotta be money."

Griffin signaled the waitress. "This isn't getting us anywhere. We might as well wait like everyone else for the police to finish their business. Meantime"—he gave Rachel a sidelong glance—"we have to do that thing this afternoon."

"That 'thing'?"

"Yes," he said with emphasis. "That *thing.*"

"Oh, *that* thing. George, I hope you'll excuse us."

He fluttered his fingers at them. "I said I'd treat you two. Run along. I'll just finish up." As they walked out, Rachel looked back to see him dragging the other plates over to his side of the booth.

When they reached the sidewalk, she stopped short. "So what is this 'thing' we have to do?"

"You wanted an adventure, didn't you?"

"Ye-ess."

"Well, the first thing you do before heading out on an adventure is prepare—that means research."

"Hey!"

"Come on." Griffin took her hand and towed her to his car. They drove up Main Street, taking a left on Lincolnville Avenue. Crossing Route One, they turned into the parking lot of the University of Maine's Hutchinson Center.

Rachel did not hide her bewilderment. "Why are we here?"

"The University of Maine happens to own one of the more extensive collections of works on the queen of Sheba. It even has Omar Masri's article."

"The one he stole from George?"

"The very one. I know the librarian, who has kindly given me permission to search the special collections."

Rachel tittered. "Did you have to flirt with her?"

Griffin frowned. "For your information, I dated Patricia when I first arrived in Penhallow. We are quite fond of each other."

Shocked by the fearsome jealousy that welled up in her, Rachel was even more astonished that another female found the big lug attractive. "Women can be so strange."

He squinted at her. "What's that supposed to mean?"

"Well, you're not exactly the Sir Walter Raleigh type."

A spasm of pain crossed his face. "No, not anymore."

Leaving Rachel to stew over the remark, he went through the double doors of the library. When she reached him, he was talking to a tall, elegant woman who knew how to wear a scarf both casually and artfully—a skill Rachel had never mastered. Griffin held out a hand. "Come on, Patricia has reserved a room for us."

She stifled the smart remark and followed them. They entered a glass-walled cubicle overlooking a belt of pine trees. Trays of papers and documents were spread out on a large work table.

Patricia smiled and said, "I'll leave you two to it. Enjoy."

Griffin sat down. "Okay, you take that tray, and I'll take this one."

For the next three hours, Rachel sifted through

articles, letters, and pictures about the queen of Sheba. Two things became clear. First, no one really knew where she came from, and second, and more important, there was no real proof she existed at all. "So, we don't even have a location for the *country* of Sheba, much less whether it had a queen."

"We've got the Bible story of Solomon and the queen of Sheba."

"Could be apocryphal. Or a metaphor or something. I don't think Solomon actually tried to cut that baby in half either."

Griffin picked up a heavy tome. "We've also got the Kebra Nagast—the Book of Kings. The whole Ethiopian national myth is based on Solomon and Makeda's affair."

"That's the book that asserts the queen had a son by Solomon, right? And that this son became the first ruler of Ethiopia, one Menelik the First?"

"Right."

"And stole the Ark of the Covenant and brought it back to Ethiopia."

"Right."

"And have they ever shown the Ark to anyone?" She waved a sheaf of papers at Griffin. "These articles make it clear that while they insist they have it, they've never made it available for viewing. Not only that, but there's not even documentary evidence of Menelik himself."

"Look," Griffin said impatiently, "we know that most origin myths have some basis in fact. Solomon and the queen crop up in legends all over the Middle East. Stands to reason there's something there. Certainly Omar Masri thought so."

"George says Masri found a clue in the Cairo Museum. I wonder what it was?"

Griffin pushed his seat back and stood up. "Next stop?"

Rachel yawned. "Not today. I'm going home."

"Fine. So that was just a lot of hot air about adventures?"

She smiled. "I'm at the age where I like to space them out."

He drove her back to Amity Landing and left her checking her mailbox. As she crossed the street, head down, she heard the squeal of brakes and a Porsche skidded to a stop in the middle of the road about ten feet from her. "There you are!"

Oh shit. "Hi, Cary."

"Don't hi, Cary me, Rachel. I've been looking for you everywhere. Did you hear what happened at the arraignment?"

"I was there."

"You were? I didn't see you. Of course, I was sitting in the front pew." He made it sound like third row center at the opera. "So you heard Noreen Fowler announce she was the murderer's wife."

"Yes."

He pulled over, turned the engine off, and got out.

"What are you doing?"

"I'm coming in with you."

"Why?"

He didn't appear to notice the asperity in her voice. "Number one, I have some news for you. And two, I haven't seen you in ages." His hand went out to her face, but she ducked in time and stuck the key in the door.

If it weren't for that intriguing word "news," she would have sent him packing. As it was, she figured she could get away with a beer and a bit of listening and then bundle him on home. "All right, you can come in for a minute. I've had a very long day and I'm tired." She took a quick look around the house for any Griffin spoor and let him in. He headed immediately for the kitchen.

"How come there are two glasses on the table?"

She snatched them from him and put them in the dishwasher. "One for juice, one for water."

"Two plates?"

"Look, I've been busy, and I haven't had a chance to put all my dirty dishes away, okay? Now, do you want a beer?"

He curled his lip. "Beer? No, I think not. Did you finish that 2007 Carillon Puligny Montrachet I bought you?"

Cary mistakenly believed he was initiating Rachel into the elite world of fine wines. She let him continue in ignorance as long as he kept her in Meursaults and Pomerols. "I believe so." She brought out the bottle and poured him a glass. After some thought, she filled a tumbler with bourbon.

They went out on the deck. "So what's your news?"

"First, where have you been?"

She could honestly say, "I've been studying at the Hutchinson Center."

"What, pottery? Needlepoint?"

She would have laughed except he seemed to be serious. "Needlepoint? Um, sure. That, and some research into the Penhallow and Moosehead Railroad for the historical society."

"Oh." He waved her activities off as so much flotsam. "So, I talked to Quimby after the hearing. He's really overwhelmed with these crimes. That detective from Augusta is busting his chops too—what's his name?"

"Blanchard."

"Don't know what the guy's problem is—he thinks us rubes can't handle a simple murder case." He took a sip of wine, rolled it around on his tongue, and swallowed slowly. "He claims he's only interested in Pinkney's connection to some old robbery, but I'll bet he's hoping to horn in on the glory after we solve the case. What an ass." He took another sip. "Ah, now that's a good wine. Buttery, fleshy, with slight notes of flint and apple. Have some."

She held up her whiskey. "Don't want to confuse my palate."

"What? Oh." He finished his glass and poured some more. "I was commiserating with poor old Tobias, and I thought to myself, 'I can help him.' So I decided to look into the woman's past."

"And he *let* you?" *Toby must be losing his touch.*

"When he hears what I've found out, he'll thank me, don't you worry."

"I see."

"Look, do you want to know or not?"

"Yes, tell me." She refreshed her drink and sat down.

"So the dame—Noreen Fowler—moved to Searsport three years ago."

"We all know that."

"Yeah, well, do you know where she moved

from?" He paused for effect. "Belize. She comes from Belize, where, according to Detective Blanchard, Pinkney and his daughter have been for ten years."

"Huh."

"Not only that—but she's not lying. She and Pinkney were married down there. Not sure if that makes it legal here, but…" He trailed off.

"It doesn't really matter, does it? The point in question is whether she's lying about his being with her the day of the murder."

"Well, he can't have been. Everyone saw him on the train. You took his ticket."

"So what would be her purpose in lying?"

Cary brooded. "It's gotta be money. It's always about money."

To you. Although she had to admit, she couldn't come up with a better motive. "Maybe she thinks she'll inherit his fortune."

"What fortune? Wait, you may be on to something. This robbery Blanchard keeps harping on. Maybe she was in on it and wants to spring him so they can retrieve the loot."

"There can't be much left after ten years."

"Maybe he didn't take it all with him to Belize. Maybe he hid it somewhere." He waved his arms expansively. "Maybe he hid some here. That would explain why they all turned up in Penhallow."

"But she's been here for more than three years. Why didn't they come back together?"

"Don't know yet. That's next on the agenda." He stood up. "I gotta go. Good thing I'm on vacation. I can really sink my teeth into this."

Rachel said a little prayer for Toby. She asked

brightly, "So soon?"

He hesitated, and she almost regretted her words. "Yeah, murders to solve. Don't know what this dinky town would do without me."

She watched him drive off. The telephone rang. "Hello?"

"Hello? Miss Tinker? This is Noreen Fowler."

Chapter Eight
The Lie

Should I pretend I don't know her? "Noreen Fowler?"

She sounded impatient—or was it scared? "Yeah. I was the one who interrupted John's hearing. You were there—I saw you in the back."

"Oh, yes. You said he was with you the day of Mr. Masri's murder." *Let's see how she reacts to that statement.*

"Right. Look, can I come over? I need your help."

Rachel checked her watch. "I'm sorry. I have…things to do this evening. How about tomorrow morning? Where are you?"

"Searsport. And you're in Amity Landing. I have your address. I'll be there about eight."

"You can come at nine."

Noreen paused. "Okay. Ten it is. And…and thank you."

Rachel had the impression those two little words rarely slipped out of the woman's mouth. She clicked the phone off and sat, chin in hand, until the unaccustomed quiet began to bother her. For a while there, her house had been crawling with bodies. Now she felt at loose ends. After a supper of leftovers, she tried to watch television, tried to read her mail, gazed at the stars a while, walked down to the dock and back, and finally went to bed.

The next morning she was up at dawn, did the three-mile walk she'd been missing, and had showered and eaten by the time Noreen pulled up across the street from her house in a battered sedan. Rust spots covered most of the lower half and the front bumper sagged. Rachel started to lead her to the deck, but the woman held back and uttered in a low voice, "Let's go inside."

"Okay."

Once in the living room, Noreen pulled the curtains closed, then sat down in a corner. "You're probably wondering why I called you."

"Uh huh."

"I know you were the one who fingered—I mean identified—John to the police."

Rachel made a surreptitious reconnaissance of potential escape routes. "Lieutenant Blanchard of the state police asked if I'd seen a couple in a photo, yes. I believe he made the photo public at the press conference. Anyone could have pointed him out."

"Sure, but you were the one who blabbed to the sheriff when you saw Mary and John on the street."

Rachel studied her. *I wonder if she knows about the purse.* "Forgive me, but where did you get this information?"

"A man named Cary Marx came by my house in Searsport asking all kinds of questions after the hearing. He told me about you."

He's even more pea-brained than I thought. "I'm sorry if I upset you. I had no idea Mr. Pinkney had…another wife. In fact, I had no idea who he was or why the detective asked about him. If I'd known it would lead to murder…"

Noreen froze. "Hey, what gives you the right…Oh, you mean to him being *accused* of murder. As a matter of fact, that's why I came over. I wanted to thank you for helping nab him."

"Pardon me?"

Noreen scratched her nose, leaving a red welt where her long scarlet fingernail bit into the soft flesh. "You got anything to drink?"

Rachel checked the mantel clock. *Ten in the morning?* "Coffee?"

"Yeah, okay."

When she had accepted the cup, poured milk and three tablespoons of sugar into it, and stirred, she said, "I'd better back up a bit. I met John Pinkney in Belize four years ago. We hit it off and got married real quick." She leered at Rachel. "His daughter wasn't too happy about it, but John didn't pay her no mind. Mary was this vapid little thing—no balls, you know? Me, Doc says I've got an extra shot of testosterone. Makes me tough. Mary, she never stood up to John. That is, except when it came to me." Noreen appeared to consider this flattering.

She sipped her coffee. "Life was great in Belize. We hung out on the beach, drank a ton of mai tais, and partied every night. John seemed to have lots of moolah and didn't mind spending it. The only—what's that expression?—fly in the juice?"

"Fly in the ointment."

"Oh, yeah. I'm no good at those whatyacallits—idioms. Anyway, everything was swell except that he and Mary had so many fights over me they finally stopped speaking to each other. Okay by me—meant I had more time with John since the little twit sat in the house all day doin' I dunno what. Then one day I walks into my bedroom and there's John goin' through my handbag. He said he was looking for a tissue, but later I noticed a check was missing from my checkbook." At this point Noreen's eyes shifted away from Rachel. Even though the words tripped smoothly off the woman's tongue, her hostess had the distinct impression that the lying had begun.

"So I started to keep tabs on my account, and sure enough, I found all kinds of suspicious deductions."

"Did you confront him?"

"Er, yeah. Yeah, I did. He threatened me, Miss Tinker. Scared the bloody hell outta me. So I skipped."

"And you came up to Penhallow?"

Here her eyes definitely went shifty. "I had no other place to go. John had told me he came from Maine, from this little town on the coast. I didn't want to meet any of his people, so I found an apartment in Searsport."

Go ahead and ask. "And you got married again?"

"Married? Um, well, sort of."

"So the gossip isn't true?"

"Look, I didn't come here to be grilled. I mean, how could I get married if I was already married?"

Answer a question with a question. She's good. "No, of course not. I just wanted to confirm the rumors were false. People can be so mean, can't they?"

That seemed to pacify her. "Damn right. Old hags in the village immediately lit into me—like they don't have no skeletons in their own closets." She sniggered. "In fact, I found a skeleton from John's closet right here in Penhallow."

"Who? Or what?"

"Hannah Sundstrom." She growled, "John din't tell me about Hannah. The fucking bastard."

Rachel didn't know what to say. This bunch seemed inclined to serial bigamy, which evidently was perfectly acceptable when Noreen practiced it, but not when one of her husbands did.

Her visitor continued to complain. "Here she is, all nice and cozy, with her own shop an' a nice house. And John leaves me without a nickel."

Should I point out that Noreen, in fact, left him? Nah. "Did you…er…talk to her?"

"Me? No. Anyway, she was just getting sick when I got here. She died a month or so ago."

"Yes, I know." *Poor Hannah. She was such a pleasant, temperate woman. I wonder if she had any sense of the depraved muck her family wallowed in?*

"Well, after she died I figured old John would show up—maybe try to get his hands on her stuff. So I hung around. Sure enough, up he pops right before the funeral. I kept an eye on him—if he tried to get his hands on her stuff, I was ready to scream bloody hell."

"To the police?"

"What? Why? No, I was going to drag my share out of him. No way I'd let him get it all."

"You mean, you wanted the money back that he stole from you."

She blinked twice. "Um, yeah, that's it. Yeah."

Hoo sister, you're a live one. "What made you go to the hearing then?"

"You got more coffee?" When Rachel had refilled her cup she said, "It was the murders." Noreen shivered. "I don't want him going after me."

"But then why did you give him an alibi?"

"Are you kidding? Did you believe me?"

Huh? "Well…no."

Noreen nodded with satisfaction. "Of course not—it was a loony explanation. Everyone knew I'd been with Stan Holiday. Plus, all those passengers on the train saw John."

"I don't get it."

"See, my little scene just made him look *more* guilty. So the judge posts a huge bail, and they keep him in custody. And I'm safe."

Rachel expected it would take her some little while to digest all this. *Better move the conversation along.* "That's all quite clever, but what do you want from me?"

"You? I want you to get that Marx guy off my back. I need some space to…I mean, I just want to live my life in peace and quiet." She started to whine. "Here I am, an innocent victim of that creep John Pinkney, and Marx keeps insinuating that I'm after something. You're his girlfriend. Pretend you're jealous of me or something. Tell him to back off."

Rachel couldn't decide which element of this incredible speech to attack first. "I'm not his girlfriend."

Noreen stared at her. "That's not what he says." Her eyes took on a cunning look. "If you're not an item, maybe that's just a line he's using to rope me in. Him and that fancy Porsche of his…" She petered out, her expression both preoccupied and predatory. She put the cup down, stood up, and shook herself.

"Well, thanks ever so for the coffee. I'll see myself out."

"Don't you want me to talk to Mr. Marx?"

"Sure, sure. No, wait—I'll talk to him myself. Yeah, well, bye." And she was off, accelerating faster than Cary's Porsche.

****

After an hour's fruitless puttering around the house in case Griffin called, Rachel drove to town. She tried to get some work done at the office, but her mind was filled with theories. Too many threads, too many stories—did they intersect? Or did a spider's web of intrigue decide to descend on little Penhallow because of some freak of fate? *El Niño*? She finally gave up and went home to put her feet up. After staring at the ceiling for a good half an hour, she grabbed a pad of paper and made a list.

First Mystery: Academic Intrigue
Omar Masri plagiarizes.
Omar Masri finds a clue.
George trails him.
Omar is killed.
Second Mystery: Robbery
John Pinkney robs a bank with his daughter.
They turn up ten years later.
His daughter dies.
His other wife shows up.

She stared at the page. "This is preposterous. Why would Pinkney kill Masri? There has to be another explanation. Or…wait a minute." She jumped up to pace. " 'Omar Masri finds a clue.' Could that clue have to do with the robbery? Could it all come down to money after all?"

She collapsed back on the couch. An overwhelming need to talk to Griffin washed over her. He would put it all in perspective. Griffin would fix it.

Stop it, Rachel. You sound like a child. Still…she wondered what he was doing now. *Probably at Durkee's grousing about the weather.* She stood up and paced the room, then went outside to gaze at the water. Sailing school was in full swing, and five little day sailers circled an orange buoy out in the bay, herded by a Boston Whaler. Margaret, the instructor, saw Rachel and waved. She waved back. *Is it lunch time yet?*

She sat at the kitchen table watching the minute hand tick slowly toward the twelve. At the first gong she was out the door and in her car heading toward town. Katie greeted her at the entrance to Durkee's. "You're early, Rachel."

Rachel tried to peer around Katie's broad back. "Anyone else here?"

"Not yet. Pick a table. Any table."

"I'll take the one facing the front door. I…uh…feel like people watching." After a few minutes customers started to filter in and the place filled up. Still no Griffin. She spooned up the cup of chowder as slowly as she dared, which wasn't hard since she had no appetite at all. She eked out an hour before admitting defeat. *Where the hell is he?*

Rachel spent the rest of the day checking her answering machine, wandering around Amity, and trying not to call Griffin. When she finally broke down about four in the afternoon, he didn't answer. So she threw on a bathing suit and rode her bike down to Kelly's Cove.

The tide was in and water filled the little crescent of shoreline. Gentle waves lapped on the rocky strip of beach. She slipped into the water and swam out toward the open bay with strong, steady strokes. She'd always loved to swim. Her muscles stretched and relaxed with the exercise, and her mind floated free of worry. As she scrambled up on the big boulder that marked the entrance to the cove she heard a halloo. "Rachel! There you are!"

"Griffin!" She thanked her stars she was far enough away to hide the elation on her face. *His ego hardly needs any more massaging.* She slid off and swam to the beach.

He stood on a flat rock, arms crossed. "Where the hell have you been? I've been all over Amity looking for you."

Goody. "I do have a life you know, Griffin."

"Yeah, well, take a sabbatical. I need you."

"Aw, that's sweet. You're turning into a real romantic."

"Huh? No, I didn't mean that. I need your help."

"And…we're back." She shivered. "Let me get my towel."

He watched her dry off, a mixture of impatience and admiration twisting his face. Rachel reflected that it must be hard work to be a crank when you're attracted to someone. *Tough bananas, big guy.*

Suddenly he stooped and picked up a pebble. Facing away from her, he skipped it out over the water. Rachel got to eleven before she lost count. *All right, so he can do two things better than Cary.* She watched him pick up another stone, his biceps rippling under the cotton shirt. *Make that three.*

"All right, I'm dry. What do you want?"

"You didn't drive?"

"No, I rode my bike. Why?"

"Damn. I walked all the way out here from your

house. Figured I'd hitch back with you."

"It's only a mile, Griffin. You can walk back."

He looked at the ancient Schwinn lying on its side by the road. "You wouldn't…"

"No."

She got on the bike and, whistling "A Bicycle Built for Two," pedaled up to the top of the hill. She waited until he drew near, then took off again. Unfortunately for her, she could only make it halfway up the next, long hill. When he reached her, she mustered enough breath to say, "All right, I'll be nice and walk with you."

"Don't spoil me." They trudged along in silence until her house hove into view. There, next to Griffin's rickety Jeep, purred the Porsche, steam rising from its hood. Cary leaned against the car. He lifted an elbow in Griffin's direction. "What's he doing here?"

Griffin snapped, "I could ask you the same question."

Cary's sneer had a practiced feel. "For a washed-up professor living on social security and under suspicion of murder, you're pretty flippant."

Griffin turned to Rachel. "What did he say?"

She pushed them aside and walked up the steps to her house. "Why don't you two settle this like dogs? I'll be in the house. Don't follow me."

She swept inside and tripped over the cat. During the ensuing caterwauling—literally—from both human and animal, she missed whatever happened between the two men. By the time she'd settled the cat and dabbed at her scratches with hydrogen peroxide, they had both left. Stifling her disappointment, she dressed and went out on the deck.

"I thought he'd never leave."

"Cary! Where did you come from?"

"Moved the car so that prick would think I'd gone. Gawd, what a jackass." He peered at Rachel. "What's he doing hanging around you anyway?"

"None of your business. Why are you here?"

"Noreen Fowler."

"What about her?"

"She came to visit you. To ask you to ask me to lay off her."

"That she did."

He looked at the drink in her hand. "Might I have one of those?"

Rachel had about had it. She wanted either to be alone or with Griffin and this oaf just stood there expecting her attention. "I'm afraid not—it's the last of the whiskey. Again, what do you want?"

"I don't want you mixed up in this, Rachel. There have been two murders, after all."

"Pinkney's in jail, isn't he? I'm perfectly safe."

"I don't think he committed the murder. At least not the first one."

Sigh. "And you think Griffin did? That's absurd."

"Masri called Tate a week before he died."

Rachel put her glass down. "How do you know that?"

Cary's manner turned furtive. "Er…I…uh…had a look at Masri's cell phone."

"You *what*! Didn't the police impound it? Cary Marx, how did you get hold of his phone?"

He pursed his lips. "I told you those guys are complete incompetents. I…uh…happened to be near the station and thought I'd drop in and get an update from Quimby. No one was around—can you believe it? There should *always* be a cop on duty. I'd better make a note of that." He made a half-hearted search of his pockets as if for a pencil and paper. "So…I'm standing there and noticed that someone left the door to the evidence room wide open. The box with Masri's personal effects lay right there on the table. How they can leave this stuff unsecured like that—"

Rachel shook her head in disbelief. "So you took it upon yourself to sift through it."

Cary had the chutzpah to simper. "Good thing I did. I found his phone and checked the call log. Right there in the list was Tate's number."

"Was the call answered?"

At this, he shrugged. "He had one of those phones you buy at the dollar store. It only showed numbers, so I couldn't tell, but what difference does that make?"

I'm not going to give him any more fodder. If he knew Griffin had spoken to Masri, he'd completely misinterpret it, and I'd have to tie him up and leave him in a closet. "It means, Cary, that Griffin may not have answered his phone. We don't know why Masri was in Penhallow, but if he wanted to connect with Griffin, he'd only have to ring his doorbell. And that didn't happen."

The man's face scrunched, reminding Rachel of a pugnacious terrier. "Well, anyway, they were in Cairo at the same time. These academic types always have longstanding feuds. It's only a matter of time before I find out what it was. I have people in Cairo checking now."

Rachel closed her eyes and breathed deeply, tamping the apprehension down. "Isn't this a job for the police?"

"Those hicks? Even the guy from Augusta doesn't know his ass from his elbow. He's zeroed in on a decade-old crime and can't be bothered with all the obvious clues—clues that point straight to your old geezer friend."

"Cary?"

"What?"

"Go home."

"Not yet." He moved closer and held a hand out. "I thought I'd take you out to dinner. Any place you like. I've been so busy with this case I haven't seen you in ages."

His wheedling tone gave her the willies. "Thanks, but not tonight. I'll see you out." She set her drink down and firmly piloted him to the door. "Good night, Cary."

His thin lips tightened in a scowl. "Don't make me regret our friendship, Rachel. You're a beautiful woman, but I don't care for...games." Somehow she knew he'd been about to say "cockteasers." Lucky for him he didn't.

When he'd gone, she changed her clothes into a sage sheath that matched her eyes, brushed her hair out, and, after a moment's thought, applied a touch of pink lipstick. Satisfied, she grabbed a can of tomato soup from the cupboard and drove to Griffin's house.

She found him staring at a cold fireplace, a bottle of beer in one hand and his chin in the other. "Here." He regarded the can with a puzzled air. She finally said, "It's soup."

"Well, duh...Oh." He laughed. "Did anyone see you come in?"

"Oh, yes. A posse of red hats drove by in a van and pointed and brayed at me."

"That would be Edna Mae Quimby and her cronies?"

"Yup. You want me to leave?"

He took her hand and pulled her down on the sofa. "Nope. I think it's about time we made our views public."

She didn't bother to make fun of his phraseology. She was too busy kissing him. When she paused for breath, she said, "You never told me what you needed me for."

"That's number two on the agenda."

"What's number one?"

"Don't play coy. You know exactly what number one is."

No point in arguing.

A while later, he murmured, "Okay, Agenda Item One, check."

Rachel stretched, aware of and reveling in how the feline movement affected him. "I guess there's no point in asking if there's a subsection B on item number one."

"Not today." At her pout he said lightly, "That's what you get for dating an old guy."

"Old is as old does." She rose and looked around for something to cover herself with. "You don't have a bathrobe?"

"Are you kidding? I'm a man. And I live alone."

She pulled a white button-down shirt from the closet and drew it over her head. "I'm going to pretend I'm in one of those movies from the fifties where the woman parades around in her man's pajama top."

He lifted the hem. "They probably wore underwear."

She backed away from him. "So…agenda item number two."

"Yes. I went back to the Hutchinson Center to do a little more research. I found something."

"What?"

"Evidence that the queen of Sheba took a trip up the Nile and left something very significant there."

Chapter Nine
The Rubbing

"I thought she went to Israel...or was it Judah? Which one did Solomon rule?"

"He was the last king to reign over a united Israel. After him his sons Rehoboam and Jeroboam ruled Israel and Judah respectively. As for the queen, hers was a trading nation. From the bits and pieces we've culled from the archaeological record, she traveled all over the Middle East."

"So, if she came from Ethiopia, Nubia would be only a hop, skip, and a jump for her?"

"If you consider a journey of over five hundred miles across the steaming desert a hop, skip, and jump, then yes."

"Closer than Israel."

"True. At any rate, I found a document that mentioned her in association with the ancient city of Meroë." Rachel sensed she was in for a lecture, so she started downstairs. "Where are you going?"

"To make some soup."

"I'm coming."

By the time Griffin arrived in the kitchen, Rachel had tomato soup bubbling in a pot and slices of French bread toasting in the oven. "What do you have to drink?"

He pulled a bottle of 2008 Meursault Les Gouttes

d'Or from the refrigerator. "Will this do?"

Eat your heart out, Cary. "It is acceptable."

Soup bowls filled and wine poured, Griffin resumed. "Okay. I'm back at the Hutch Center going through more boxes. I'd about given up on finding anything interesting and started putting the stuff away when a scrap of paper fell out of a big atlas of the Horn of Africa."

"Horn of Africa?"

"It's the big pointy part of East Africa that juts into the Arabian Sea, comprised of Eritrea, Ethiopia, Somalia, and Djibouti. The butt of many a bawdy joke." He fixed her with a professorial glare. "You're an anthropologist—you're supposed to know your geography."

Rachel stared him down. "That's just silly. Why should I have to know anything about Africa? I specialized in Australian kinship. You know, eight-section, twelve-section systems, that sort of thing."

"Huh?"

She put down her glass and explained patiently. "Kinship. How humans classify the people in their community. It's a way to regulate social behavior."

"Huh?"

Patience, Rachel. "Every group sets up a system in which they define how each person interacts with the others."

"Why?"

"In order to maintain a harmonious society. A kinship system places each of your relatives in a certain category, so you know how to behave when in his or her company. Cuts down on internecine warfare."

"Lemme see…" Griffin swallowed a spoonful of

soup. "So…it's like how you treat your cheapskate maiden aunt when she sends you a one-dollar bill for Christmas *again*?"

"In your case, that would merely be bad manners, but it's true that American kinship is very fluid."

"Fluid? As in viscous? Like snot?"

"Yuck! No. More like…er…syrupy. I'm talking about the interplay of relationships in a particular family. Say a man divorces his wife. Here in America some families still consider her a relative. She gets Christmas presents, birth announcements, that sort of thing. Other families will cut her off, whether they like her or not. In Australia, kin relationships are much more structured and quite intricate. In some aboriginal communities, your conduct is so circumscribed that you're allowed to talk to your father's sister, but not to your mother's brother. In other societies…"

"Fascinating. Now stop interrupting and let me continue."

"Yes, *sir*."

"Okay." He hesitated and shot her a wary glance. "Anyhoo, the scrap of paper came from a news article about this treasure hunter named Lars Svendigen. He had explored Axum—the ancient royal city of Ethiopia, as well as an earlier civilization called Meroë that existed in Upper Egypt, near the fifth cataract of the Nile. Now the Meroitic empire, which was a major trading nation, flourished from the fourth century BC to the third century AD, but there is evidence of habitation in the area as early as the ninth century BC. In its early period it copied all things Egyptian—it had pharaohs and pyramids and used hieroglyphics. Then somewhere around 295 BC there was a major break with Egypt and it adopted its own language—a script which has never successfully been deciphered."

"No Rosetta Stone?"

Griffin shook an unhappy head. "Not so far."

"Cool."

"*Shh*. Most of the Egyptian monuments were destroyed and the hieroglyphs defaced, so not much is known about Meroitic culture or history."

"Sounds like a good setting for an Indiana Jones movie."

"Will you be quiet or do I have to gag you?"

Rachel licked the last bit of soup from her spoon and blew him a kiss.

He leaned over and wiped her lip. "Okay. If I may *continue*. Svendigen claimed to have discovered a tomb somewhere near Meroë, but off the normal travel routes. It dated from the tenth century, and still had legible hieroglyphic writing on its walls. Remember, according to various sources, Makeda ruled Sheba in the tenth century BC." He stood up and paced. "Here comes the good part. Svendigen didn't understand any of the inscription, but he recognized its antiquity, and— bless his pointy little Scandinavian head—made a rubbing of it. A rubbing which happens to be in the special collections of the Queenstown University."

"A rubbing!"

"Yes."

Rachel took her bowl to the sink so she wouldn't have to look at Griffin. "That would be great if you were still on good terms with said university."

"I may not be, but you are."

She twirled around. "Me? You want *me* to go down and take a look at it?"

"What good would that do? No, I need to see an actual copy." He cleared his throat. "I happen to know that Bruce Mills, the curator of special collections, was always sweet on you. I want you to ask him to send you a copy. Will you?"

She stared at him. "How on earth did you know that?"

Griffin spoke into his soup. "You weren't entirely unfamiliar to me when you moved here to Penhallow from the university."

"You're kidding. So that was you skulking behind the trees on campus? Who knew?" Rachel stopped giggling when she saw his face.

"I...uh...followed your...career from afar, if you must know." His voice dropped another octave. "You were always surrounded by beaux. Never thought I'd have a chance with you." He stopped, then, drawing in a deep breath, barked, "Now I know what a silly git you are, I wish I hadn't bothered."

Pitty pat. When her heart had stopped trying to bang a hole in her chest, Rachel said meekly, "I'll call Bruce tomorrow."

Griffin picked up his dish and added it to the pile in the sink. "Time is of the essence."

"Yes, Indy."

****

After all the excitement it seemed strange to come back to an empty house. Spot didn't even bother to greet her but raised a weary head and emitted a disconsolate mew. Rachel took a minute to look at the stars, then headed to bed. As she lay under the cool sheets she thought about Griffin. *He surely is an odd duck.* If she didn't know better, she'd think he didn't like her at all. Abrupt to the point of churlishness, focused on the problem at hand, he didn't seem to see her as a woman when he was discussing dry, ancient, African history. Called her names too. Could "silly git" be his version of a term of endearment? Or an attempt to obscure his real feelings? *How did he put it? He followed my career from afar.* He'd caught her eye many times on the university grounds, but she'd assumed he was uninterested, if not unattainable. *Who knew?*

On the other hand, tonight, after his pseudo-confession, he'd been as surly as ever. *Yes, but as I left, he touched my lips with his fingers, smiled into my eyes, and patted my bottom.* She pulled a pillow over her head and sighed. "Damn."

Between a stopped-up sink and a visit to the vet so he could dislodge the fish hook from Spot's paw, Rachel didn't get a chance to contact Bruce Mills until after lunch the next day. She booted up the computer, found his phone number, and called him. Overnight she'd come up with the story that a former student of hers, now at the University of Maine, was doing a paper on Meroë and had heard about the document. Bruce was more than happy to oblige.

"How's retirement treating you?"

"I'm not retired, Bruce. I'm the director of the Penhallow Historical Society."

"Oh, I see."

What was that? A snicker?

"You know," he said cheerfully, "Queenstown University would welcome you back with open arms if you chose to return. The anthropology department hasn't been the same without you."

153

"No more wild parties? Social calendar empty?"

"Dreary is the adjective I'd use to describe the place. They've been sucked into that awful Chicago school of thought. No one does field work anymore— they just sit around the pub and critique other people's work."

"Sounds depressing. So, can you send me that rubbing as an attachment?"

"It'll take me a couple of minutes to retrieve it."

"Thanks so much, Bruce. I owe you one."

"You do indeed."

She called Griffin. "It's on its way."

"I'll be right over."

Rachel had printed out the file by the time Griffin arrived, and together they pored over the smudged copy. "I can only make out the signs for water and daughter. There seems to be a cartouche at the bottom."

"That's the name of a king, correct?"

"Or queen. For some period Meroë was jointly ruled by a king and a queen or queen mother. In Greek texts the females were called Candace." He chuckled. "Big, brawny mamas from the looks of the carvings left behind." He tapped the page. "I'm hoping the cartouche belongs to our queen and not Candace."

Rachel stood up and poured herself a glass of water. "We need help."

"Yes. How do you feel about bringing Hamdani in?"

"I don't know. I mean, I can't really believe he killed Masri, but what if he did?"

"We can't solve this ourselves. And besides, he deserves to be included—he did most of the legwork."

"Agreed." She put down the glass and walked out

of the kitchen.

"Where are you going?"

"To get my BB gun. Just in case."

Hamdani answered on the third ring. Griffin spoke with him briefly, then put down the receiver. "He can't come over until tomorrow. Evidently he has a conference call with Harvard."

Rachel tried to ignore her disappointment. "So what do we do?"

He rolled up the paper and set it on the counter. "We wait. I've got some things to do around the house." He checked his watch. "It's only three o'clock. You might, for once, want to earn the piddling sum they pay you at the historical society."

"Thank you for releasing me." She zipped out the door ahead of the expected caustic remark.

Rachel—her mind on the queen of Sheba—had completely forgotten about John Pinkney until she found Toby waiting for her at the entrance to the historical society. "What's up?"

He stood, pulling at his rumpled uniform shirt. "I thought you'd be interested in the latest glitch in my murder case."

"Which one?"

"Ah, there's the rub. Let's go inside."

Rachel led the way to her office. "Is the wretched Blanchard still hanging around?"

"Unfortunately. I must say, he's not much fun. He's really pissed that Pinkney's languishing in my jail."

"Maybe he could come up with the bail."

Toby harrumphed. "He's got more problems than that. The medical report on Mary Pinkney came back."

"Oh? Was it suicide after all?"

"Nope. Definitely murder."

"Oh dear."

"It gets worse. She wasn't killed by Pinkney. In fact, she wasn't killed by a man."

Rachel sat heavily. "A woman murdered her?"

"I'm tempted to say, no, a horse did. But I can't. Johnson—he's the medical examiner—found female DNA under the victim's fingernails and in the scratches all over her face and arms. He thinks there was a struggle."

Noreen. "Have you arrested her yet?"

"Who?"

"Noreen Fowler of course. She's the obvious suspect."

"We police don't actually work that way, Rachel," Toby drawled in his best *Heat of the Night* accent. "We have procedures. We're required to do stuff like have solid evidence of someone's guilt. And as yet we haven't found it."

Rachel flipped a pencil, tapping first one end and then the other on the desk. "I suppose you've taken a sample of Noreen's DNA."

Toby rolled his eyes. "You're beginning to sound like Cary Marx. That would be part of the protocol. Duh."

"And?"

He shook his head with some reluctance. "We haven't, no. We would if we could. She seems to have disappeared."

"What?"

"Car and purse gone. Blinds down in her apartment. Empty space where a suitcase should be.

We've got an APB out on her." He took the pencil from Rachel and put it carefully in his shirt pocket. "One interesting item."

"Yes?"

"Stan Holiday is missing too."

I guess Cary turned her down. "By the way, Noreen came to see me."

"We are aware of that."

"You are?"

Toby said patiently, "We're investigating two murders, my dear. After Noreen Fowler made a spectacle of herself in the court room, we were inclined to monitor her movements. She visited you yesterday morning. What did she want?"

Rachel told Toby all about Noreen's visit and her obviously fictitious story.

The sheriff pulled out a small pad of paper and jotted down some notes. "The part about inventing an alibi no one would believe rings true. She must think Pinkney has money here."

"The cache from the robbery, of course. She tried to locate it but wasn't successful. Then when John and Mary turned up she panicked—"

"And murdered Mary? Why?"

Rachel warmed to her theory. "She had to get rid of the two of them, see? So first she tried to frame John for Masri's murder."

Toby mulled that over. "Are you postulating that she just picked a guy at random to kill?"

"I'm not saying she killed Masri—just that she took advantage of it."

"First of all, we know she was with Stan the day of the murder, so how on earth would she know about

Masri's death on June fifteenth?"

"She didn't have to. When she heard you'd arrested Pinckney she saw her opportunity."

"That would make sense—if she hadn't tried to give him an alibi."

"We both know why she did that." A fly buzzed around Rachel's head. She swatted at it. "I've got it. She didn't try to frame John for *Masri's* death. She tried to frame John for *Mary's* death."

"Killed Mary, huh? A little more likely. But"—he shook his head—"she knew John was already under suspicion for Masri's death. Why not just let matters take their course?"

Rachel remembered Noreen's hostility toward her husband's daughter. "Mary had always been a thorn in her side. She may have planned to get rid of her anyway."

The sheriff's eyebrows went up. "You think she's that callous?"

A blowsy carrot top with chilly eyes rose before her, strident voice yammering on about mai tais and mayhem. "Yep." Rachel stood up and gestured at the pile of papers on her desk. "I appreciate you keeping me informed, Toby, but I've really got to get some work done."

"Fine, fine." Toby jumped up and backed out of the tiny room. "Let me know if you hear from Noreen again. She may not know we're hunting for her. I'd like to keep it that way."

"Okey doke." He left, but when Rachel tried to settle down, she found herself staring at the wall. By six she was pacing. By seven, she was ready to go home. By nine she was in bed.

****

The phone rang at ten the next morning, waking her up.

"Hello, stranger."

"Maude! Where have you been?"

"I could ask the same question. Thought maybe I'd check in and see what you were doing for lunch."

"Nothing." Rachel's spirits soared. *Something to take my mind off Grif—I mean, the mystery.* "How about we go up to the Ice Cream Barn?"

"Didn't you hear? They've gone out of business."

"Oh dear, not another restaurant!"

"I know—at the height of the tourist season too. No one can afford the property taxes anymore. A place just opened across the street from it, though—you know, where the old cemetery used to be? They're calling it Hallowed Ground. Cute, huh? Want to try it?"

"Sure. Let's hope it's only haunted by waitresses."

"I'll pick you up at noon."

As they drove across the Passagassawaukeag, Rachel looked out her window and down to the old bridge, now transformed into a fishing pier. "I wonder what Mary Pinkney was doing there that night."

"That's the usual spot for suicides. Remember young Henry Tottle?"

"She didn't commit suicide, though. She was murdered."

Maude braked suddenly. "Oops, sorry. You know that for sure?"

"Toby told me."

"Was it John Pinkney?"

"No, it was a woman. They found female DNA under her fingernails."

Rachel noticed Maude's hands gripped the steering wheel so tightly her knuckles showed white. "Have they identified it?"

"The DNA? No, not as far as I know." She waited, not sure why.

"Strange. It makes so much sense that Pinkney would kill her. Whether because she wanted to turn herself in or for some other reason. Just because they found another woman's DNA on her doesn't mean that woman killed her. Maybe she had a quarrel with Mary and John killed her later."

"Why would you say that?"

"All those scratches on her face and arms. Sounds like a cat fight." She snickered. "Maybe she went a round with Bert Weems's latest girlfriend."

"How did you know about the scratches?"

"Huh? Oh, it must have been on the news. You know this town—can't keep any secrets." She gave Rachel a sly glance. "Like a certain historian spending a *lot of time* with a certain professor."

They arrived at the restaurant before Rachel could think of a response. As they walked toward the deck, Maude stopped at a table occupied by two women. "Ingrid Sundstrom—is that you? I haven't seen you since the funeral."

A big-boned woman with unnaturally blonde hair looked up, a frosty expression on her heavily made-up face. "Oh, Maude…Maude Jewett, isn't it?"

Her inhospitable tone didn't deter Maude. "Yes." She waved a hand at Rachel. "This is my friend Rachel Tinker—she's from away." Rachel tried to remember where she'd seen the woman before, but gave up. *It's probably only that she bears a resemblance to Hannah.*

"How are you holding up? It was so sad to see Hannah pass."

The woman did not appear grief-stricken. "Yes. Sad." She started to turn away, but Maude persisted.

"So you think you'll stay around here? Are you living up on Bluff Road in Hannah's house?"

"For now." That seemed to be the end of the conversation.

Rachel took Maude's elbow and steered her to a table on the other side of the room. "You are the biggest busybody."

Maude shrugged. "Never liked that woman. I just wanted to see if she had any feelings for her sister at all. She never came to visit when Hannah was ill." They ordered mussels and moved on to other topics. "So, the Maskers are putting on *Arsenic and Old Lace* as the final offering of the summer. Audrey thinks I should audition for one of the sisters."

Rachel licked her fingers. "I thought you only did costumes and the box office?"

"Oh no. Didn't I ever mention it? I was one of the founding members of the Maskers, back in the nineties." Maude picked at her coleslaw. "Boy, we've gone through some rough times since then. Plenty of bodies buried in that old railroad station." She laughed a trifle shakily. "I guess that makes *Arsenic and Old Lace* the perfect season finale."

"Bodies? What kind of bodies?" Rachel leaned forward, eyes alight. She was expecting some more juicy gossip, but instead Maude blushed to the roots of her hair and beckoned the waitress.

"I've got to get back. I…I forgot I had an…appointment." She didn't look at Rachel and walked quickly out of the restaurant, not even pausing to glare at Ingrid. Rachel followed.

Maude dropped her off at the corner of Main and Church and drove on out Belmont Avenue. Rachel had almost reached her office when she saw Cary's Porsche coming down the street. Ducking into an alley to avoid him, she came out on Washington Street. The whole waterfront spread out before her. A launch was slowly pulling up to the pier. She watched as a young man threw lines from the bow and stern to secure it, then handed a woman out. Even from that distance, Rachel could make out orange hair and a matching tube top the woman should never have been allowed to buy. *Noreen.*

Noreen waited while a man in the bow jumped out with a duffel bag, and the two of them set off up the hill to a dusty Buick. Rachel recognized the flannel shirt that Stan never changed, winter or summer. *Hmm.* She turned back into the alley and walked the three blocks to the police station.

Toby was on the phone. "Well, he may be absolved of Mary Pinkney's murder soon, but we haven't finished our investigation. Even so, we're still planning to charge him with Masri's death...Yes, I'm aware of Mr. Marx's activities...No, I do not condone them...Yes, I will speak to him...No, there's no need to come to Penhallow just yet. Yes." He looked up. "Oh, sorry, I have a visitor. Yes...yes...I'll be in touch, Blanchard."

He threw the receiver on the desk with a loud *thunk.* "He's driving me crazy. The man's obsessed with a robbery that may have taken place—if it took place at all—years ago. The bank doesn't even exist anymore. Why does that take precedence over a murder case? I ask you."

Rachel understood that he wasn't really asking and decided to be tactful. "I guess some policemen can't let a cold case go."

"You'd think Blanchard had a personal vendetta against Pinkney." He stopped and wrote a note on a pad. "I might just do a little sleuthing on that."

"Toby?"

"Yes? Oh, sorry, Rachel. What can I do for you?"

Don't beat about the bush. "I just saw Noreen. She was with Stan and they were getting off a bay boat at the wharf."

"Are you sure?"

"Absolutely. They had a suitcase. I'm guessing they may have gone on a weekend getaway."

"So she didn't skedaddle."

"It would appear not."

"I'll cancel the APB then." He stood, his belly showing a crease where he'd leaned into the desk. He saw her looking at it and sucked in his gut.

Rachel giggled. "Better watch out, or I'll tell Edna Mae you've been flirting with me."

"She'll take that as a happy sign I'm still alive."

Rachel watched the squad car roll off toward Searsport and went to her car.

****

"Where the hell have you been? We've been waiting hours for you. It's almost two o'clock!"

"I love you too, but I wish you'd desist from breaking and entering my house, Griffin. I may have to call the gendarmes."

"I have a hall pass from Toby."

"That's only for the john. Don't abuse your

privileges."

He kissed her nose. "Okay. I have a surprise for you."

"Just so long as it isn't a puppy."

"Well, close."

George chose that moment to appear from the bathroom. "There you are, Rachel. Where have you been?"

"Not you too!"

The poor man looked confused. "I beg your pardon?"

In response, Rachel punched Griffin in the ribs. "Why are you here?"

"You forgot, didn't you?"

"Forgot what?"

Griffin rolled his eyes. "We were going to bring George in on…on…" He leered at Rachel with ponderous significance.

"Oh! On the rubbing." Despite herself, she blushed. So did Griffin.

George looked from one to the other of them. "Rubbing?"

This time they both broke out in gales of laughter, leaving George to scratch his head. Finally, Griffin took the Lebanese's arm and led him to the dining room. "We have found something and we thought we'd let you in on it. Also, we need your help."

George was staring avidly at the twelve by sixteen sheet of paper on the table. "Those are hieroglyphics."

"Yes."

He bent closer. "From about the tenth century BC, I'd guess."

"You're on a roll, George."

He turned to Griffin. "Where did you get this?"

Griffin described his discovery.

George whistled. "So there *was* a second copy."

"Second copy? You mean of the rubbing?"

"Um…er." He blinked rapidly, a sign Rachel now knew meant he was prevaricating.

She had a sudden inspiration. "The item you found in the Egyptian Museum. It was a rubbing, wasn't it?"

His brown skin took on a pink glow. "No. Or rather, yes," he added hastily, "but I never saw it. I found a reference in the catalogue to a rubbing donated by some Swedish traveler. I thought nothing of it until I had returned to the Institut d'archéologie and organized my notes. Once I realized its importance, I tried to go back to the museum, but my research permit had expired. They are very strict there. I had to reapply. By the time I had cut through the morass of Egyptian red tape, Masri had found the rubbing and…and…" He nearly broke down, his chubby cheeks quivering. "…stolen it!"

Rachel gasped. "He stole a document from the Cairo Museum? Why didn't they arrest him?"

A tear dripped from one coal black eye. "I fear Egypt is not as modern as Lebanon and corruption is still rampant there. Masri's family is very powerful—no lowly curator of document collections would dare impugn his honor. Masri simply walked out with it and took off for Sudan. Again, there was nothing I could do."

Griffin rapped a fist on the table. "Well, we can do something now. We have the inscription right here."

George rubbed his hands together. "Let's get started."

It turned out that the word "let's" was rhetorical. George spent the afternoon poring over the page, emitting intermittent squeaks and trills. He held a magnifier in one hand and wrote rapid notes with the other. Finally he looked up. "I've done the best I could. Unfortunately, this is only a partial copy of the original inscription."

"Oh really? What's missing?"

"The top half—plus some of the words are impossible to make out. It is likely the original is eroded. I have tweezed out some interesting information, though."

"What's that?"

"First, may I have something to eat? I missed elevenses. And now lunch and tea as well."

"Elevenses?"

George appeared flummoxed. "Elevenses. Surely you partake of a midmorning snack here in America? However could you carry on without a bit of toast and jam between breakfast and luncheon?"

Rachel grudgingly went to the refrigerator, pulled out five containers of food, and laid them out on the counter. She handed George a plate and after a nod from Griffin, one to him. For a frustrating twenty minutes the two men ate, chatting amiably.

Finally, over their strenuous objections, she grabbed both plates and took them to the sink. Griffin finished off his iced tea and wiped his mouth. George followed Rachel and tried to lick his plate. She cuffed him. "Tell me what you found. Now."

"So I shall, mademoiselle." He bowed.

Back in the dining room, they circled the table. George smoothed out the rubbing. "First off, and most exciting, the cartouche is not of Candace. It is Makeda's."

"Oh my God. That's the queen of Sheba, right?"

"She's the only Makeda I know. She was called Bilqis by the Arabs, but her Ethiopian name is Makeda. If you need additional proof, the rest of the cartouche says, 'Queen of the lands of Shaa Baa in the southern mountains'—Shaa Baa likely being Sheba."

Rachel's pulse raced. "What else does it say?"

"Let's see… The rubbing starts mid-sentence, but I think it refers to the queen. '…of all the mountains and desert between the great blue water and the river that kills men, built this temple.' The 'blue water' must refer to the Red Sea."

"And what's the 'river that kills men?' "

"I presume the Nile. Meroë is south of the fifth cataract. Many a boat and life have been lost in the rapids there. That's why it took so many decades to discover the source of the Blue Nile."

"The Blue Nile? There's more than one?"

Griffin leaned in. "The Blue and White Niles are the major tributaries of the Nile. The White flows north from South Sudan or possibly from as far south as Burundi, to Khartoum, where it joins the Blue. The Blue meanders down from the highlands. The landscape there was too rugged for the early visitors to track."

"And where is its source?"

"In Ethiopia—Lake Tana. John Speke and Richard Burton were the last of the great explorers to search for the sources of the Nile. They never made it, but R. E. Cheesman, the British Consul for northwest Abyssinia, managed to chart the course of the river back to the lake in the 1920s."

"So what are these mountains and desert that the rubbing refers to?" Rachel's eyes were bright with curiosity.

Griffin answered. "Western Ethiopia consists of ranges of highlands—plateaus and mountains. Between that and the sea lies the Danakil depression—a sere place of salt flats and volcanoes."

"So, from left to right: Nile, mountains, desert, Red Sea."

George nodded. "If I am right, the land of Sheba lay in what is now northwestern Ethiopia."

Griffin half rose, his cheeks flushed. "Axum?"

"Possibly. But of course, predating the Axumite Empire by centuries."

Rachel looked from one intense face to the other. "Axum was the empire that conquered Meroë, wasn't it?"

"Yes."

"So, where—"

Griffin interrupted. "Enough background. Let's get on with it. She built a temple in Meroë? The one Svendigen discovered."

"Duh." Rachel refused to be left out.

"Not exactly in Meroë. This temple must have been built some distance from the other sites."

"Other sites?"

"Meroë has several cemeteries—large sites filled with funerary pyramids. Sheba's temple wasn't discovered during the extensive excavations by George Reisner in the first decade of the 20th century."

"So you surmise that the temple isn't in the cemeteries?"

"Yes. It's more likely to be in a rather remote spot,

since it survived the destruction of the Egyptian-influenced buildings." He broke off. "I wish we knew exactly where the temple is situated." His eyes closed and he thrummed a fat finger on the table. "*Hmm.* Maybe…"

Rachel tapped the rubbing. "What else does it say?"

"Give me a moment. '…built this temple to the glory of Israel's god for my daughter'—I think it says 'Judith'—'child of my burning love and a gift from the great king who lives across the sea….' " He stopped and peered closer at the paper. "Wait, I was wrong. The word is not 'temple,' it's 'tomb.' " He threw his hands in the air. "It's a tomb! This is it! This is Makeda's tomb! Svendigen found it!" He began to gallop around the room, reminding Rachel inescapably of Disney's Fantasia and the dancing hippos. She hated to burst his bubble, but she had to do something before he ran through the wall and punched a silhouette-shaped hole in it.

"George! Cease and desist."

"Besides, you've forgotten something." Griffin's words fell like hot stones on the poor man's joy. "It says *she* built the tomb, and for her child. Not for her."

Poor Brutus. George slumped on his chair, producing an alarming sound effect. A new thought occurred to Rachel. "Wait—the story of Solomon and the queen of Sheba. According to the Kebra Nagast, she bore Solomon a son. Not a daughter."

"Menelik. Yes. *Hmm.*" Griffin stood up to pace. He stopped at the window and spun around. "This gives a whole new slant to the story. If the great king who lives across the sea is Solomon, and she built the tomb to honor 'Israel's god,' isn't she implying the daughter is his?"

Rachel said, "That would kind of put a damper on Ethiopia's national origin myth, wouldn't it? I mean, according to the book, the emperors of Ethiopia descended in an unbroken line from Menelik to Haile Selassie."

"And not only would it mean Menelik didn't exist, but that the daughter died before she took the throne."

"No, no, no! You silly people." George jumped up again, this time knocking the chair over and hitting his elbow on the table. While Rachel righted the chair, he nursed the bruise, a wounded look on his face.

She put some ice in a towel and handed it to him. "Would you mind explaining why we are all of a sudden 'silly people?' "

"Thank you. I am so sorry—in my enthusiasm I fear I employed disparaging language. Please accept my apologies."

"Fine, fine, but what were you going to say?"

"That Makeda could have borne two children to Solomon. It doesn't change anything." Hamdani held up a finger and wagged it at his audience, who were busy doing a fair interpretation of fish out of water. "But allow me to finish translating." He sat down and pored over the paper. "It goes on. 'Unable to bring my child home as she wished, I have built this tomb, but…'—the next few words are illegible—'I have inscribed a map, so that the great god Osiris may guide her back to me, to reside next to me forever in the afterlife.' "

A low hum indicated that the committee was ingesting this news. Rachel couldn't help herself. "I guess she wanted to cover all her bases."

"You mean invoking both Osiris and Yahwe? That was very common in the ancient world."

Griffin flicked at the paper. "Is there any sign of a map on the rubbing?"

"No."

"Could it have been on the rubbing Masri stole?"

"Possibly. It's not clear where she put the map."

Rachel said, "If Masri's document contained the map—"

"If it had, why did he run off to Sudan? For that matter, why would he have wandered around Europe? What was he looking for?"

Griffin clucked his tongue. "I'm guessing Masri's document was just as fragmentary as ours. He went to Meroë to see the original inscription."

"And discovered something that led him to Europe."

"Yes."

"But what?"

In the silence, George suppressed a small burp. "I believe we've done enough for today. I shall take my leave."

"Off to get some supper?"

His attempt at indignation failed. "I intend to partake of a small salad and a light beer. That is all." He smiled proudly. "I have shed two pounds so far in my endeavor."

Rachel felt a glimmer of affection for the large Lebanese. "I meant to remark earlier that you were looking quite svelte."

"Thank you."

Three hours later Rachel had a call from Griffin.

"Do you know where George is?"

"He's not my toddler, Griffin. No, I don't. I thought he was with you."

"Damn. I think he's decamped."

Rachel had a sinking feeling. "To Meroë."

"To Meroë."

"Damn."

Chapter Ten
The KO

"Talk about a flight risk. What were you thinking?" Griffin and Rachel sat like truant children in Toby's office. "You were there when I asked Mr. Hamdani to stay in town until the case is settled, and you let him go."

"Well, in all fairness, we weren't deputized, Toby. You should have taken him into custody if you were so worried."

"I had nothing to be worried about until you two hatched this ridiculous scheme and lured him into it."

His rebuke galled Rachel. "It wasn't a *scheme*, Toby. It was a mystery. And besides, we were helping you out. We now know what Masri was doing here and what he was looking for."

"We don't know any of that for sure. This is all pure speculation—of the typical ivory tower, armchair quarterback variety." He must have sensed a growing insurgency in the ranks, for he added hastily, "Besides, your work simply strengthens the case for Hamdani's guilt. You've given me motive and opportunity."

Rachel grasped at the straw. "But no means?"

She was gratified to see the arrow struck a soft spot. "Yes. Well. No, we haven't found the gun yet, but that's the least of our problems. We don't 'habeus corpus.' "

"Doesn't that refer to the victim?"

Toby rolled his eyes. "Don't you recognize police humor?"

Silence greeted this remark. After a minute Griffin asked, "So, do you have someone going after Hamdani?"

"Of course. You said Meroë is in the Sudan, right?"

"One hundred forty miles north-east of Khartoum, yes."

"We sent word to Bangor International and to Logan to look out for a George Hamdani wanting to board a plane for Khartoum." He drew in his breath. "We've got one thing in our favor—he's hardly inconspicuous."

Griffin pounded a fist into his palm. "I wish we had more specifics. Does he have a French passport? A Lebanese one? Would he be knowledgeable enough to drive over to, say, Knox County airport and then to Boston? Did you check the buses?"

Toby threw up his hands. "Oh my God, whatever would the police do without the help of citizens such as yourselves. Buses—now why didn't I think of that?"

"There's no call for sarcasm, Toby." Rachel rose. "If you've finished berating us, we'll be off."

"By all means. If I find myself wallowing in doubt as to standard police procedure I shall call—I have you both on speed-dial."

"Right below Cary's I suppose."

"No need. I rarely, if ever, have to call him. He's always in touch." He sighed, then twisted his lips into a grin. "I did, however, manage to send the incredible Mr. Limpet off on a fool's errand. He's in Searsport harassing Noreen's mechanic."

"Noreen! Did you pick her up?"

"She's being interviewed as we speak. By a real policeman. Oh, and by the way, the DNA sample came back negative—she didn't kill Mary." Toby showed them the door. "I'm going back to Edna Mae and the newspaper. I can't thank you enough for ruining my Sunday morning. *Again*."

Griffin and Rachel ambled slowly down the sidewalk, loath to go their separate ways. There was so much to discuss, so many winding paths to follow. And yet, Rachel found herself concentrating on how Griffin's elbow kept rubbing against hers. The touch sent a tingle up her arm to her throat. She coughed.

"You okay?" He put a hand on her shoulder, which had the effect of closing off her throat entirely.

"*Urgle*."

"I see. So…what do you want to do now?"

Quick, quick. "I…I…I'm hungry?"

She felt him relax. "A little brunch perhaps?"

"That would be swell."

"I'd suggest the Captain Nickels Inn in Searsport, but we might run into Brother Marx."

"Oh, the inn sounds wonderful—their breakfasts are to die for." She stopped. "Er…"

Griffin took pity on her. "Tell you what, you duck and run into the restaurant—I'll camouflage the car."

"Sounds like a plan."

They saw no sign of the intrepid Cary until they were leaving the inn. A silver Porsche roared down Route One, its driver staring straight ahead. Rachel swore she saw spittle spraying from his open mouth.

"No dear, that was his dog." Griffin looked after

the car. "I fear not only poor Toby's morning, but his afternoon, will be ruined."

They spent their own afternoon at the annual Isleborough regatta. Sailboats big and small tacked up the bay and around the island that lay directly across from Amity Landing. Conversations had to suspend every few minutes when Hermione Ruddles blew the air horn to signal another finisher. Holding hands, more than half the time concentrating on each other and feasting upon visions of forthcoming snuggles, neither Rachel nor Griffin minded.

As the sun set and the breeze picked up, they trudged up the hill to Rachel's house. She checked for errant Porsches and signaled to Griffin when it was safe. He hunched over and slid through the door. At that moment thunder boomed and the sky went dark. In the gloom Griffin held his hands out in front of him. "I can't see you—where are you?"

Rachel slipped around the corner. "Over here."

She heard stumbles and curses going into the living room, then coming around the other hall into the kitchen. "Where the hell are you, wench?"

She suppressed a giggle. "Right in front of you."

He grabbed at thin air, then lunged, catching the end of her shirt tail. She tugged at it, but he held on and twirled her, wrapping the shirt around her body. His arms squeezed tight. "Ha. You are mine."

Before she could retort, he put his lips to her hair and whispered it again. "You are mine."

Okay.

****

Rachel lay awake, thinking. Both the rain and Griffin had gone, the latter leaving behind a kiss on the forehead and a question. "When can I stay over?"

She wasn't thinking about the question. The answer to that was obvious. *Just do it.* She wasn't even thinking about the kiss, although she'd spent some fifteen minutes after he left reliving it. She was thinking about Omar Masri. Despite her words, spoken with such assurance in Toby's office, they really didn't know why he had come here. He wrote that he wanted Griffin's help—but with what? The excuse that Griffin's sterling reputation would facilitate the introduction of Masri's find didn't hold water. Masri had kept all his research to himself before then—why reveal it to a total stranger? Hamdani believed he came to Penhallow to see a person. Could it have been Griffin? Or someone else? Someone at the Hutchinson Center? Who else could it be? Unless…he'd gone on the train ride. Why? Just to kill time while he waited to hear from Griffin or the other person? Or…

She sat up in bed. *Or to meet someone? John Pinkney?* Aha! Pinkney was a bank robber. And a banker. Either one—*or both*—might be of use to the Egyptian. The object of his search could be in a bank vault. Or perhaps Masri needed cash to buy the object? *Yes!* He entered into a contract with Pinkney—Pinkney would lend him the money from his stolen loot to buy the object, and in return would get a piece of the action.

She sank back on the pillows. *But what action would that be?* What did Masri intend to do with his find? And what was he looking for? The map? Or the place on the map? With a heavy sigh, she rose and padded to the bathroom. A nice long shower later, she headed downstairs. Cary stood outside on the front porch.

"Hey, I was just about to ring. Can I come in?"

He sounds chastened. How unlike him. "Sure."

He sat down in the massage chair. "I had an interesting afternoon."

Not as interesting as mine. "Oh?"

"Yes. The sheriff sent me off on what he expected to be a wild goose chase—don't know why he doesn't just admit I have a nose for ferreting out information—"

Thank God Griffin didn't hear that. The urge to make the obvious analogy would surely be too much for him.

"—serves him right because I did learn something about Noreen Fowler."

His words jolted Rachel back to the present. "Oh really?"

"Yes." He broke off. "Look, can I have a drink? It's been a long day."

Why not? "Whiskey okay?"

"As long as it's single malt Scotch."

"Not a problem." She went into the kitchen, pulled the jug of Old Sly Dog Canadian out from under the sink, and poured him a tot. She got herself a shot of Jack Daniels, returned to the living room, and handed him his glass.

He sipped, making appreciative noises. "Ah, you can't beat that peaty flavor, can you?" When Rachel didn't respond, he went on. "So, Noreen. First off, I discovered that, although she did in fact come here from Belize, before that she spent a few fun-filled years in the women's prison at Hazelton, West Virginia. After she was released she went to Belize, presumably to start a new life."

"What was she in for?"

"Aiding and abetting a robbery. She drove the getaway car."

"*Hmm.*"

"*Hmm* is right. So we know she's already got felonious inclinations. Probably sought out like-minded people in Belize."

"Like John Pinkney."

"Like John Pinkney." Cary chortled. "They must have hit it off—so much in common."

"Ha, ha…Wait." Rachel's eyebrows went up. "You know about the bank robbery?"

"Yeah. I told you I overheard that dickhead Blanchard yelling at Quimby about it."

"I mean, that it was of the Penhallow Bank and Trust?"

"Of course." He hesitated, sipping his whiskey. "Actually I only learned today that Pinkney pulled it off right here in Mayberry." The belated revelation seemed to embarrass him.

"So…go on. Noreen goes to Belize and meets John…"

"Yeah. Well, three years ago, she left him and came up here. Not long after, she started nosing around asking about the Penhallow Bank and Trust. No one remembered much."

Rachel thought of the conversation with Bert Weems. "Nobody in town knew the money was stolen, you know. They were told PB&T went bankrupt."

Cary's put his glass down. "Really? How did the police keep it a secret?"

"I don't think anyone ever went to the police. Old Crocker claimed the losses were poor business decisions and he was allowed to close up without a lot of questions."

"That doesn't make sense."

Rachel shrugged. "Maybe it was true. We only have Blanchard's word that a crime was committed."

Cary pursed his lips. "You think he's making it up? That he has an ulterior motive? Interesting…" He took another sip of whiskey and frowned. "At any rate, *Noreen* believed it. Which means Pinkney told her. He must have hinted that he'd left some of the swag behind—that's why she raced up here. Then, when the Pinkneys arrived, she killed Mary and framed John for her death so she could have it all."

Shall I tell him? "Great scenario. Except that the DNA found on Mary doesn't belong to Noreen."

"What? Whose is it?"

"They don't know yet. They only know it was a woman."

"Huh." He tossed off his drink. "Has anyone checked to see if John Pinkney is really Jane Pinkney?"

Rachel made a quick decision. "You know, Cary, that's an intriguing idea. Why don't you run it by Toby tomorrow?"

He rose. "I think I will. It's about time he listened to me."

Rachel saw him off with a secret grin.

****

"Another coffee, Rachel?"

"Thanks, Katie." Rachel turned to Griffin. "Why did you go back to see Toby this morning?"

"Wanted to see if they'd run George to ground."

"And have they?"

"No. You should have seen his face, Rachel. I

didn't know complexions came in that rich ochre color."

"Even if they didn't catch George at the airport, it's no secret where he was headed."

"That's right, but Toby wanted to apprehend him before he left the States. Now we have to contend with the Sudanese police."

"Our fine sheriff still thinks George is guilty of Masri's murder?"

"He has nothing else to go on."

"You know," mused Rachel, "I'm not sure what George expects to find in Meroë. Masri came to Maine for a reason. Whether it's a map or an object, he needed it first."

"You mean, he needed a key of some sort in order to find the queen's grave?"

"Yes. If what's his name—the Sven guy—or Masri—"

"Or any of the thousands of other archaeologists who have swarmed over the tombs there."

"—didn't find the map, then what makes Hamdani think he can?"

"Agreed. So we're not going to worry about George's defection?"

"No." She finished her coffee. "We stay here and look."

Griffin leaned over the table and kissed her. He didn't seem to notice the gasps that went up from the other booths, the bar patrons, and the bartender. In the sudden silence, Katie came out from the kitchen. "What's going on?"

No one said a word.

After a suitable interval to allow the herd to settle

down, they walked out, maintaining a conspicuous distance between them. When they reached the street, Griffin said, "What now?"

"Uh…" Up to that point Rachel had felt terribly decisive. Now it struck her that she had no notion of what to do next.

Griffin turned toward his car. "I'm going back to do some more research."

"Well, that's what you're good at."

"As for you—you just stand there and look pretty." Her swat missed his head by inches. "Okay, do you have a better idea?"

I can't let him see me waffling like some ninny. She said the first thing that came into her head. "I'm going to Searsport."

"Why?"

She said carelessly, "Oh, I've been meaning to visit Ned at the sailing museum. Haven't seen him for a while."

"Ned?" His brows knit. "Wait—Ned Turner. The volunteer coordinator. The one you dated. I thought you didn't volunteer there anymore?"

Rachel chose to disregard the venom in his voice and merely said, "Now and then. Not as much as I used to." *Before I met you and began to waste whole days daydreaming.* "I need to think some things through." She may not have actually run to her car, but there was a decided spring in her step.

She drove across the bridge and up Route One. As she passed Perry's Nut House, she slowed. The parking lot was full of minivans with license plates from Nebraska, Ohio, and Indiana. The huge stuffed gorilla still stood out front, a vestige of the original emporium and exhibits. When she was a child, her family had always stopped there on their way north. The store sold penny candy out of huge bins, and all kinds of nuts and fudge, but the real treat was the quirky museum in the back room. Crammed with life-sized stuffed animals, tropical shells—"Found Only on the Island of Bora Bora"—antique toys, and unidentified dusty, round objects labeled "From Deepest Africa," it had lured Rachel into an exotic world. Her brother James maintained the objects were just dried-out elephant poop, but Rachel knew otherwise. "Foolish boy—they're betel nuts, like the ones the Polynesian chiefs chewed before they went into battle. And those fuzzy things over there—they're frangipani blossoms that the beautiful brown-skinned maidens wore in their flowing, black hair, preserved here for eternity."

When James pointed out that Polynesia was not in fact in Africa, Rachel would toss her hair and assert, "Nevertheless," in her best Katherine Hepburn voice.

As she passed the store, a family of four came out wearing matching T-shirts and carrying boxes of salt water taffy made in Virginia. *Too bad it's just a souvenir shop now.*

She reached the outskirts of Searsport and slowed down for the inevitable crawl through the tiny town. Being the height of the summer season, tourists from all over the country swarmed up and down the coast of Maine in their SUVs and campers. TripAdvisor listed the Penobscot Sailing Museum as a must-see, and the place was jam-packed. Rachel found a spot in the volunteer lot and showed her badge to the teenager lolling by the gate.

"Oh, hi, Rachel. Long time no see. Are you coming

in to work? We could use your help."

"Wish I could, Hedwig, but I'm swamped at the historical society." *Another white lie. Sorry, Mother.* "Is Ned around?"

"He's gone to lunch. He'll be back in half an hour."

"I'll just wander around then. And yes," in answer to Hedwig's silent query, "I'll be happy to field any questions from visitors."

She left the administration building and wandered down the road past various nineteenth-century edifices housing artifacts from the shipbuilding and sailing industries. She stepped into the exhibit on the China trade and stood admiring the intricate carved ivory pieces and silks the Maine merchants brought home from their far-flung travels. A tap on her shoulder made her turn around.

Expecting to see a tourist, she jumped back at the woman's savage expression. "Noreen! What are you doing here?"

Her eyes glittering with malice, Noreen didn't reply. She grabbed Rachel's elbow and dragged her out of the building and down an alley to a back lot piled with scraps of lumber. She scoped the place out, then spun Rachel to face her. "You fucking whore."

"Excuse me?"

"You sicced that fucking Marx on me—and after I *asked* you to get him off my back."

Should I remind her that she changed her mind when she realized Cary would make a good mark? A quick peek at Noreen's face told her that rational discussion did not rank high on her current list of priorities.

184

The woman spat out, "The bastard went and pulled my prison records. Look, that was six years ago. I did my time and I've stayed clean. But no, he has to slink off to the sheriff and try to get him to go after me—like I had anything to do with that bitch Mary's death. She was no threat to me. She did anything her Papa said. Feeble-minded little rabbit."

Without thinking, Rachel blurted out, "Are you after the money?"

Noreen's eyes opened wide. "Me? Money? What money?" Her expression morphed into sly. "Nah. I broke up with John back in Belize. He wouldn't share. Said I'd run through all his cash, but I didn't believe him."

"So why *did* you come up to Maine?"

Noreen dropped Rachel's arm. "It's here. I can feel it. His stash."

I'm thinking consistency is not her strong suit.

As if sensing Rachel's sentiment, Noreen shook her head. "I had nothing to do with any robbery anyway. John told me he'd inherited the money. I'm entitled to half his stuff, you know. I'm his wife."

"What about Hannah Sundstrom?"

"She's dead, ain't she?"

The fact that Hannah wasn't yet dead when Noreen married Pinkney didn't appear to enter into her calculations. *She's waded so far into the swamp of lies she doesn't know she's drowning.* "What about John?"

"John? He's still in the slammer, ain't he? I have a free hand." Her face darkened. "Or I did, until you and your precious Marx started sticking your honkers where they don't belong. Damn you! Now I'm on the sheriff's radar again." She reddened. "If he lets John out, I'm screwed." The woman grabbed her arm again and squeezed painfully. "It's all your fault. Why couldn't you just let well enough alone?" Her voice rose. "Why are you persecuting me? I never did nothing to you. You Yankee snobs and your self-righteous hi-de-hos. I hate all of you."

Rachel took a step back and Noreen lunged forward, baring her teeth. "Don't you run away, bitch. You need a lesson in minding your own business, you do." She drew closer, her hands balled into fists. Rachel took another step backward, but her right heel hit a stack of wood and she fell over. As she tried to push off from the rolling logs, Noreen loomed above her. "This'll teach you." She drew her arm back and smashed her fist into Rachel's nose.

Everything went black.

****

"Rachel? Rachel! Oh good, you're awake."

Rachel looked up into the concerned brown eyes of her friend Ned Turner. "Where ab I?"

"You're in Waldo County Hospital. I found you in the maintenance yard and came with you in the ambulance. How are you feeling?"

She struggled to get up. "Ded, what habbent to me and why ab I talking like this?"

A nurse bustled in. "All right, Mr. Turner, time for Rachel's pain pill. Let her be."

Ned drew back and the nurse's face came into view. "Just let me check the dressing first." Her hand hovered between Rachel's eyes. "Looks good. Dr. Wilberforce says it was a clean break, and you should be healed in no time. There will be some bruising of course."

"Bruisig?"

Ned leaned in. "From the punch. Somebody punched you and broke your nose."

"Doreed."

"Doreed? Doreed who? You know who did this to you?" His face hardened. "No one was in the yard when I found you."

"Do! Do!" Rachel made a supreme effort. "D...Noreed. Doreed."

Ned shook his head. "We'll leave it for now. The sheriff called and said he's sending a deputy over to your house for a statement. You can write it down then."

The nurse pushed him aside and handed Rachel a Dixie cup of water. "Now take this pill and—"

Maude's voice rose from behind Ned. "Rachel, I'm here, hon. I heard about your accident from Katie and drove down as fast as I could."

Ned spun around. "Accident? No—it was—"

A commotion at the door drowned him out. "Where the hell is she?"

For once, the anger in Griffin's voice warmed Rachel's heart. "I'b here, Griffid."

The assemblage parted to reveal a very large, steaming man, his blue eyes dark with fear. "What did you say? Griffid?" His eyes brightened and began to twinkle. He bit his lip. "Do you have any idea how peculiar you look?"

This was too much. "Ged out, Griffid. I don't deed your ridicule."

"Oh my sweet, it's just that...that..." He looked helplessly at Ned.

The latter did not sympathize. "For your

information, Tate, her nose is broken. She's in a lot of pain. Have some respect."

"She's also bloody funny looking." He bent down and kissed her forehead. "I came as soon as I heard. Who did this?"

"She says Doreed somebody. Do you know her?"

"Doreed? No idea. Wait..." He pinched his nose between two fingers. "Doreed." He released his fingers and shouted, "Noreen, right?"

Rachel nodded.

"Noreen Fowler hit you? Why?"

"Because Cary Barx has been houndig her and she blabes me for it."

A white-coated man with a brisk manner entered. "Would the visitors please leave the room? I need to examine the patient." The trio trooped out in less than military order. The man bent down to Rachel. "Hi, Rachel, remember me? Bill Wilberforce? We met at Maude Jewett's New Year's Eve party. How are you feeling?"

Rachel considered a simple grimace adequate response.

The doctor prodded her nose, eliciting a yelp. "You're going to be black and blue for a while, but I think we can take the bandages off now. Nurse?"

"Yes, Doctor Wilberforce?"

"Where's the release form?"

She handed it to him. "Okay, after Judy removes the bandages you can go. I'm writing a prescription for pain. When you get home, I want you to rest for the remainder of the day. Got that?"

"Yes, sir."

"And keep ice on the injury as much as possible."

"Yes, sir."

"Who's taking you home?"

Maude poked her head in. "I am."

"No, I am." Griffin shouldered Maude aside. "I'll bring the car around."

Maude stared at him. "Griffin Tate, who do you think you are?"

"I'm…I'm…" He petered out, his hands dangling helplessly by his sides, his face a deep scarlet.

Their friend looked from one to the other and said slowly, "I…see." She bent down, kissed Rachel's cheek, and whispered, "Good for you."

Chapter Eleven
The Thief

"What do you mean, she says she's innocent?"

"She claims she was nowhere near the museum on Monday. Says she has a girlfriend who'll vouch for her."

"A girlfriend who's looking at jail time then."

"I don't know." Griffin handed Rachel a sippy cup. "Here. Maude gave me this. It's her granddaughter's. I'm tired of cleaning up your spills."

Rachel took a sip and wrinkled her nose, remembering too late what a bad idea that was. "Ouch! Apple juice? If I have to drink from a baby cup, couldn't you at least have put wine in it?"

"Bill says not while you're on the oxycodone."

Rachel grumbled. "I'd rather have an alcoholic painkiller. It's a lot more fun to swallow."

Griffin lightly touched her forehead. "Does it hurt?"

"A little. Doctor Wilberforce says I should be healed in a week."

"And when will the bruising go down?"

"If you giggle one more time when you say that I swear I'll…I'll break *your* nose." She sipped. "Soon. I hope."

Griffin gave her a once-over. "It's getting better. I may be willing to kiss you within a fortnight."

She shrugged to hide her distress at his words. "Don't need your kisses."

"Oh, but I need yours."

She looked up quickly to see an odd expression cross Griffin's face. *Does he really care for me?* Her heart thumped. She took a stab at indifference. "Well, maybe someday, if you're good. And add whiskey to the juice."

He laughed. "I'm off. I thought I'd do some more research."

"What about Noreen?"

"Toby told her not to leave town. I gather he's having the lab cross-check DNA from the maintenance yard with the sample they took yesterday. Maybe we'll get lucky."

"What are you studying?"

"I've been going through sources on Meroë in the journals of European explorers, looking for any further reference to Svendigen's tomb. Bruce, Samuel Baker, Burton, Speke, that sort of thing. George Reisner spent seven years at the site. I thought he may have come across it."

"Svendigen? Oh, yes, the Swedish treasure hunter. Didn't he say it was off the beaten track?"

"Yes, but it's worth a try. You get some rest. I'll be back later."

"We're still on for tomorrow, aren't we? I want to see the fireworks."

"We'll see." He left before she could reply.

Rachel set the juice down and lay back on the couch to indulge in her daily whack at gauging the scope and temper of Griffin's affection. *His comments are so cryptic. I can't tell if he runs them up the flagpole to see if I salute or if he really is interested.*

The man had hardly danced attendance on her in her convalescence. He turned up every other day, griped about waiting on her hand and foot, made fun of her nose, and stomped out. Just about the time she'd convinced herself he'd moved on and that she might as well too, he'd turn up with a bunch of wilted wildflowers he pretended a little girl had thrust into his hands. "What could I do? I couldn't very well throw them away. So I figured I'd unload them on you."

Her glance moved to the water glass filled with asters. "I know you picked them yourself, you bastard. Why can't you admit it?" *Because he's just being nice. Doing what his mother taught him. Bringing flowers to the elderly and infirm. Sigh.*

She swung her legs off the couch and stepped on Spot. He let out a yowl and streaked toward the kitchen. Rachel limped after him. Through the dining room window she could see Phineas tacking up bunting on the playground monkey bars. In the distance, Hermione Ruddles directed young Fred as he wobbled on the yacht club roof attaching red, white, and blue lights. There would be the usual Independence Day parade through the village tomorrow, and the boat race, of course. *I hope Griffin will at least take me into Penhallow for the fireworks.* She pressed her lips together in an effort to stop the tears and went upstairs for a nap.

She woke in the dark. The light on the answering machine did not blink. No messages showed on her cell phone. She fixed herself a sandwich and uttering a rebellious expletive, pulled a beer from the refrigerator and went out to the deck to listen to little Ida Fitzwater practice her recorder. The eleventh attempt at "Frère Jacques" having failed to launch, Rachel sought out other distractions. When the cat refused to cuddle and reruns of Saturday Night Live fell flat, she went back to bed.

****

"You awake?"

"Wha?"

"I *said,* are you awake?"

"I am now. What do you want?"

"It's not what I want, it's what you demanded." Griffin planted himself at the foot of the bed. "I'm here to take you to the damned fireworks. Get up."

Rachel threw off the covers. "I was only taking a nap. It's been a long day." *Without a peep from you.* "You missed a marvelous parade. Old Turtle Dinkins rode his horse and the Gigliano girls decorated Big Mel's pickup as a float."

"Did the fire department make an appearance?"

"Of course. They stopped in front of the inn and let all the kids take a ride on the truck."

Griffin picked up a lacy, pink bra from the bureau and played with the ribbon. Rachel snatched it from his fingers and stuffed it in a drawer, her cheeks burning. His voice suspiciously neutral, Griffin asked, "So, who won the race?"

"The Hills as usual."

"That's because they've got all that high tech sailing stuff. Cheating, I call it."

"It's just for fun, Griffin. Nobody cares. Besides, Josh Hill sails in races all over the world—*of course* he's going to have the latest gear."

"*Hmmph.*" He watched her brush her hair. "I

couldn't make it today because I was busy."

"Oh?"

"With Toby."

"Oh?"

"He let me go along to Searsport with him."

"I thought he'd finished his investigation at the museum?"

"He did. He went to arrest Noreen."

Rachel dropped the hairbrush. "Arrest her! So they found proof."

Griffin picked up the brush and handed it to her. His finger traced a blonde curl, and tucked it behind her ear. "Conclusive proof that she attacked you, yes. Her DNA finally matched something."

She nodded. "Those samples Toby took from me."

"Yes. Noreen still maintains her innocence, but the evidence of an altercation in the maintenance yard and her DNA on your nose, plus your unassailable reputation for honesty—not to mention her lack thereof—combined to give Toby enough to charge her with assault and battery."

"Is she in jail?"

"Yup. In the cell right next to John Pinkney."

"Oh dear." Rachel almost laughed, but then thought of something. "Might they not conspire together?"

"Excuse me? 'Conspire together?' You sound like one of those asinine historical romances. Have you been reading trash again?"

Hands on hips, Rachel lifted her chin. "'For your information, Jemimah Heartsleeve is a very fine writer. She has a 'voice.' "

"A voice?"

"Yes. Her dialogue and settings are quite authentic for the time period. Steampunk is a very exacting genre."

Griffin stared at her, wide-eyed. Finally, he stammered, "So…are the sex parts good?"

"Oh, for heaven's sake, Griffin. Go downstairs while I freshen up, will you?"

He risked a hungry leer and backed quickly out of the room.

As they drove into Penhallow, a rocket shot up and burst into red and gold streams, raining down on the spires of Church Street. Another zoomed out over the harbor, lighting up the pleasure yachts and Penhallow's twin tugboats. They could hear shouts and applause. "Hurry, we're missing it!"

They parked behind her office building and climbed up to the top floor. From there a spiral iron stair led to the roof. Rachel knew from experience that you could see the entire city from here. "It's the perfect spot to view the display." She pulled out two folding chairs and they sat, heads back, watching. Rachel oohed and aahed at the flashes of color and jumped at the loud bangs. She only realized that Griffin had fallen asleep when a gentle snore split the stillness between rockets. She shook him. "Griffin!"

"What? Oh, very nice. Loved the show."

"Oh, Griffin." Instead of the expected exasperation, Rachel felt an overwhelming desire to kiss him. As she leaned over him, a siren began to squeal. He sat up quickly and the chair fell backward. "Ouch." Rubbing his back, he struggled to rise.

Rachel helped him up. "What's that noise?"

"Police. I wonder what's going on?"

"Probably just juvenile delinquents shooting off illegal fireworks. Go back to sleep."

"I doubt it. They usually wait until the official fireworks are over to get the most bang for their allowance. And I wasn't asleep." He stood and pointed. "Look, there's the squad car. It's heading toward Bridge Street."

"Are you worried about your house?"

"Rather. Malcolm Hilgartner—you know, Derrick's kid? He's a total klutz. He was supposed to mow the lawn today and I wouldn't put it past him to have spilled gasoline all over the shed." He headed toward the stairs. "I'm going down there."

Rachel followed him. Instead of taking the car, Griffin strode down High Street and turned right on Bridge Street. They could see a red light flashing a couple of blocks away. "It's not your house, Griffin. It's too close."

"Let's go see anyway."

They had reached the Trinket Shoppe when Toby staggered out of the door with another officer. Between them sagged Maude.

Rachel's hand went to her mouth. "Maude?" She glared at the sheriff. "What the hell do you think you're doing, Toby?"

"Hi, Rachel. We had a report of an alarm going off at Hannah Sundstrom's place. When we got here, Maude was rummaging around inside in the dark."

"You let go of me, you nitwit." Maude seemed to have recovered enough to be angry.

Rachel cried, "Toby, let her go. She has every right to be in Hannah's shop. She's covering for LuAnne this month."

Maude blushed. "Well, not this month, actually. Just June."

Toby straightened. "Do you want to tell me what you're doing here then, Maude Jewett?"

Before she could respond, a tall, blonde woman in full sail descended upon them. Her wig was slightly askew, as though she'd just plopped it on her head. In the blinking light, her pancake makeup—also likely done on the run—would have put a clown to shame. Her shrill voice carried easily over the bangs and pops of the fireworks. Pointing an orange fingernail at Maude, she shrieked, "Sheriff, arrest this woman. She's trespassing on my property."

Toby kept a tight grip on Maude's elbow. "Are you Ingrid Sundstrom?"

"I am."

He regarded her, an enigmatic expression on his face, and spoke soothingly. "Before we do anything rash, I'd like to ask her a few questions. Maude Jewett is usually an upstanding citizen of Penhallow. Maude? Do you want to tell us why you were in *Hannah's* shop at nine o'clock?"

Rachel noticed the stress on the name "Hannah."

The older woman ran a shaking hand through her thick, gray hair. "It's true. I was supposed to watch Hannah's place until LuAnne returned from vacation July the first. Well, she called this afternoon and said she'd been delayed a couple of days. She asked me to go turn the security system on, since the shop would be closed over the holiday. So I trundled over, let myself in, and set the alarm. Then I...I...walked out, but I realized halfway down the block that I'd forgotten my purse. I came back and without thinking opened the door."

"And the alarm went off."

"Yes. Stupid, I know."

Ingrid snorted. "Bullshit. You were breaking in. I know you had your eye on that brooch, the one with the peacock feather. You figured no one would suspect you. Upstanding citizen, my ass."

Toby bit his lip. "Maude? Do you mind if we search you?" He added hastily, "Standard procedure. Then we can all go home."

Maude, who towered over the stubby little sheriff, beetled her brows. "Tobias Quimby, how dare you impugn my integrity? I taught you algebra, for God's sake."

"Er." He looked at the officer. "Tom, would you…?"

Tom blushed. "Um." Finally he turned to Maude. "Would you mind awfully?"

"I would."

"Maude, please." Toby's voice grew firm. "Otherwise we'll have to take you down to the station."

As the tall, gaunt old lady stood, arms stretched out and eyes squeezed shut, Tom patted her down. "Ouch!" He sucked his thumb. Maude dropped her arms, her face purple with embarrassment. Tom slipped a hand inside her pocket and drew out a rainbow-colored feather attached to a pin.

"Aha! I told you!" Ingrid's triumph shot through the general dismay.

Tom handed the pin to Toby. He held it up. "Do you have anything to say, Maude?"

She hung her head. "It's true. I mean the whole story is true—I did forget my purse and did set off the alarm accidentally. And…and I did steal the brooch."

Toby looked at Ingrid, who had been surreptitiously adjusting her wig. "Do you want to press charges?"

"Sure do. S'my property. She had no right to go inside. There are…er…valuable items in there."

Toby gave the brooch a dubious look. "Surely this isn't worth very much."

Ingrid tossed her head, dislodging the hair again. "She'd only start with that. What's to stop her stealing me blind?"

Rachel had to intervene. "She wouldn't be stealing from you, Ingrid." She paused to absorb Griffin's sharp glance. "I mean, if she *were* to steal. It's not your property."

The woman leveled a look brimming with malice at Rachel. "What?"

Maude, having recovered some of her usual aplomb, said, "I happen to know the estate is not settled yet. The store may have to be auctioned off."

Ingrid's mouth dropped open and stayed there for a long minute. When no one else said anything, her eyes narrowed and a cunning smile crossed her lips. "Yeah, well. The stuff *inside* the shop must belong to me. My sister had insurance."

Griffin spoke. "If I understand the situation correctly, even the *stuff* doesn't yet belong to you. John Pinkney is still her husband. Technically, he may have first dibs on it."

The woman turned the full force of her disagreeable personality on the hapless Toby. "John Pinkney is a murderer. He has no right to my sister's property. You tell 'em."

Toby responded mildly. "John Pinkney is a *suspected* murderer, innocent until proven guilty. As such, he continues to have the rights of every American citizen. Including property rights." Ingrid began to bluster, but he cut her off. "However, since the assignment of legal rights has yet to be determined, you may prefer charges as the closest kin."

Ingrid settled down a bit, malicious satisfaction coating her painted features. "I do."

"All right. Maude, come with us. Ms. Sundstrom, you too."

Cursing and mumbling, the two women got in the back of the squad car. Rachel and Griffin watched them go.

"I can't believe Maude would do something like that. What possessed her?"

Griffin shook his head. "I don't know. You know her better than I do."

The fireworks finale—a barrage of gold and silver and green and blue and red missiles—cascaded over their heads. They started to walk back to the historic society building, but Griffin took her hand and stopped. "No, let's go home."

"Home?"

He spun around and headed back down Bridge Street. "Home."

"Okay." *First things first. We'll deal with Maude and murder tomorrow.* She let him lead her to his house, and up the stairs, and into his bed, but before she succumbed to his charms, she giggled.

"What? My technique? My physique?"

"No, my dear. I'm just thinking. Penhallow's lockup hasn't seen this many prisoners since the

Whiskey Rebellion."

"The Whiskey Rebellion?"

"Yeah. According to Katie, it was five years ago. The Jack Daniels truck broke down in Bath, and Joseph's liquor store ran out of whiskey. She'd never seen the good citizens of Penhallow so up in arms."

****

Rachel woke to a loud thump.

"Hey!"

She rolled over and peered down at the floor. "Did I knock you out of bed?"

"Yes, you did, you stinker. God, I'll never get used to sleeping with you."

With some difficulty, Rachel dismissed the painful twinge that came with his words. "You don't have to."

His head rose up over the mattress. "I don't?"

"No, you're perfectly free to sleep alone." She tried to pull the covers up and turn away but he ripped them off.

"Okay, if that's how you feel, I get one last swan song."

A while later they lay in a rather convoluted tangle of limbs and hair. Griffin remarked lazily, "What kind of song do swans sing, anyway?"

"I think they're mute."

"You should be so lucky. Okay, I think I'll crow instead."

"Go for it."

He glanced down at her. "Crows don't have last songs. In fact, once they've chosen a territory, they stay around forever. You can't chase them off with a stick."

Rachel nestled under his arm. "Good."

He lay back.

A while later, Rachel woke again, this time to a huge sun shooting beams that ricocheted off the dew. She stretched. "What a glorious morning!"

For answer, Griffin rolled over and covered his head with a pillow. "Go away."

She obliged. Finding only half-empty Chinese food cartons and a suspicious brown object in the refrigerator, she set up the old-fashioned percolator and sat down to wait. When Griffin appeared in the kitchen half an hour later, she gave him a bright Donna Reed smile. "Coffee? So, how did the research go?"

"Thanks. I forgot to tell you in all the excitement, didn't I? Before I went to Searsport with Toby, I came across a very interesting item in the library."

"Another one?"

"What? Oh, yes. You know I went back to check primary sources—letters, journals, books of European explorers, right?"

"Right."

"I read through Speke, Burton, and Baker without any luck. Then I came across a French mineralogist named Frédéric Cailliaud who explored the Meroë site in the early 19th century. In his book *Voyage à Meroë*, he left very detailed charts of hundreds of early tombs and steles with hieroglyphic carvings. Unfortunately, none of them mentioned the queen of Sheba. So, without much optimism, I checked his footnotes. On page 242 I came across a reference to the diary of an Italian explorer." He stopped to pour more coffee into his cup. "Didn't you make breakfast?"

"No. Go on."

He shrugged. "You know that Mussolini dreamed of ruling over an African colonial empire?"

"Really?"

"Oh, yes. He wanted to play with the big boys, you know, strut around Europe wearing a lion skin and a necklace of shrunken heads, gifts from his adoring subjects. It didn't last long."

"Neither did Mussolini, as I recall." Rachel pulled a jug of dark liquid from the refrigerator and sniffed it. "How long has this juice been in here, anyhow? If it is in fact juice?"

Griffin gently pried the pitcher from her hand and poured the contents down the drain. "I shall continue, despite your attempts to dwell on more mundane subjects."

"Me! I—"

His voice rose an octave. "Italy had maintained rather precarious control of Libya since 1911, but Mussolini yearned to expand the empire, and invaded Ethiopia in 1935. He only held it briefly, and that was the first and last time the country was ever colonized."

"Enthralling." Rachel found a crust of bread in the pantry and chewed it slowly. "Forgive my ignorance, but what does this have to do with the problem at hand?"

Griffin watched the bread as it disappeared into Rachel's mouth. "Patience, child. During that period, Mussolini sent lots of geographers and scientists to map and explore their new colony."

"Like Napoleon in Egypt?"

"Yes. Napoleon was his hero. Anyway, one intrepid fellow named Straniero followed the Nile north and practically fell into the ruins of Meroë, apparently unaware that he'd crossed the border into Sudan and risked capture and imprisonment by the British authorities. He recorded his find in his diary. A diary which, as luck would have it, made its way into Cailliaud's book as an appendix."

"And you read it." Rachel rose and gave the refrigerator one last desperate inspection. "Don't you ever go to the grocery store?"

"I have Durkee's for that."

"Let's go to Durkee's then. I'm hungry."

"Don't you want to hear the grand revelation?"

"I can't listen when I'm starving. Tell me there."

They arrived at Durkee's, Griffin champing at the bit and Rachel grinding her teeth. Once settled in the booth, eggs and sausage on the way, Rachel let her fuming friend talk. "The diary?"

"Yes. Thanks for asking."

"You're welcome."

Griffin was not amused. "Okay. According to Cailliaud, Paolo Straniero was part of a team Mussolini sent out to explore his new colony of Ethiopia in the early 1940s. At some point he found himself cut off from his group, and wandered around, finally stumbling onto the ruins of Meroë. He tried to drive back across the border, but a sandstorm hit and he was forced to find shelter. After the storm passed, he became disoriented and headed west instead of east."

"Wouldn't he run into the Nile then?"

Griffin accepted a glass of orange juice from Katie. "The simple answer to that is yes. A hundred kilometers north of Khartoum, the Nile makes a broad curve around a peninsula of land, in the center of which stood Meroë. Ancient texts mistakenly identified it as an island. So this pinhead drives in circles around and around, hitting water at every turn, until the Fiat runs out of gas. He wrote that he was trying to fill his canteen from the river when he fell in."

Rachel giggled. "Really? Did the crocodiles eat him?"

"If they had, he wouldn't have been able to write his diary, now would he?"

"No, I suppose not."

"Anyway, he floats downstream for a while, finally fetching up on a little sandbar. He crawls up the bank to a tumbledown mud brick building and falls, exhausted, inside."

"Poor baby."

"Poor baby, my ass. The fellow was a complete nincompoop. When he woke up, he discovered he was in a tomb, but one unlike any of the tombs he'd seen in the pyramid fields of Meroë."

Katie refilled Rachel's cup. Rachel took a sip. "Svendigen's tomb."

"I think so. It appeared to have features of both Egyptian and Ethiopian architecture. On one wall he says he found an inscription in a strange form of picture writing."

"Strange? As in not hieroglyphics? So this wasn't the Swede's inscription after all?"

"Actually, I think it was. Straniero just didn't recognize the writing. He was supposed to be exploring Ethiopia, remember? He might know South Arabian script or Ge'ez, but not necessarily Egyptian."

"Wait a minute." Rachel took another sip. "If the land of Sheba lay in northwestern Ethiopia, she would have used her own language, wouldn't she? Why would she leave an inscription in hieroglyphics?"

"Simple. Because she wasn't in Ethiopia. She was

on a trade mission—she would have written in the language of the region so travelers would be able to read it."

Her head beginning to ache from both hunger and an overabundance of facts, Rachel welcomed the approach of her breakfast with relief. "Oh, here comes Katie." She took one large plate from the waitress and set it in front of Griffin. As she reached for her own meal, she asked idly, "Did this Straniero recognize the age of the tomb? Did he agree that it was tenth century?"

Griffin jumped up, knocking Rachel's plate out of Katie's hand.

"Griffin! How could you?" Rachel gazed in despair at her breakfast spread out in lumps all over the floor. Katie joined her.

"I'm sorry, Katie." He grabbed Rachel's hand, yanking her up. "We've got to go to the library. Come on."

Recognizing an irresistible force when she saw one, and not wanting him to consider her an immoveable object, Rachel grabbed a piece of toast with her other hand and followed him to the car.

Griffin spoke to himself as he drove. "Tenth century. Tenth century. Meroë, fourth century. Ninth century—close. Not close enough."

"Griffin?"

"What? Oh, you reminded me of something. This is great." He stepped on the gas and leaned forward, gripping the wheel. Rachel regarded his profile. His lips twitched, and he blinked rapidly. Something tugged at her chest.

When they reached the library, Griffin strode

through the doors four paces ahead of Rachel, yelling for Patricia. "I've got to see Cailliaud's memoirs. Now."

Rachel came up to them. "If you don't mind." She added what she hoped was a dazzling smile.

Apparently Patricia was used to Griffin's ways and didn't quibble. She indicated a carrel. "I'll get it."

Five minutes later they were poring over a dusty quarto volume, its pages dog-eared and yellowed. Griffin skimmed the pages, flipping them quickly. Finally he stopped and pointed at a footnote. "Here."

Rachel read. " 'Francillon, on the other hand, believes there was a settlement prior to the Meroitic kingdom in the bend between the fifth and sixth cataracts. Not much more than an outpost, it would have been a stopping point on the trade routes between Sudan, Ethiopia, and Nubia. He claims to have found two small structures that resembled Ethiopian tombs ten miles downstream from the main city. He didn't have time to record their inscriptions, but he theorized they could be as old as the tenth, possibly the eleventh century BC.' " She looked up. "Straniero's tomb?"

"Yes. And it dates from the time of the queen of Sheba."

"Do you suppose George knows about this?"

Griffin shook his head. "I don't know. But in a way, we're still not any farther along."

"What do you mean?"

"Straniero and Francillon both mention a tomb some distance from Meroë. We have Svendigen's rubbing telling us that Makeda buried her daughter there and left a map to her own gravesite. I'm thinking Masri must have found the tomb, and George may at least have an idea where it is."

Rachel said slowly, "But we still don't have the one thing everyone's looking for."

"The map."

Her stomach grumbled. "I'm going home. I need food."

"I'm going with you."

"No, you're not. I need some down time."

"But what if the dread Marx is sitting on your doorstep?"

"I'll step over him."

Griffin frowned. "I—"

"No, Griffin." She kissed his nose. "I'll miss you though."

A set scowl on his face, he drove her home. When they discovered the front stoop uninhabited, he perked up. "Okay. I'll leave you with this, then. There's only one explanation for Masri's arrival here."

"Only one?"

"Yes. He believed the map to be in Penhallow."

Chapter Twelve
The Date

Her hoped-for siesta didn't go as planned, even on a mercifully full stomach. Griffin's theory kept nibbling at her brain. She finally rose, poured herself some lemonade, and went out on the deck to stew. *If he's correct, the answer to Masri's quest is right here in Penhallow. Somewhere. But is it the answer to his murder? Did someone murder him for it? That would mean someone else knew about his mission.* She sipped her lemonade. That didn't necessarily mean the person would know where or what Masri's find was. George knew about his mission, after all. *Was George lying to us? But…but…if he was, he'd have taken the map long ago…*

She spoke to the lilac in her front yard. "Did George perhaps not go to Sudan at all, but to some hiding place to hole up with his map?" She pictured the fat man, black, silky moustaches drooping over his full lips, his hands as usual holding a knife and fork. *Could he be a murderer?* "Impossible."

To clear her head, she went for a long swim at Kelly's Cove, then walked all the way down Coast Road to Shaman Heights. Early supper, early bed. She was out the minute her head hit the pillow.

As the sun peeped through the dotted Swiss curtains the next morning, her phone rang. "Rachel?"

"Maude! Are you all right? Where are you?"

"Can you come get me? I'm at the police station. Ingrid dropped the charges. I'm free to go." Her voice cracked.

"I'll be right there."

Maude waited on the sidewalk. Rachel opened the car door for her. "You look terrible."

Her friend slid onto the passenger seat. "Thanks. That's all I needed to hear. Oh Rachel, it's been so horrible! I had to share a cell with Noreen." She shuddered. "She's not very ladylike."

Rachel rubbed the bandage on her nose. "She does, however, pack a heckuva right cross."

"Oh, I forgot. I'm sorry. How are you feeling?"

"Improving, thanks. How about if I take you out for breakfast? The Stray Cat's open."

"Sounds perfect. Thanks."

As they pulled out and headed down Waldo Avenue, Rachel asked, "So, what made Ingrid drop the charges?"

Her companion stiffened, then, after a lengthy pause, replied, "Not a clue. She was so furious Thursday night I felt sure I was facing a trial. Elmer had even started preparing the paperwork."

"Elmer?"

"Elmer Bucket has been my lawyer all my life. He was Dad's lawyer as well."

"He must be getting on."

"Eighty-one and still ticking. He would have gotten me off of course. He taught Clarence Darrow everything he knew."

Rachel laughed. "Why am I not surprised? Still, it's a good thing she dropped the charges. She didn't ask for anything in return?"

"Oh," Maude fumbled with something in her purse and muttered, "just a token sum, acknowledging my guilt. A private transaction. No need for Toby to know."

Blackmail. Great. "How much?"

"*Mmm.*"

"How much?"

"Five thousand dollars."

The car veered, and Rachel slammed on the brakes. "Five thousand! Maude, how could you?"

"Look, I did steal the brooch after all. I just wanted the whole thing over with."

Rachel examined the older woman's face, on which pain and embarrassment vied with stubborn defiance. She decided to let it go. *For now.*

They found a parking spot in front of the restaurant, but Maude made no move to get out. "You know what? I think I'd rather go home. Do you mind?"

Rachel thought that was a good idea. She didn't want to make Maude feel any worse than she did already, and she knew she'd be hard-pressed to avoid the subject of the money if they spent any more time together. "Okay." She started the engine and headed back to town. A few minutes later they pulled up in front of Maude's neat, yellow cottage on Elm Street. "Do you want me to come in?"

"No, thanks. I just want a hot bath and a cup of tea."

"Sounds very sensible."

"I'll see you later." Maude turned toward her house and called over her shoulder, "Thanks again for picking me up."

Rachel drove slowly down Amity Avenue, thinking about Ingrid. Was she just another mercenary female like Noreen? Or was her strident reaction to the theft based on family allegiance? No one knew much about her, and she certainly didn't go out of her way to be friendly. If word got out that she'd demanded that much money from Maude, the townsfolk would string her up from the nearest elm. Didn't she care?

On a whim she turned around and drove to Bridge Street. The door to Hannah's store stood open. She pulled over to the curb and went in. Ingrid stood, hands on generous hips, in the center of the room. Canvas tarps covered most of the furniture. A man in white overalls was brushing samples of paint onto a wall. Ingrid pointed to one. "The taupe, I think. With white trim."

"Okey doke. I'll get started this afternoon."

"No, don't start yet. I want to box up all the crap."

"My crew can take care of that."

"No!" Her voice rose a notch. "I want to go through it. Weed a bit. I'll see you tomorrow." She turned around and almost ran into Rachel. "Who the hell are you?"

Rachel took a step back. "Rachel Tinker. We met the other day at Hallowed Ground. And a couple of nights ago...here."

Her face showed no sign of recognition. It did soften however. "Oh. Can I help you? I'm not open for business yet."

"Are you planning to reopen the Trinket Shoppe? That's nice." *Apparently legal niceties such as ownership don't factor into her world view.*

"Working on it. Now that I've got a little money to

spend on renovation."

Huh. So maybe it was *loyalty to her sister.* Rachel warbled, "We all loved this place. It's got so many…interesting items." She waved her hand vaguely at the dresses and kitsch, large and small, piled in the corners. "Is that a totem pole over there?"

Ingrid looked. "I believe so." She moved toward the door, propelling Rachel ahead of her. "I'll be going through the inventory in the next few days. Maybe have a big sale."

Rachel took the heavy hint. "Wonderful! I'll let everyone know."

As she reached the car her cell phone buzzed. Toby texted, "Hearing set for ten a.m. Monday." *What hearing?* The cell buzzed again. "For Noreen." *Oh, the assault. I suppose I'll have to show up.* She didn't really look forward to seeing the woman again. *I wonder if I'm allowed to drop the charges?*

She punched in the question to Toby. The answer came back swiftly. "No."

Sigh.

Rachel spent all Saturday afternoon and Sunday making more lists—lists of suspects and lists of possibilities. *If there is a connection between John Pinkney and Omar Masri, will we ever find it?* Only if Pinkney confessed to it. Setting the Masri mystery aside, she tackled the robbery. She thought back to her encounter with Mary Pinkney. The woman had been afraid—that was clear. But did she fear her father? Or jail? Or something else? Could she indeed have been swept up in the robbery against her will? *Or am I being too easy on her?*

According to Blanchard, John and Mary were

alone in the bank together—*no, not entirely alone.*
There was the security guard…what was his name?
Fred something. *If she saw her father hit Fred, why
didn't she scream? Why go along with it?* And why did
she stay with him in Belize all those years? Noreen had
called her a mousy little thing—perhaps she didn't have
the nerve to defy her father. And once in Belize, she
couldn't find any avenue for escape until they came
back to Penhallow.

Noreen. Aha. That's what she was afraid of—
Noreen. She saw her on the street and knew she was
after the loot and…*Wait.* Rachel pulled her mind back
to the scene at the bank and the underlying question of
Mary's guilt. It couldn't have been serendipity that she
was there when her father broke into the vault. Or could
it? *The deposit slip. That's it.* She'd have to ask Toby
about it. Or Griffin. If he ever showed his face again.
Not that I care.

As the sun teetered on the ridge of the mountain,
unwilling to give up on another day, Rachel sat gazing
at the dark island across the water. Inhabited solely by
people rich enough to afford their own helicopters, its
thick pine forests and empty beaches practically
screamed No Trespassing. Howard Jones, her neighbor,
called up to the deck from the road. "Hey, stranger,
where you been?"

"Hi, Howard. Haven't you been following all the
excitement?"

"Excitement? You mean Maude Jewett collared for
burglary? Nah. I've been down at the garage in
Lincolnville. Almost got the Harley running. I'll take
you for a spin next week if you like."

What Mainers chose to consider an important event

never failed to mystify Rachel. Petty theft by one of their own far outshone the untimely dispatch of a couple of strangers. *Sigh.* "I'd love that. What's Tanya doing?"

"Making suet cakes for the birds. I swear to God she spends more time feeding them than feeding me."

Rachel laughed. "You don't look the worse for it."

He patted his stomach. "You're right. Oh, by the way, she'll be dropping off a blueberry pie. We went picking up on Darling Mountain the other day and came back with four gallons."

Rachel loved wild blueberry season in Maine. "How kind of her. I'll have to give her some of my famous…er…"

"Never mind," Howard interrupted hastily. "Your thanks are more than enough." He loped on down the street.

By eight o'clock Rachel had begun to wonder where Griffin was. She checked her phone and her email. Nothing. *Hmm. Oh, yeah, I told him to leave me alone, didn't I?* She wasn't about to crawl to him now. No, sir. She turned on the television. Channel 10 featured *Survivor*, channel 20 *Celebrity Chef.* When she got to channel 30 and *Naked Dating*, she turned it off. *I'm going for a walk.*

She wandered down the hill, past a couple of teenagers taking advantage of the last few minutes of daylight to finish off a game of Horse on the basketball court. She reached the dock to find the bay at high tide, waves shattering on the gravel beach. In the waning light the moored sailboats seemed to float a few inches above the surface. Farther out, the Werners' motor launch chugged toward the marina, the sound of laughter and chink of glasses wafting across the whitecaps. A pale moon danced on the water.

It all seemed so peaceful, so normal. For a short minute she wished she could go back a few weeks—to a time before the murders, before the unexpected houseguest, before the mysteries that had begun to consume her. *Before Griffin made love to me. On second thought...As Mother used to say, "You can take the good with the bad, the bad with the good, or complain about both and never have any fun."* She marched back up the hill, poured herself a nightcap, and checked her email one more time before going to bed.

*****

She almost missed the hearing. As she entered the courtroom, she heard Judge Smithers say in his deep bass voice, "...released on her own recognizance. Ms. Fowler, you are directed to be present for sentencing on Monday, July 15. That is all." He banged his gavel.

Noreen turned around, the vestiges of a smug smile still on her face, a smile that disappeared when she saw Rachel. "You."

Rachel brushed past her and sat down next to Toby. He looked up from his papers. "There you are. Luckily, the judge didn't need your testimony. We had enough evidence without it."

She nodded at the retreating back of her erstwhile sparring partner. "What's going to happen to her?"

"She'll probably be fined and receive credit for time served. With any luck, she'll take it as a cue to get her butt out of Maine."

"I hope so, but that would mean she'd have to give up on finding what she came for."

"Pinkney's stash?"

"Yes."

Toby shrugged. "That's not my problem. It's going to be Blanchard's as of Tuesday."

Rachel opened her mouth and closed it. "He got the authorization to take Pinkney back to Augusta?"

"Yup. And to tell you the truth, I'm happy as a clam. Edna Mae wants to clean out the cells—it's been grand central station at the jailhouse."

"How is Pinkney's mental state? How did he react to the death of his daughter?"

Toby rubbed his chin. "Funny you should ask. He never bothered to declare his innocence, you know. Seemed angry, then almost broken-hearted. Kept mumbling about 'his Mary.' Kinda sad."

His words reminded Rachel of her musings from the day before. "Toby, I've been thinking about the Pinkneys. Did Blanchard mention the specific date of the robbery?"

"Date? Didn't he say sometime in 2005?"

"Yes, but I want the actual day."

Toby's brow furrowed. "I know Crocker filed for bankruptcy a month after Blanchard claims Pinkney robbed it. Wait a minute—it might be in my notes." He ruffled through the file on the desk before him. "Yes, here it is. Crocker filed for Chapter Eleven on September 10, 2005. Blanchard puts the date of the robbery at August 2, 2005."

Rachel nodded with secret satisfaction. "Thanks. So...do you still think he had something to do with the Egyptian's death?"

"No idea. We've pretty much closed the books on that case. No motive that makes any sense. I couldn't keep him much longer, and Blanchard was on my case day and night to release Pinkney."

"I didn't know you could stop investigating a murder."

"Sometimes you just have to. And no next of kin have come forward—no one pressuring us to solve it."

"That's odd. I heard his family is quite powerful in Egypt."

"Yes, but by all accounts he was a bit of a troublemaker. The Cairo police chief told me in confidence that they considered themselves well rid of him."

"But the man was murdered!"

He waved his hands around the room. "Look, Rachel. It's not like we've been sitting around twiddling our thumbs the last few weeks. I've got to set priorities."

Rachel rose. "Still, it seems a shame. You never found the gun, right?"

"Right. We did find a bullet lodged in the car's ceiling, so we know it was a forty-five caliber, but that's all we have."

"Can't you—what's that called—identify the riflings on the bullet?"

"Could, but what would we match it to?"

"I don't know—you're the gun expert."

Toby led the way out of the courtroom. "I'm sorry, Rachel. We just don't have enough to go on."

On the street outside, Rachel caught sight of a familiar hulking silhouette. "S'okay. See you later." She left Toby and ran down the street. As she reached the little bookstore called Grandfather's Attic, she called breathlessly, "Griffin!"

He turned, his eyes lighting up. "So you've finally

figured out you can't live without me?"

"Fat chance." In her excitement she missed the shadow that passed over his eyes, darkening the cerulean blue to near black. "Noreen's out of jail."

"I know."

"Oh." *Damn. Well, I bet he doesn't know this.* "Lieutenant Blanchard has secured permission to take John Pinkney back to Augusta."

"I know."

Insufferable bastard. "And I know why Mary gave me the purse."

He stopped. "Really?"

Ha. "Yes." She began to walk down High Street away from him.

"Hey!"

She turned and said coolly, "Yes?"

"Come here."

"Why? I'm busy. And hungry. Thought I'd hit Ripleys for a burger."

He lowered his massive head, his piercing eyes sending darts in her direction. She raised a hand to fend them off. "Come…here."

She hated to give in, but her steps turned inexorably back to the handsome, gray-haired man who stood, legs planted, on the sidewalk. When she reached him, he pulled her to his chest and gave her a great thumping kiss. As she melted into him, she heard a gasp. Then another. *I bet a hundred dollars that's Edna Mae and Audrey Carver. So much for discretion.*

Sure enough, a small crowd had gathered on the sidewalk by the shop. And they weren't looking at the books in the window. Rachel contrived to appear serene and indifferent, even though she knew her cheeks were flushed and her eyes glazed. She stepped back from Griffin's arms and twirled, striding purposefully down the street. Only the red light impeded her progress, and only for a minute. She presumed Griffin would follow her and was not disappointed.

He slid onto the bench next to her, a broad grin on his lips. "Priceless."

"I don't know what you're talking about."

"I should have done that a long time ago. It would have kept the old biddy matchmaking machine off my back all these years."

"Excuse me?"

He drew back. "You didn't know? Edna Mae and her barbarian horde have been throwing damsels at me for ages. I had to set up a force field around the house."

"And one around your body. To think all this time I thought it was your sour disposition."

"Well, I admit that helped."

She put a hand on his knee and squeezed, knowing what his reaction would be. He jumped straight up, banging his other knee on the table and smashing his head under Wanda's elbow.

"Griffin Tate—you idiot!"

"Sorry, Wanda. Uh, Wanda, could I get a beer?"

"No."

Rachel leaned in. "I'm really thirsty, Wanda. Might I have two Lobster Ales? And a couple of burgers?"

"For you, Rachel, anything." Wanda tossed a frosty glare at Griffin and swept away.

Griffin rubbed his kneecap. "That's…what?…the third time you've roughed me up in as many days. Mind telling me why you're the temptress all of a sudden?"

"Just wanted to get your attention. You claimed to be aching to hear how I solved the mystery."

"I suppose." He pretended to yawn.

She waited until Wanda brought the beers. "I have proof Mary Pinkney was not an accessory to the bank robbery. She was an innocent bystander."

He shook his head. "Makes no sense. For all the reasons we talked about."

"You're forgetting one thing. The deposit slip."

"What deposit slip?"

"The one Mary gave me. The day before she was murdered."

"So what?"

"Toby told me that Pinkney robbed the bank on August 2, 2005. The slip Mary gave me was dated August 2, 2005."

"I repeat, so what?"

"Well, why on earth would Mary Pinkney be depositing money into a bank she was in the process of robbing?"

Wanda slid two plates piled high with burgers, fries, and coleslaw under Rachel's nose. Griffin waited till she left and dragged one plate toward him. He also picked up one of the beers and took a long swallow. "Huh."

Recognizing reluctant agreement, Rachel poured ketchup on her hamburger and bit into it. When she'd finished chewing she went on. "This is my theory. Mary entered the bank just as her father broke into the vault. He came out with the money, found her there, and forced her to run away with him."

"Why didn't she scream? Why didn't she refuse?"

"Because by all accounts Mary was a very timid

girl. John Pinkney purportedly browbeat both Hannah and his daughter. She wouldn't have had the nerve to say no."

"And so she stayed with him in Belize for ten years? My god, the creature must have been made of mush."

Rachel drank her beer. "Some people are."

Griffin touched her nose. "You *could* be slightly more malleable, you know."

"And ruin your fun?"

He grinned. "So, should we take this theory of yours out for a spin?"

"After I finish my lunch. I'm tired of only getting halfway through a meal before you pull me off on some wild goose chase."

"Fine."

An hour later they strolled over to the police station. Toby stood in his glass-walled office, clearly in a heated conversation with Lieutenant Blanchard. He flailed his arms, his mouth open wide. The state policeman stood before the sheriff through the onslaught, lips pursed, then turned on his heel and marched out. He saw Griffin and Rachel and spat, "This blasted town needs to secede from the state. I've had it."

They both gave him buoyant smiles and held the outer door for him. Toby came out, slamming his door, his face disfigured by fury. "What the hell do you two want?"

"Er."

"Er." Griffin for once seemed abashed. "It can wait I guess."

"No, it can't. I've got to go get the paperwork

started so that asshole can have his man. What a prick."

Rachel was shocked at the unusual language emanating from the old sheriff's mouth. Finally Griffin spoke. "Rachel has a theory about the robbery."

"Will it give me an excuse to hang onto Pinkney?"

"We don't know." Griffin led the way back into Toby's office, and related Rachel's idea.

Toby listened quietly. "Interesting. But moot."

"Why?"

"It makes no difference at this point. Mary Pinkney is dead—we can exonerate her memory, but that doesn't do much for her. John Pinkney may still be guilty."

Rachel's stomach flipped. She saw Mary's terrified face again. *If only I could help her after all.* "Can't we at least enter it in some record? That she was forced to go with her father? That she tried to confess?"

Toby must have heard the desperation in Rachel's voice, for he patted her hand. "Sure I can. And I can inform her mother's sister. At least someone in the family will know what happened."

Rachel wasn't so sure the delightful Ingrid would take the news in the spirit in which it was intended, but it was better than nothing.

On the way out, Griffin tapped her shoulder. "I'm off to Bangor for a day or two. Will you be okay?"

Something clicked in her chest. "You are? How come?"

"Have to see a man about a dog."

"So you're not going to tell me. Are you following a lead?"

Griffin paused, then in a tone that did not fool Rachel, said, "Why, yes."

"Griffin! What are you keeping from me?"

He straightened and placed an offended expression on his mobile face. "Excuse me?"

The clicking accelerated. *He's got a girlfriend there. Oh God.* "Never mind. You're...you're a free man. Do whatever you want."

He hesitated, opened his mouth, but then closed it. "Yes, I think I will. I'll be back Wednesday." He walked quickly away.

A black cloud about the size of her head settled on Rachel's shoulders, spreading gloom over her breasts and down to her stomach. She fought her way out of it and slowly trudged to the historical society.

Three hours later she filed the last sheet of the Drinkwater genealogy and closed the cabinet. She wasn't sure how she had managed to get anything done with the black cloud continually veiling her eyes, but nonetheless she felt a sense of accomplishment. It had been days since she'd worked on the genealogy. *Wasted days. I couldn't help poor Mary. And I...I...squandered so much precious time on a man who doesn't care. How stupid, how naïve can I be?* A tear dropped on the desk. *Griffin is way past relationships. He's too old.* She stood and rapped her fist on the desk. *He's way too old for me. And set in his ways. And...and mean.* She got her purse and marched out of the building. *I'm well rid of him.*

She lasted all the way home, but as she fit the key in the lock, her resolve disintegrated and a great weight pressed on her chest. She managed to push the door open and went down on her knees in the hall. Ten minutes later, she wiped her face and plodded up to her bedroom. Falling face down on the bed, she fell instantly asleep.

The insistent ding-a-ling of the cell phone finally penetrated. Rachel pulled it from her jeans pocket and swiped it. "Yes?"

"Rachel? Are you all right?"

"Oh, hi Maude. I was just taking a short nap." Her voice sounded clogged and raspy to her ears. "What's going on?"

"Well, I've got good news and bad news."

Come on, Maude. "I'll bite. The good news?"

"Okay. You don't have to worry about dealing with the joyless Noreen Fowler anymore."

"And the bad?"

"Because she's dead."

Chapter Thirteen
The Third Death

"What?" Rachel rolled over. The clock blinked 2:00 in bright neon numbers. She checked the window. Pitch dark. *It must be two in the morning. I've been asleep for six hours!*

"I said, Noreen Fowler was found dead in Freeport."

Rachel couldn't resist. "She died waiting for L. L. Bean to open up?"

"Very funny. They just announced it on the radio. WXRQ says it was an apparent overdose."

"Maude, can I ask you a question?"

"Sure."

"What the hell are you doing up at two a.m.?"

"Me? I'm a night owl—didn't you know? Haven't slept more than two hours at a stretch since I was fourteen."

"Really." Rachel rose and, keeping the phone to her ear, began pulling off her rumpled blouse. "So what else did they say about Noreen?"

"Not much. She'd checked into the Windmill Motel—you know the one just north of town on 1A?"

"Uh huh."

"Came in late, seemed kinda wobbly, and went to her room. Night watchman heard a crash and went to investigate. Found her shaking and wiggling on the

226

floor. Died before the ambulance got there."

"Oh dear. I hope it wasn't suicide."

Maude's tone was dry. "She didn't strike me as the suicidal type."

Too true. "Thanks for letting me know. Are you feeling better?"

"It's amazing what a cup of Darjeeling tea and an Agatha Christie whodunit can do for a body. Yes, much better."

"Meet me at Durkee's for breakfast?"

"You got it." She hung up. Rachel took a quick shower and fell back into bed.

The sun, tiptoeing across her cheeks with little warm feet, woke her up. Without thinking, she laid her arm down on the other side of the bed. Instead of the muscular back she expected, she landed on a round ball of fur, a ball which hissed and scratched. "Ouch. Sorry, Spot." *How long did Griffin say he'd be gone?* Her lower lip trembled. *Two days.* The hours stretched ahead of her like a long, lonely highway across the dead, flat plains of Kansas in winter.

Her stomach rumbled, bringing her back to reality and the new day. *That's right—Maude. And Noreen.* She turned on the television. The local news show was reveling in the tragedy.

"Lou, what've you got for us?"

The same reporter, this time in a stained pink button-down shirt and sneakers, came on the screen. He wiped his damp forehead with a flabby hand. "The press conference just finished up here, Andrew. Victim's name is Noreen Fowler, about fifty years of age. From away, but rents an apartment up beyond Searsport. Found by night watchman at approximately twelve-thirty p.m. in her room at the Windmill Motel. Preliminary examination points to cause of death as a lethal dose of potassium chloride."

"What's potassium chloride?"

"According to the doc, it stops the heart." Lou checked his notes. "It's the third part of the drug cocktail they use in executions."

"So was it murder?"

"Police are calling it an apparent suicide, but I have a contact in the ME's office who says she doesn't think it could have been self-administered. She wouldn't tell me why until the results are official."

"Was the woman with anybody?"

"Not that the hotel clerk saw. Word is, she checked in, then left for dinner. When she came back, he says she seemed ill and said she was going to bed. Asked for a wake-up call for seven."

"Yeah, that's when the big Bean sale starts. Probably why she was down there."

"No confirmation on that." Lou made the statement with just the right touch of journalistic conceit.

Rachel turned off the television and was on the road to Penhallow in ten minutes. She met Maude in Durkee's parking lot. Her friend led the way in. "First eat, then we'll talk."

"Got it."

They ordered the special—two eggs over medium, Jen McGillicuddy's homemade sausage, and pumpernickel toast. Rachel spoke first. "The reporter on Channel 8 says that it may have been murder."

Maude dropped her toast. "Another one? What, is it in the water or something?"

"It *is* weird, isn't it? I mean, we've now had three

in the last three weeks. They must be connected."

"Why?"

Rachel stared at Maude. "Stands to reason, doesn't it?"

Maude sipped her coffee. "Not really. The first one—that Egyptian or Ethiopian or whoever—was just passing through. Someone could have followed him here and knocked him off when it was convenient."

Rachel thought of George. *Possible.*

Maude continued. "The Pinkneys return because Hannah is dead, and he hopes to get the store—"

"You know, I hadn't thought of that." *Maybe the case isn't as complicated as I thought.*

"—and then Mary trips and falls off the bridge. An accident."

"What about Noreen?"

Maude grinned. "Not a problem. Hoping to reconcile, Noreen follows John Pinkney here, and when he's arrested, her hopes die and she kills herself."

"Interesting." Rachel mopped up the last bit of egg with her toast. "Except that Noreen arrived first. And Noreen—pardon my French—was a pig."

"Well, two out of three ain't bad." Maude raised her hand for the check. "Where's lover boy today?"

Rachel fought off the cloud. "Gone to Bangor."

"What for?"

"I don't know."

Maude must have sensed that the question was not a welcome one and changed the subject. "You going to work today?"

Rachel sighed. "I guess so."

As she walked up the hill, she noticed a state police cruiser and a van parked in front of the police station.

She wandered over. The door opened and Blanchard appeared with a state trooper, John Pinkney in cuffs between them. He sagged just the way Maude had done, with a similar expression. Rachel felt oddly sorry for him. He'd lost his daughter, his wife...and his other wife in the space of a month. *On the other hand, maybe he's getting what he deserves.*

Toby came out and watched as the men shoved Pinkney in the back of the van and slammed the doors shut. His voice—full of repressed anger—carried all the way to where Rachel stood. "If I come into any new evidence concerning the Masri murder, we're agreed I get another crack at Pinkney, right?"

Blanchard got in the cruiser before he answered. "Yeah, sure. Thanks for your help." The two vehicles roared off.

Toby stared after them, then shook his head and went back inside. On an impulse, Rachel followed him. She caught him before he could pick up the telephone. "Toby, are you working on the Noreen Fowler case?"

"Me? No—that's in Freeport's jurisdiction."

"But they'll keep you informed, right?"

"If I ask them to. Why?"

"I can't help but think her death is connected to Mary Pinkney's."

Toby slammed the receiver down. "Rachel Tinker, as far as I know you're not a sworn deputy, so just buzz off, will you? I've had enough of these murders for one day. And of the state police." When she didn't reply, but continued to stand in front of him, he blew out his cheeks and sat down with a plop. "Look, the DNA evidence cleared Noreen. You can't convict a person of murder just because you don't like her."

"It's not that. I'm convinced Noreen came up here to find John Pinkney's money. He may have followed her, or maybe not. If he didn't already know she had come to Maine, they must have met when he and Mary arrived, or at least run across her. Noreen then tried to horn in or negotiate for a cut."

"And when Mary refused, killed her using someone else's DNA?"

The image of Maude's hands tightly gripping the steering wheel as they talked about Mary's death rose before Rachel. *Could it be possible?* "No, no. I think they were afraid Mary would confess and blow all their plans to hell. Mary wanted out—that's why she gave me that deposit slip."

"Deposit slip?"

"Remember? It was from the bank, the Penhallow Bank and Trust. And it was dated the day the two of them disappeared. The day of the robbery."

"If there was a robbery."

Rachel goggled at him. "What are you talking about?

Toby poured himself a cup of coffee. "I've been thinking. All this time we've been going on the assumption that Blanchard is telling the truth."

"What! You're saying he made it up? Why?"

"Haven't a clue. But Old Crocker never claimed to have been robbed. He closed the bank in August, ostensibly for reorganization. In September of 2005—a full month after the supposed theft—he filed for bankruptcy. He never spoke to the police. I checked all the documents in the records office. Everything was in order. Crocker left town and hasn't been heard from since. There is no way to corroborate Blanchard's claims."

"But…"

Toby scowled. "Look. Blanchard shows up here with orders to investigate Masri's murder. Suddenly he gets this bee in his bonnet about some ancient crime, but he won't divulge the details. If he won't give me the back story, I'm not prepared to believe him. At any rate, we've found nothing to tie either Noreen or even John to Mary's death."

"Murder."

"Maybe. Could've easily been an accident."

"Aren't you even looking for a suspect then?"

Toby rose. "I reiterate, when you are sworn in as my deputy I'll let you participate. Right now, I've got work to do." He showed her the door.

Out on the street, Rachel checked her watch. She'd successfully used up a whopping two hours. Only twenty-two plus another twenty-four to go. She looked around for the cloud and wrapped herself in it.

The day drifted by. Rachel puttered around in the museum room, then went home and puttered some more. The clock had apparently slowed, all on its own, to a crawl. It finally slouched up to six o'clock. Rachel took this as permission to mix herself a cocktail and sit down to the news.

"So, Lou, I understand there was another press conference today on the Fowler death. Any developments?"

Lou appeared on the screen. "Police have now confirmed that Noreen Fowler was drugged. My source was correct that the potassium chloride was not self-inflicted because"—his lips closed tightly, evidently in an attempt to hold back the superior smile—"it was injected into her left buttock."

"What did you say, Lou? Her what?" Rachel heard giggling in the background.

The reporter replied primly, "You heard me, Andrew. Her left buttock. She probably never saw it coming."

The anchor interjected, his voice trembling, "Probably *not.*"

Lou squinted into the camera a moment, then went on in a severe tone. "Police are talking to everyone who was at the Hot Potato—that's a roadhouse near the motel. The victim spent the evening there. She arrived about seven and made the rounds of the available guys until someone she apparently knew showed up."

"Time?"

"Around eleven, eleven-thirty."

"Have they located the man?"

"No, but they know his identity."

"Oh, yeah? What is it?"

"Lessee…Stan…" He checked his notebook. "Stanley Holiday."

Rachel leaned forward. *Stan Holiday? At the murder scene?*

"Do you have a photograph?"

"Yeah. Some guy at the bar snapped a picture with his phone." A picture of a man, hawk-nosed and bald, clad in a faded flannel shirt, loomed onto the screen. Stan did not look happy, even though an obviously tipsy Noreen was mashing her lips onto his cheek.

"How come they have his name?"

"He paid for their drinks with a credit card and the bartender remembered it. Says he always jots down unusual names. Says his niece is writing a school paper on names. Says—"

"Lou? We only have thirty seconds."

"Okay, okay. Here's the juicy part. Bartender says the couple was about to leave when this other woman comes in and starts yelling at them. Bouncer thought it might be Holiday's wife." Lou tittered. "The three of them evidently put on a great show."

"Did they leave together?"

"No one's sure. Their scuffle set off a free-for-all in the bar. Once things calmed down, one of the women went off to the bathroom and the other one followed her a few minutes later. The second they were gone, Stan the Man hightailed it out the door. People drifted back to their drinks after that."

The anchor turned to another camera and began to talk about the upcoming legislative session. Rachel switched off the television. *Stan the man. Huh. Could he...?* She considered the lean, wiry Stanley Holiday. An old Mainer, he had the typical reticent demeanor of a lobsterman. She couldn't imagine him killing a person—or for that matter, having two girlfriends. Stanley didn't have a wife as far as she knew. *So who was the other woman?*

The phone rang. She answered it.

"It's me."

She waited for her throat to open up, then, after a gulp of air, she replied. "Oh. Hi, Griffin. What's new?"

"Just calling to see how you were."

"Are you...are you still in Bangor?"

"Uh, yes. By the way, I heard that Blanchard took Pinkney away."

"Yes. Toby's not happy. Do you know he's beginning to doubt the whole robbery thing? And now with the Fowler murder—"

"Ah yes. The news is that the ineffable Noreen was with Stan Holiday the night of her death. And that he'd been two-timing her. What a tangled web, huh?" When she didn't respond, he asked, his tone suspiciously casual, "Oh, by the way, what's your favorite color?"

"Me? Why?"

"Oh…er…just wondering. Saw a pretty scarf in a store here. Wasn't sure if it would be something you'd wear. So?"

Who is this guy and what has he done with my petulant professor? "Um, I guess sort of a sage green—"

"Like your eyes?"

"Yeah. Or copper."

"*Copper*? That's weird."

"Why?"

"Oh. Um, never mind. How about blue—do you like blue?"

"Sure."

"Dark blue? Light blue?"

"Griffin, what are you talking about?"

He paused. "Just that scarf. They…um…had a lot of different shades. Okay, well, thanks. I'll see you day after tomorrow."

Her throat closed back up, and she could only gurgle. "I thought you said you'd only be gone two days! When are you coming home?"

She heard an intake of breath. "Why, Rachel Tinker, do you miss me?"

I'm too old to dither. "Yes."

He paused again. Then, in a very low voice, he breathed, "I miss you too."

****

Somehow Rachel made it through another day without falling apart. She weeded her tiny garden, chatted with every single person who passed the house, went to the co-op and bought a pound of cheese she didn't plan to eat, and waited for sunset. Just as she began to relax, knowing that her ordeal was coming to a close, what increasingly appeared to be a feature of Penhallow life entered the picture.

She had stepped into Ripley's to get out of the rain and noticed Bert Weems on his usual stool. She sat down next to him. Wanda sashayed over. "You wanna beer, Rachel?"

"Sure."

A man in overalls yelled, "Hey Bert! Yur oughta see this." Wanda turned up the volume on the one screen that wasn't showing the Red Sox game. The ubiquitous Lou stood under an umbrella—from the looks of his shirt a little too late. He was offering a ten-dollar bill to a police officer. When he realized he was on camera he swung around quickly, pocketing the money.

"Oh, er, hi, Andrew. State police are trying to downplay the escape, but the egg on their face is a dead giveaway. My sources tell me the prisoner John Pinkney simply walked away from the police van at a stoplight and disappeared. He's still handcuffed, so if you see a guy in his fifties wearing a wet orange jumpsuit walking down Route One, please call his mother. If she doesn't answer, call Lieutenant Blanchard of the Maine State Police, who was supposed to be babysitting him."

Bert didn't react, but Rachel fell off her stool. He

turned to her. "Hey, you're that friend of Maude Jewett's, ain't ya?"

Rachel dusted off her bottom and pulled it back on to the stool. "Yes, Rachel Tinker. You're Bert Weems, right? You knew the Pinkneys, didn't you?"

His face closed down. She laid a hand on his elbow. "I'm sorry about Mary, Bert. I think she was a good girl. All those rumors were just that...rumors. I met her, you know."

He jerked. "You did? Here?"

"Uh huh. The day before she died. She asked me for help." *Well, sort of.* "Bert, I think she was forced to go with her father. I think she wanted to stay here. With you." *What the hell.*

The eyes that up to now had been stony black and almost lifeless began to spark. "You think so?"

"I do. In fact, I think when she caught her father in the act of robbing the bank, he took her hostage."

He stared at her. "What the...the...dickens are you talking about? Pinkney robbed the bank? Penhallow B and T?"

Too late Rachel remembered the accepted story about Crocker's bankruptcy. "Um...er...I've heard rumors that John and Mary didn't run away together because... because...you know."

He spat into his beer. "That was a bunch of bull...hockey. Edna Mae Quimby and her cronies spread it around, but I bet Ingrid started it. Bitch hated her sister and took it out on the kid."

"You mean Hannah's sister Ingrid? What did she do to Mary?"

"Yeah, Ingrid. She was for sure jealous that Hannah inherited the shop and got the guy. She never forgave her sister, but couldn't go after her because Hannah was the *nice one*. So she picked on Mary. Told her she was ugly and no man would ever like her. Told her she was dumb." He stopped to wipe an eye. "After a while the poor kid began to believe it." He set his mug down hard. Beer sloshed out and spilled onto the bar. "It was that witch what told John Pinkney I was no good. That he shouldn't let me take Mary to the prom."

Rachel tried to steer Bert back to the issue at hand. "That is too bad. So unfair. I'm sorry, Bert. So…you never knew about the bank robbery?"

"First I heard of it. We all just assumed old Crocker ran through that fellow's millions."

"A policeman from Augusta—"

"That one they talked about on TV?"

"Yeah, him. He claims John Pinkney robbed the bank and Crocker never told anyone."

"Why not?"

"No idea. And now Pinkney's escaped, we may never know."

"Oh, they'll catch him again."

"How can you be so sure?"

Bert finished off his beer. "Because he'll come back here."

Rachel reflected as she crossed High Street that Bert was a lot brighter than anyone gave him credit for. *Of course he'll come back here. This is where his stash is.* If only she could figure out where it was hidden. Had to be some place public or open. Otherwise, he would have picked it up already.

Musing on the latest mystery, she ran head first into a hard chest. A rough voice snapped, "Can't you be bothered to look where you're going?"

She raised her head. Somewhere between the open collar of the flannel shirt and the top of a salt-and-pepper brush cut, she found a mouth and clung to it. When she was satisfied he'd been properly kissed, she said, "Where the hell have you been?"

To her surprise, Griffin blushed fiercely. "Busy. I'm back. Isn't that enough?"

She started to argue but thought better of it. "Come on." She locked onto his hand and started to pull.

"Whoa, sister. I have to go home first. Haven't showered yet today. And I need a beer."

Seeing her hopes for a reunion—complete with physically gratifying details—fading, Rachel groped for something to counter with. "I have a shower." *So lame.*

"I know you do." He gently pried her hand off. "But I have some things to do. How about if I bring a lobster by in an hour?"

Don't be needy. She tossed her head. "I have things to do myself. Maybe tomorrow."

"I see. Until tomorrow then." Before she could open her mouth, he turned and strode off.

Well, this is a fine how-de-do. She stared at his retreating back, stiff with anger. When he'd disappeared around the corner, she plodded back to her car and went home. No word came from Griffin that evening. She thought about calling him, but she was supposed to be otherwise engaged. She stared at the blank screen of the television, then moved to her study where she stared at the blank screen of her laptop.

About nine o'clock she drove to Durkee's. Katie was closing up. "Oh, Rachel, it was so quiet we figured we'd shut down early."

"Oh, that's okay. I'll go home then."

She must have looked so forlorn that Katie went behind the bar and poured a mug of pilsner. "Here. I think I've got some pot pie left—I'll warm it up." She bustled around and put a plate before Rachel. She let her eat for a while, then dropped her elbows on the bar. "So, what's up?"

"Nothing."

"That's what my twelve-year-old says when it's something. Is it Griffin?"

Rachel froze. "Griffin? Why would you think that?"

"You've always been sweet on each other. He is a handful, isn't he?" She grinned.

"Does everybody know?"

"Well, Edna Mae and her crowd suspected, but when you put on that display of totally unacceptable PDA it went out over the APB lines within seconds."

"APB?"

"All points biddy."

What would happen if they knew we'd slept together? The thought cheered Rachel immensely. That, and the pot pie. She scraped the bottom of the bowl. "Well, for your information, Griffin and I are not an item. In fact, I haven't seen him in three days. I'm much too busy for any…complications."

"Yeah, right."

Rachel slid off the stool. "What do I owe you?"

"It's on the house." As Rachel left, Katie called, "Give Griffin my love!"

****

Rachel resolved not to go anywhere but the historical society the next day. If Griffin wanted to see her, he would have to come and find her. Her will power only flagged fifteen times as the day wore on. By four o'clock she had had it.

As she came out of the parking lot, a squad car went roaring past, lights flashing. She followed it to the end of the block and saw it turn down Bridge Street. *Griffin. Griffin's hurt. He needs my help.* She walked quickly to the intersection, then began to skip and finally to run.

She pulled up short when she saw where the car had stopped. *The Trinket Shoppe.* What now? *I think I'll just take a stroll down the street.* As she neared the store, a uniformed policeman yanked the door open and went in. Toby followed him, gun drawn. She heard a shot, and then silence. She waited, fists tightly clenched. *Please God, don't make it another death. Penhallow has had enough.* A voice behind her startled her. "What's going on?"

She turned to find Griffin standing in the road.

"I don't know."

"Well, why don't we ask?"

"I don't want to interfere with a police action. Toby wouldn't like it." *Besides, I'm not sure I really want to know.*

"Well, if you won't, I will." He strode down the sidewalk. At that moment, Toby emerged. Behind him, Jeff shouldered his way out the door dragging a man. A disheveled, dirty, sodden man in an orange jumpsuit. John Pinkney.

When he saw Rachel and Griffin, Toby smiled with grim satisfaction. "Got him."

Rachel dragged her eyes from Pinkney. "How did you know to look for him here?"

"There are times when I love my wife."

"Huh?"

"Edna Mae. On her daily patrol through the neighborhood, she saw a figure in the shop. She happened to know—don't ask me how—that Ingrid was at the beauty parlor—"

The policeman interjected, "Havin' a maneecyur."

Toby gave him a disgusted look. "Getting a manicure. So Edna Mae figured it was an intruder and called me."

"Edna Mae has a cell phone?" *Who'da thunk it?*

"Are you kidding? No, she uses a walkie talkie. Set the other one up in my office. Beeps me whenever she sees something out of the ordinary." He indicated his prisoner. "She's usually right." Jeff pushed Pinkney into the back of the squad car, and the two policemen took off.

Rachel kept her face averted from Griffin's. He said nothing, but after a minute touched her shoulder. "Rachel? Are you still cross with me?"

Many years later, she would describe to Maude the effect his words had on her. "It was like the bottom part of my heart dropped into the pit of my stomach, leaving this hole in my chest just big enough to hold all the love he could pour into it."

"No, Griffin."

"Good. I have something to show you." He walked briskly toward his house, leaving her to follow.

The entry hall was empty, as was the living room. "Griffin?"

"Out here."

She went through the kitchen to the tiny deck that overlooked the harbor. Griffin had pushed the two chairs and patio table to a corner and stood in the center. The sun glanced off his hair and shimmered in his azure eyes. Even with the dented nose and bristly chin, Rachel suspected he could have knocked Jude Law, Robert Downey, Jr., and even Colin Firth out of the ring with his little finger. He said nothing, his expression intense but unreadable.

"Well? You wanted to show me something?"

"Oh, er, yes." He put a hand on the chair to steady himself and slowly, awkwardly, went down on one knee. "Rachel…wait, what's your middle name?"

Oh dear. "Um…er…Annabelle. It's actually my first name."

"What? Did you say…" His lips quivered. "*Annabelle?*"

"Griffin Tate, if you're going to laugh at me, why don't you do it on your own two feet? Face to face?"

He ground out, "I would, but I can't get up."

"That's because you're an old fart." When he didn't respond, she asked brightly, "Anything else? Place of birth? Social security number?"

He grunted. "Hold your horses, woman. I'm still pondering the folly of allowing women to choose their baby's name." Rachel turned back toward the kitchen. "Wait!"

She stopped. In the silence, she could hear her stomach growl.

"Annabelle Rachel Tinker, will you…" He held out a black velvet box.

She stared at it. He stared at her, then down at it. "Oh, shit. Forgot." He opened it. The most beautiful ring she'd ever seen lay inside. Gold and silver and copper had been intertwined in an intricate braid. Tiny diamonds peeped out between the strands, and in the center, a deep blue sapphire sparkled. Her hand went to her mouth. After a minute, Griffin nudged the box toward her. "Rachel?"

"What?"

"Will you marry me?"

The telephone rang.

Now, if Rachel and Griffin had been twenty-one they would have let it ring and continued to gaze reverently into each other's eyes. Age and experience forced them to act. Griffin picked up the phone.

"Hello? Oh, hi, Toby. What's up?...Yes, she's here...Okay...We'll be right there." He hung up, snapped the box shut and put it in his pocket. "We've got to go to the station. Pinkney wants to confess, and he says he wants to confess to you."

Chapter Fourteen
The Confession

"Um, Griffin?"

"Yes?" He had started to walk out, but paused.

"Did you want an answer?"

He shrugged impatiently. "Of course I do—and it sounds as though Pinkney's going to give it. I wonder what he's going to confess to. And why to you? *Hmm.*"

"I meant to *your* question."

"Oh! Oh, yeah. Out with it." He waited all of a second. "It's yes, right? Good. Let's go."

Rachel reflected that she had better get used to being shunted aside for more important things. She followed him.

They arrived at the station and were led into a small room occupied by three people, a battered wooden table, and two chairs. Toby and Jeff, the sergeant, stood by the door. Griffin moved over to stand next to Jeff. John Pinkney sat, head in his hands, at the table. Toby helped Rachel to a chair opposite the prisoner. "Thanks for coming. This is John Pinkney."

Rachel regarded the man at the center of so much pain. "I know."

Pinkney raised his head. His faded gray eyes were bloodshot and blurry. Rachel wondered if he'd been crying. "You are Rachel Tinker?"

"Yes."

"You're the one my Mary gave her purse to."

"Yes."

He dropped his head down again. "She thought you could help. She told me she'd left a clue in the purse. She...she wanted to confess. She wanted to take the rap for me. She wanted it over."

Rachel sat down and reached a hand out to the man. "She was a good girl, John. Tell me all about it."

He mumbled something.

"I can't hear you."

He stared at the wall behind Rachel and spoke hesitatingly. "I...robbed the bank...the Penhallow Bank and Trust. In 2005."

Rachel heard a tiny click and assumed Jeff had turned a tape recorder on. "Go on."

"I prepared the groundwork for a whole year." His voice grew more animated. "My plan was perfect. I'd thought of all contingencies." He leaned forward eagerly. "See, the staff always used birthdays as an excuse for a three-hour lunch celebration. Helen Burberry's birthday fell on August second, a Monday. Since the bank closed at two on Mondays, I knew they wouldn't be back that day.

"I waited until everyone had left. I thought I had the place to myself, so I unlocked the vault. Crocker had put two million dollars in the big deposit box. It didn't take me long to find the combination—he'd hidden it in his personal safe." He paused. "Thought he was too clever by half, old Crocker. Moron."

"The robbery?" prompted Toby.

"Oh yeah. I'd picked up the moneybags and started to go out the back when I heard Fred Ellerby—he was the security guard—in the lobby."

He shook his head. "I'd counted on the bank being vacant the entire afternoon. Never did find out why he didn't go with the others, but I knew he'd check the vault and discover the open safe deposit box. If he raised the alarm, I wouldn't have the extra time I'd allotted for my getaway. So I slipped out to the waiting area and picked up one of those stanchions. You know, the heavy post you hook the velvet rope into. I snuck up behind Fred and knocked his legs out from under him. He landed hard on the floor." He looked at Toby. "I didn't kill him, did I? That's always bothered me."

"No, but he had a concussion." Toby gazed speculatively at Pinkney. "I guess it didn't bother you enough to come back and find out if he was okay."

Pinkney grimaced. "It's true. I'm a weak man. Just ask Hannah. Oh no, you can't. She's dead." He put his face in his hands again. He spoke through the fingers. "She was a good wife. She didn't deserve me."

Rachel peered at the sheriff. "How did you know about the concussion?"

"When I went through Blanchard's file, I noticed that Ellerby had gone to the hospital on the day of the robbery." He looked thoughtful. "There was no mention of foul play. He claimed he'd slipped and fallen."

Pinkney didn't appear to be listening. As a tear dripped down his dirty cheek, he continued to ramble. "Mary was a good daughter. She was always so obedient."

Rachel touched his arm. "She just happened to be in the bank that day, didn't she?"

He nodded. "When Fred fell, I saw her standing at the counter. She had a deposit slip in her hand. I'd...I'd forgotten to lock the front door, and she must have walked in and started to fill out the slip when I attacked Fred."

So the plan wasn't so perfect after all. "And you grabbed her and made her come with you."

"What else could I do? I had the stanchion in my hand and the moneybags on the floor beside me. She knew what I'd done."

"You took her to Belize."

"Yes." His thin smile held no warmth. "First, we had to hightail it back to the house and to…to…another place, so Mary could gather some things together and I could hide a portion of the loot. She meant to take her handbag and the deposit slip with her, but forgot it in the rush to make the airplane—"

Rachel held a hand up. "Wait. She left her flowered bag here in Penhallow?"

"Yeah—too bad, because she had over two hundred dollars in it. I had to pull some of the stolen cash out to buy a second ticket." He nodded to himself. "That was a close one. I'd transferred it to this big stuffed bear—"

"Stuffed bear?"

"Yeah. See, I had devised this great cover about how we were going to adopt a little Belize…Belizean?…kid, and I was bringing him this big Gund bear as a welcome present. Then, when we got to the airport, Mary realized she'd forgotten the purse with the cash. So I had to rip open the bear to get at the money for the ticket. Luckily, Mary had a big safety pin in her carry-on and pinned it back up. She was always so prepared, my Mary…" He lapsed back into a reverie, pain etched in his face.

Toby broke his silence. "So how come when she

came into the historical society to see Miss Tinker, she had the purse with her?"

"Huh? Oh, she found it when we came back. Hannah had left everything in her room just as it was when we escaped." A second tear followed the course of the first one down his cheek. "Poor Hannah—I hated to leave her in the lurch, but what could I do? Mary had to come with me for her own protection."

"Really." Toby's tone was dry.

Pinkney reddened. "She would have been charged as an accomplice for sure. Plus, I didn't want that Bert Weems to get his hands on her. Ingrid told me what a sicko he was. Without me there, who would keep her safe? Lord knows Hannah didn't have the gumption."

Rachel let that one pass. "Is that when Mary decided to turn herself in? When she found the purse with the deposit slip in her room?"

"I guess so. Wish we'd never come back." A strangely serene smile crossed his lips. "We were happy in Belize, you know. Mary was so helpful and sweet. We made a life there."

Toby interrupted. "Aren't you forgetting something? Or rather, someone?"

"You mean Noreen." It surprised Rachel that he didn't bother to lie about her. "Sure, we had a fling. But that was it. A real slick chick—she used to go through my stuff when I wasn't around."

Rachel recalled shifting eyes and ruby-painted lips hissing about John going through her purse. *Yes, a real slick chick.*

"And somehow she learned about the robbery. So she finds some stooge to forge a fake marriage license, and claims we got hitched when we were both drunk as lords. Then she proceeds to milk me dry. A year later I'd about had it and was going to dump her, when Mary let slip that we had left some of the money here in Penhallow. The next day she hopped a plane to Maine."

"And you followed her."

"Nah. I knew she'd never find the dough. We considered ourselves well rid of her."

"Apparently not." Everybody jumped at Griffin's voice. "She must still have constituted a danger to you. Why else would you kill her?"

Pinkney's elbow slipped on the table, and his face smashed onto the hard wood. When he lifted it, his eyes were wide with astonishment. He cried, "Kill her? She's dead?"

Toby leaned forward, hands planted on the table. "Don't tell me you didn't know!"

The prisoner shook his head. "I haven't exactly been hanging out in sports bars listening to the news. What happened?"

"She died of a drug overdose two days ago."

The news didn't faze him. "I'm not surprised. She was a cokehead."

Rachel spoke. "It wasn't cocaine. Someone injected her with potassium chloride."

He seemed more nonplussed than frightened. "Potassium what?"

Toby pulled a sheet of paper from his back pocket. "This is the medical examiner's report." He read, " 'Deceased died of 100 milliequivalents of potassium chloride, injected into left buttock approximately one hour prior to demise. Death due to heart failure.' "

Pinkney tried to stand, but Jeff put a heavy hand on his shoulder and pushed him back down. "I…I didn't…I didn't kill her. How could I? I was on the lam—I've been hiding in a dumpster behind Hannaford's until I could get to Hannah's shop."

Toby put the report down. "Okay, we'll leave that aside for the moment. Now—"

Griffin interrupted, "If you weren't chasing after Noreen, why did you come back to Penhallow?"

"I wouldn't have. Sure, I'd left part of the money here as insurance if we needed it in the future, but we could have lived on what I took with me for another twenty years." He broke off. "Belize has a very low cost of living."

"Aren't you lucky." Griffin's dry tone mirrored Toby's.

Pinkney didn't seem to notice. "Yes, we were. But then I heard Hannah was dying. I knew her sister Ingrid would try to get her hands on the store." He made as if to spit but thought better of it. "Bitch. I had to get back before she got there."

Rachel had an inspiration. "Your money's hidden in the store."

"It was. It's not there anymore. Hannah found it and put it somewhere else. We turned the place upside down and all I found was a key and an envelope addressed to Mary."

"Envelope? What was in it?"

He shrugged. "I don't know. Mary wouldn't show it to me. Claimed it was just a note."

"A note?"

"Yeah. Ever since she was a little girl Hannah would leave Mary messages—in her lunch box or under her pillow. You know, poems and prayers, that sort of thing. To buck her up, encourage her." He wiped an eye. "Mary was picked on a lot at school. She was such a wispy, fragile thing."

"Do you remember what she did with the envelope?"

"Stuck it in her purse."

Griffin waved an impatient hand. "You said there was a key as well. What did the key go to?"

"I've been trying to figure that out for weeks. At first I thought it went to a safe deposit box, but it didn't fit. It's one of those old-fashioned types." He held up an index finger. "Small with lots of fancy curlicues."

"You mean filigree?"

"I guess."

Toby rubbed his hands together. "What did you do with the key?"

"I left it in its hiding place."

"You did? Why?"

The man shrugged. "Seemed safest there. No one but me and Mary knew where it was." Toby pointed at Jeff, who made as if to leave. "*But*...but when I broke in today it was gone." Jeff halted on the threshold.

Rachel remembered her conversation with Hannah's sister. "Ingrid's been inventorying—maybe she found it."

"Really?" Pinkney's mouth opened wide, revealing stained and yellowed teeth. "Has she taken over the store? She has no right…"

Toby was unexpectedly mild. "Given your situation, she's Hannah's only other surviving relative. I think she gets it by default."

"My situation?" He turned suddenly sly. "You know, I think the statute of limitations on the robbery has expired."

"Actually, it hasn't. Since you fled the state, the statute extends for another five years. By my calculations, we have a whole year left. Besides, there's no statute of limitation on murder."

Pinkney fell back in his chair. "I told you! I didn't murder anyone."

"I'm not sure we can take your word on that."

A commotion outside the door drew their attention. Voices rose in anger. The door opened with a bang and Blanchard barged in. "What the hell are you doing, Quimby? That's my prisoner you're interrogating."

Toby gave him a broad smile. "Why, hello there, Lieutenant. Mr. Pinkney here has just confessed to robbing the Penhallow Bank and Trust in 2005. We have it on tape and will soon have a signed confession."

The detective's jaw dropped. "He told you about Eddie the Falcon?"

Everyone else's jaw dropped. "Who?"

"Eddie the Falcon. The Chicago mafia boss. It was his money."

"What was his money?"

Blanchard surveyed the company, his face mottled with fury. "Are you folks all imbeciles? I'm talking about the two million dollars Pinkney stole. It belonged to Eddie the Falcon. He'd stashed it at the bank while it was still hot. Two million smackers from a heroin sale in Vegas. What, did you think I was after this little twerp for *robbery*?" He shook his head in disbelief and swung on Toby. "I assumed you knew that. God, you're a fool."

Dead silence filled the room, unless you count the sound of a few mouths quietly closing.

Pinkney spoke slowly. "So...you're saying the

cash I stole belonged to a gangster?"

Contempt spewing across his face, Blanchard snapped, "Don't play dumb, Pinkney. You knew what you were doing. You were Eddie's mule. You were supposed to hide the stuff for him. Instead, you decided you could put a couple mill in unmarked bills to better use than a guy whose virtues do not include generosity. Or mercy. It was your dumb luck that the Feds brought him in on racketeering charges before he could send his gorillas after you. He's been in the slammer ever since."

Toby knit his brows. "Well, if he's in jail already, what do you need Pinkney for?"

The detective blinked rapidly, clearly trying to recover his composure. "Last month one of my snitches told me that word on the street was Eddie had bribed a member of the parole board. It looked like he might wangle his release from prison. We thought we'd lost him, but then the news of the train incident crossed the wires. The chief sent me to investigate, and up toddles Pinkney, the guy I'd been after for ten years. Checkmate. Eddie is handed to us on a silver platter." He waved at the man slumped at the table. "So you see, Pinkney has to come back to testify so we can nail Eddie."

Pinkney's eyes were wild. "But I wasn't this Eddie person's anything! I wasn't mixed up with any mob. Crocker told me the money belonged to an investor. That he'd left it at PB&T in escrow. It sat in the vault for two years. I figured it belonged to some billionaire who'd forgotten about it and wouldn't miss it. If I'd known…"

"Cut the crap, Pinkney. The jig's up."

"Wait." Everyone looked at Rachel. "What about Crocker?"

"What about him?"

"Didn't it seem strange to anybody that he didn't report the missing money?"

Blanchard's lips worked. "He did. He reported it to the state police. We kept it under wraps while we concentrated on finding a way to use it to collar Eddie."

"Yes, but why didn't he report it to the local cops first?" Rachel pursued her line of thought. "He lied to John about the investor. He didn't tell anyone here about the robbery. Why fabricate the fiction that he was going bankrupt if he didn't have something to hide?" When no one responded, she asked, "I mean, who's to say he wasn't the…the mule?"

Griffin, his voice shaking with excitement, jumped in. "And when he discovered the theft, he knew he was toast. If he'd reported it right away, Eddie the Falcon would have been on him like a ravenous pit bull. So he waits a month, goes Chapter Eleven, and beats a hasty retreat just ahead of the hit men."

Rachel warmed to the theme. "Or tried to. Did anyone see Crocker again after he closed the bank's doors? No? For all we know, he may be at the bottom of Penobscot Bay, wearing cement shoes."

Griffin added, "Concrete socks."

Jeff chimed in. "Sleeping with the fishes."

"And…*and,* Fred the security guard was in on it. That's why he told the hospital he had fallen. They couldn't risk anyone knowing what happened." Rachel clapped her hands.

Both Toby and Blanchard rolled their eyes. "When you're finished, could we continue our interview?"

"Oh, but there's nothing more to ask, is there? Shouldn't you be trolling the bay for a body?"

Toby snorted. "You think the fishes have left anything of Crocker to find?"

"N…no. I guess not."

"If Crocker's your man"—Toby turned to Blanchard—"John Pinkney is of no use to you. And I can investigate him for the Fowler homicide."

Blanchard's lips contorted in a snarl, but he said only, "This isn't over, Quimby." He stalked out, slamming the door behind him.

The last of the color left in Pinkney's face drained out of it. "But I didn't kill Noreen! I didn't even know she was dead."

Toby faced him. "Until we have proof of that, you're the prime suspect. John Pinkney, I am charging you with the murder of Noreen Fowler." He gestured at Jeff. "Read him his rights."

"Wait! Wait! At least tell me where and how I'm supposed to have done her in."

"You had some kind of falling out. You lured her to Freeport and drugged her."

A bit of the pedantic banker surfaced and Pinkney sniffed. "I did no such thing. Didn't you say she was injected with the potassium whatever? I wouldn't know which end of a syringe to use."

Rachel spoke loudly to drown out Toby's next words. "Well, if you didn't kill her, who did?" No one responded. She sat down again. "Let's recap. We now have three murders in the space of one month in what used to be an unobjectionable little town. Omar Masri was sitting peacefully in a train car when he was gunned down. Mary Pinkney was attacked and pushed off the bridge to her death. Noreen Fowler was poisoned."

"*Hmm*." Griffin rubbed his chin. "Three methods. Three venues. Doesn't sound like a serial killer."

"Why not?"

"Are they related in any way?"

"Noreen and Mary are obvious."

"Really?"

She gestured at Pinkney. "It must have something to do with the money."

"And Masri?"

"Same thing. Has it occurred to you that Omar Masri may have been on the train to meet Pinkney?"

"What on earth for?"

Rachel shrugged. "Pinkney had money. Maybe Masri needed money." She gave Griffin a meaningful look.

"To buy—?" He shut his mouth quickly. "Still, what would that have to do with Noreen and Mary?"

Quick. Deflect. She pretended not to hear Griffin and touched the sheriff's hand. "Toby, have you located George Hamdani yet?"

Toby started. "Oh, are you talking to me? The sworn police officer here?"

"Yes," she responded, keeping her impatience at bay. "Has Interpol found him yet? He'll be in southern Sudan near the fifth cataract of the Nile."

He gave her shoulder a jovial pat. "Well, I sure do appreciate you tellin' me that, ma'am. As a matter of fact, I have my latest deputy working on it."

"Deputy?"

"Cary Marx. He graciously offered to use his contacts in the Middle East to track him down. And just as graciously offered to go get him. They're leaving Khartoum as we speak." He checked his watch. "Should arrive at Logan tomorrow."

So that's where he's been. "Are you going to charge Hamdani with Masri's murder?"

Toby stuck to his avuncular act. "Now, little lady, we don't want to get ahead of ourselves. Right now, I have to book this man for the murder of Noreen Fowler. When we bring Hamdani in, I'll reopen that investigation. Why don't you two civilians skedaddle for now? We'll be in touch." He tipped his hat.

Griffin surprised Rachel by taking her hand and pulling her up. "Happy to. It's been a pleasure." He pushed her out the door and led her to the street still clutching her hand.

"Griffin, stop! You're hurting me." He let her go but continued to march down the street. "Griffin!" He didn't turn around. After a minute, Rachel gave up and headed toward her office. She had started going through some files when her cell phone rang.

"Rachel, where the hell are you?"

"At work. Where else would I be?"

"Here. We have some unfinished business, in case you've forgotten."

His words did not warm her heart. In fact, she was pissed at him. *That had to be the most unromantic proposal I've ever heard. What kind of a guy asks for your hand and then doesn't even wait for an answer?* "I have some work to do. I'll be along later."

The phone went dead.

She lasted a grand total of forty minutes before packing up and heading to Bridge Street. Behind her the sun lingered on the horizon, exhaling a final gasp of chartreuse light before yielding to the inevitable. Griffin didn't answer her knock, so she walked around the back of the house to the deck. Her quarry was nowhere to be seen. She sat down to wait, admiring the boats clipping back and forth across the bay. After a bit she went in search of a drink. As she poured herself a glass of bourbon, Griffin's Jeep roared up to the curb, its tires squealing. He pounded up the steps and through the door. "There you are. My God, woman, you're harder to find than a flea on a St. Bernard."

"Huh?"

"I've been sitting on your front porch for an hour."

"You could have called me," she said crossly. "I've been here—where you told me to come—for twenty minutes."

He looked at the glass in her hand. "Make me one of those. I'll be down in a minute." He leapt up the stairs to his bedroom.

When he came back down, his hair shone wetly and his face was freshly shaved. He wore a pressed white oxford shirt and chinos.

Rachel looked him up and down. "Are you playing Cary Grant?"

"Cary Grant?"

"In *Arsenic and Old Lace*. The Maskers are putting it on."

He seemed confused. "No. I thought—well, I thought I'd clean up so I could do it properly."

"It?"

He pulled the black box from his pocket. "Now, where were we when we were so rudely interrupted?"

She took the box from him. "You were waiting for my reply."

"I thought you said yes?" His chin wobbled. "You did say yes, didn't you?"

She took a deliberate sip of whiskey, then, when he began to fidget, slipped the ring on her finger. "No, I didn't. But I am saying it now."

****

After all the excitement, it was strange to have a day go by without some earth-shattering event, let alone two days, but that's what happened. Maybe nature needed a nap. Rachel sure did. Nonstop making up for years of unrequited admiration took its toll, and Sunday morning found her in her own bed, alone, trying to read the newspaper. She had to stop every paragraph or so to smile secretly to herself or answer a text from Griffin, so it took her a full two hours to get through the front section. *No matter*.

As a mature adult, she knew she should be working or being productive in some fashion, but she didn't want to. She wanted to stare out the window or maybe just up at the ceiling and gloat over her good fortune. In fact, she planned to do just that for another twenty-four hours.

By Monday, she had had enough. By Monday all hell would break loose again anyway.

As she parked the car behind her office, her cell phone tinkled. "Hello?"

"Rachel, I'm back!" Cary's excited voice floated over the bandwidth.

Rachel paused, not sure how soon or by what means to burst his bubble. "Hi, Cary."

"Where are you?"

"At the society."

"Working?"

Duh. "Yes, I am. I have a pile of stuff to do after the last few days."

"Oh? What's been going on?"

Rachel discovered to her surprise that she wasn't ready to tell Cary her personal news. She wanted to keep it to herself for a while longer. *I might not even tell Maude yet.* "Well, the state police took John Pinkney away and then lost him. Toby found him and he's back in jail. Noreen Fowler was murdered—"

"I know all that." He managed to make the statement both condescending and aggravating. "I'm heading to the station now. I'll pick you up at twelve-thirty for lunch." He hung up before she could refuse.

Griffin called. "How did you sleep?"

"Oh, extremely well." She allowed the grating sound that indicated irritation to ebb before continuing. "Guess who's back in town? Cary Marx."

"The fifth brother. The unfunny one. He's taking you to lunch."

"How did you know?"

"Saw him on the street. He told me."

"Should I refuse?"

"Do what you want. I promised Patricia I'd help her with a manuscript. We'll probably have a working lunch."

I guess things don't change just because you're engaged. "Fine. I'll find out whether he retrieved George."

She could sense his interest spark by the quickened breath. "Ooh. Um. I'll have to stop by the station and see."

Not if I get there first. "Oh, would you mind picking up some hamburger…and some wine for me

261

first? Just drop it at the house. I thought we might grill out tonight."

"I guess so. You wouldn't by any chance be planning to do an end run around me and weasel the news out of Toby first?"

"*Moi*? Are you saying you refuse to do me the teensiest favor?"

He spluttered, "You'll regret this, doll face."

She hung up and sprinted out the door and up the street to the sheriff's office. It was crowded with people. The sergeant, Toby, and Cary took up one corner of the office, and George Hamdani took up the rest of it. Rachel sidled in. "Hello, George."

He kissed her hand. "*Bonjour, ma chère amie. Comment ça va?*"

"*Bien, merci.* It goes." She looked at the other three men crushed together in the corner. "I just thought I'd drop in and see my old friend." She waited expectantly.

Cary broke from the pack first. "I nabbed him, Rachel. He tried to get away in Khartoum and again in Frankfurt, but he was no match for me. Took me an extra day, but I found him hiding at the Frankfurt Hilton." He faced Toby and almost saluted. "Didn't I tell you I'd catch him?"

Toby shook his head wearily. "You did, Mr. Marx. Thanks." He turned to George. "You want to tell me why you skipped town when I expressly told you not to?"

The fat man looked down his bulbous nose at the sheriff. "Of course, Sir Sheriff. I was pursuing a lead. I believe Omar Masri was killed because he was after an extremely valuable piece of information. Professor Griffin Tate and I are working together, attempting to solve the mystery and thus find Masri's killer."

A booming baritone cut through the hubbub that followed this announcement. "Except that George here scampered off to Sudan all by his lonesome to find the tomb, leaving me to sift through crumbling manuscripts in the bowels of the Hutchinson Center." All eyes went to Griffin, who stood in the doorway—mainly because he couldn't fit inside the room.

In a puzzled voice, Toby asked, "The tomb?"

George interrupted. "Never mind that. I found something, Tate! That's why I came back."

Cary hunched his shoulders as though he thought that would make him look taller. "Bullshit, Hamdani. I had to drag you back kicking and screaming."

The big Lebanese contrived to look affronted. "You did no such thing. I came of my own accord. Sheriff, you should arrest this man for molesting me."

Toby raised his eyebrows. "Molesting you?"

"Yes. Snapping at my heels. Trailing me across the globe. I managed to give him the slip in Germany, but this…this *blackguard* found me and hauled me away from my hotel in Frankfurt." He paused for dramatic effect. "*Before room service arrived.*"

Rachel gasped. Did Cary know how close he came to being strangled?

George continued to complain. "And then he insisted that he be seated next to me in the airplane. He was most offensive."

Toby glanced from one to the other. "Hamdani, I expect you to stay put at your hotel this time. Now get out, all of you."

All eyes turned to the sheriff. "But…"

"But…"

"But…"

"But…"

"Out!"

It took a while, but at last, the four ersatz Hercule Poirots made it out of the room and the building. They huddled on the sidewalk, not sure what to do next. Finally, Cary checked his watch. "I'm hungry. Come on, Rachel."

Tossing a smirk at Griffin, Rachel let Cary lead her away. Out of the corner of her eye, she saw Hamdani take Griffin's elbow and start talking fast. *Damn, I'm going to have to beg Griffin to tell me what he found out. Unless I can winkle it out of George.* She began to tick off the contents of her refrigerator in her head.

She let Cary chatter on through the long meal, her mind on George's discovery, if indeed he'd made one. When Cary had finished both extolling his own ingenuity and perseverance, and half of her sandwich, she broke in. "Thanks ever so much for lunch, Cary, but I'm afraid I really have to get back to work. Can you give me a lift?"

He stopped mid-sentence. "I thought we'd spend the afternoon together."

Oh Gawd. I'm going to have to tell him after all. "I really can't. And besides, Cary, I think you should know. I'm…I'm dating someone else."

He rocked back so fast the chair fell over, taking him with it. The waitress ran over and helped him up. Rachel couldn't help but notice the look on her face, at once adoring and anxious. "Oh, Mr. Marx, are you okay? Can I get you anything? Anything at all?" She stopped, out of breath.

He must have sensed the girl's attraction to him,

for he squeezed her hand a little too warmly and simpered, "My dear Sheila, I'm fine. Don't you worry about me."

Sheila beamed and Rachel thought, *yes! Now to give the inclination a little push.* She spoke enthusiastically. "So, Sheila, how's school going? Are you getting close to finishing that master's degree in business?"

The waitress's eyes lit up. "Only one more course to go! I'm so excited."

Cary waxed expansive. "Great. Well, then, when you have that little piece of paper in hand, you should apply for a job at Sloane and Marx. I'd be happy to put in a good word."

"Oh, Mr. Marx, that would be swell." She batted her eyelashes at him. Rachel cringed, but it came as no surprise that Cary's chest inflated to the size of a medicine ball.

"Just let me know when you're available, and I'll get my secretary to set you up with an appointment at the Human Resources department."

After much fawning and gibbering, they finally escaped Sheila's clinging ambition, Cary with visible reluctance. Rachel was proud of herself. With any luck, the budding romance would blossom, and she'd be off the hook. Cary dropped her off on Market Street. "I'd better tell the office about Sheila Andrews before it slips my mind." He drove off.

Rachel quit about five-thirty and headed home. She longed to talk to Griffin, but since he hadn't called, she suspected he was closeted with George. She'd find out soon enough what the Lebanese had been doing—*he'll tell me anything, as long as I promise him a nice juicy*

265

lamb chop.

She stopped off at the co-op butcher on the way—*just in case*—and climbed up the back stairs. The two men sat waiting for her. George lumbered out of his chair. "I understand congratulations are in order."

Rachel looked in surprise at Griffin. "You told him?"

"Well, of course I told him."

"But I thought we were going to keep it quiet for a while. Find the right moment to announce it."

"Announce it? No, we need to get the article in shape before we make any announcements. I want to publish as soon as possible."

Rachel stared at him blankly. "Huh?"

"Our discovery."

Hamdani chimed in. "I thought I'd impress Professor Tate that I'd found the tomb, but he says you two had already ascertained its location. Very fine detective work, I must say."

"Oh. Oh, yes. Thank you."

George patted his stomach. "Before I relate my latest and most important news, I wonder if I could prevail upon you to rustle us up a spot of dinner? I took the liberty of bringing steaks and a pleasant, if understated, bottle of Pinot Noir."

Rachel knew that to quibble would be useless, so she went to the kitchen. Griffin graciously offered to fire up the grill, and she slathered the thick, juicy strip steaks with mustard, then sliced some onions for him to cook with them. Luckily, she had a bag of fresh greens from the farmer's market, and made up a large salad of arugula, mâche, butter lettuce, and spinach, garnishing it with nasturtium flowers from the garden.

As usual, George finished his food in record time. He sat back and watched with amusement while the others enjoyed the meal at a more leisurely pace. When Rachel had taken the dishes to the kitchen and come back, he said, "Now, I shall tell you of my adventures."

Rachel put down her wine. "You tore off to Sudan looking for Masri's tomb."

"Yes." He grinned at Griffin. "And just like your hapless Italian, I lost my way, fetching up at a small beehive structure about ten miles from Meroë. I immediately recognized both Ethiopian and Egyptian elements in the architecture."

Griffin poured more wine. "George concurs with our other sources that the structure was much older than the complex at Meroë, probably part of a trading post on the Nile."

The big man leaned forward, his eyes impassioned. "Imagine my sensations when I found the very inscription from our rubbing there."

Griffin took up the thread. "He could easily tell the inscription dated back to at least the tenth century."

"The queen of Sheba's time."

"Precisely."

"Unfortunately, the inscription was in even worse shape than our rubbings, so it was of little use." George stood up with many a creak from his knees and planted his hands on the table. "But…but I made my most important discovery after that."

"Which was?"

He poured the last of the wine into his glass. "I made my way back to the highway, where my rental car unfortunately balked at further movement. I managed to flag down a passing bus"—here his features expressed extreme distaste—"which took me to Khartoum. The bus driver directed me to a passable little hostel near the Omdurman souq." He smiled fondly. "The mistress— her name is Leila—seemed rather taken with me and shared many a toothsome dish while I was there. I told her of my quest." He stopped for effect. "She was aware of the little tomb."

His audience rewarded him with excited squeals. "She was?"

"Yes. She also knew that it had been looted."

"Like every other tomb on the planet."

"Ah, but in this case, the looter was an...er...acquaintance. He told her where he had sold some of the artifacts. A small shop on Walad Garbur. I strolled over to it one evening and spent a pleasant hour with the shopkeeper. I must say Sudanese tea is not as good as Turkish. I should probably stick with *qat.*"

"*Qat?*"

Griffin leaned forward. "*Qat* is a plant native to the Horn of Africa. It produces a mild stimulant effect when chewed, equivalent to coffee."

"Go on." Rachel felt restless. She wished now that Griffin had told George of their engagement. She was tired of the suspense and wanted to go back to sweet talk.

George blew out his cheeks. "The shopkeeper showed me many interesting pieces, both Nubian and Egyptian, but he said his most prized item had been a stone stele from my tomb, a column carved with a mix of hieroglyphics and a strange script unfamiliar to him."

"Did he show it to you?"

"No. He had sold it several years earlier, but before he gave it up, he had carefully copied the inscription on it in case a brilliant archaeologist—"

"Such as you."

"Such as I, came into his store and could read the writing. He brought it out for me."

"Could you read it?" *Out with it.*

He shook his head. "I had no trouble with the hieroglyphics, of course. The other script resembled a very early form of proto-Sinaitic, an ancient alphabetic system discovered in the Sinai peninsula. It's a complex system, probably a precursor of the Phoenician or—"

Griffin leaned forward, his face inches from George's. "*Could you read it?*"

The big man huffed a little, but replied, "A very little. I had not brought a lexicon with me, but I did make out the words 'Balkis,' 'daughter,' 'map,' and 'wood.' "

Rachel, after a brief intermission to dwell on Griffin's profile, returned her attention to the discussion. "Balkis?"

"Balkis or Belkis is one of the names given to the queen of Sheba."

"I thought it was Makeda?"

George clarified. "I believe I told you Belkis is her Arabic name. She is called Makeda in Ethiopia."

"So," said Rachel, thinking aloud, "do you think this stone column repeated what the inscription said?"

"Probably. One would have to study the stone itself, with a key to the script. At least now we have the added information that the map was on wood."

Griffin rose and paced. "If it was on wood, it would have disintegrated long before this."

"If it were exposed to the elements, yes…but what if it weren't? What if it had been looted along with the stele?"

"Then the shopkeeper would have it." Rachel turned to George. "Did he?"

"Allow me to finish. No, he did not. He had only acquired the stele, and he had sold that maybe ten years ago. She—"

"She? A woman bought it?"

"Yes. An Austrian. She seemed to appreciate the historic nature of the piece and paid a great deal of money for it. The shopkeeper remembered her being quite exuberant. She said something about it solving a mystery for her."

"Was she an archaeologist?"

"He didn't think so. She left him her card. She owned an antiquities shop in Vienna."

Rachel exclaimed, "Vienna! Masri explored antique shops in Vienna, didn't he?"

"Had he visited the shop in Khartoum then?"

"Yes. However, the man had misplaced her card, and only found it after Masri had left."

"So he knew the stele was in Europe, but not exactly where."

"Yes. When I spoke with the Sudanese dealer, he gave me the card. He'd been holding it, hoping Masri would return." George smiled wickedly. "I told him I knew Masri and would be sure to deliver the card to him."

"Ha."

"So..." George gave a little hiccup. "I came back to ask you to accompany me to Austria."

"To find the stele?"

"To find the map."

Chapter Fifteen
The Day-Noo-Mon

"The map? What makes you think the map is in Vienna?"

"*Because...*" George began to exhibit the early signs of impatience. Past experience told Rachel to open another bottle of wine and a few sips restored him to his normal equanimity. "Thank you, my dear. Because otherwise the woman would not have been in such a fever. Remember, she said the stele cleared up a mystery. What else could she be referring to if not the map? Ergo, she already had it, but couldn't decipher it. Or needed a key of some sort..."

"A key!" Rachel could feel the thrill of the hunt start to course through her veins. "Masri said he'd found 'the key.' And he went to Vienna. You may be on to something, George."

"Of course I am. When can you be ready?"

She rose and started toward the stairs. Griffin held out a hand. "Where are you going?"

"Why, to pack, of course. And I suppose I'd better find my passport...and make reservations...and—"

"Stop!"

One foot on the stairs, she paused. Griffin walked over, took her arm, and brought her back to stand before George. "I'm afraid we can't go just yet."

George blinked. "Really? I thought I was being

surpassingly generous by offering to include you."

"Sorry. I'll—we'll…be busy."

"What could be more important than finding the tomb of the queen of Sheba?"

Griffin took Rachel's left hand and showed it to George. "Getting married?"

After the initial shock had dissipated, George was able to congratulate his two friends, although not without a lot of heavy-handed teasing and artificial sighs. "To heal my broken heart, I shall be forced to take total credit for the discovery. I shall mention you in a footnote, but that's all I can promise at this time."

"You don't know whether you'll find the map in Vienna or not, George. It could have been sold long ago. You said the woman purchased the stele ten years ago."

Rachel added, "If she already possessed the map, she might have sold it and the stele by now. It's not like she was a collector. In fact, she may have been on commission."

"That's right. It could have been a confidential sale. We might get all the way over there and she won't be able to tell us anything."

George tossed off his wine. "Regardless of your pessimism, I intend to make the attempt."

"You're not climbing Mount Everest, you know." Griffin gave him an amused pat.

Rachel was less sanguine. "Besides, Sheriff Quimby might not be too keen on letting you leave again."

His large, flat face crumpled. "I'd forgotten about the good sheriff. Perhaps we can enlist him in the chase?" His childlike expression, full of unrealistic hope, depressed Rachel.

"Perhaps. Still, you should talk to him. He continues to believe you're involved in Omar Masri's death."

"True. I shall explain that I am incapable of murder. That should suffice."

"It's worth a try."

After George left, Rachel took a stab at engaging Griffin in wedding planning, assuming she'd have little success. In fact, she had no success. Apparently, his participation was confined to the exhibition of Rachel's ring to George. After that, as he told her gruffly, she was on her own.

She waited until the next morning to try again.

"At least tell me *when* you want to get married."

"Now."

"Come *on*."

"Okay. Later."

"Fine. I guess I'll call Maude. She'll take it from there."

"You wouldn't dare."

"Wouldn't I?" She marched to the phone and picked up the receiver.

Instead of reacting as she expected, Griffin picked up his own phone and dialed. "George? What did the sheriff say about your going to Vienna? He did? You're where? I see. Well, I'll just have to go by myself then." He hung up. "Sheriff Quimby did not greet George's proposal with the warm reception it deserved. Our Lebanese friend is currently languishing in jail with only Edna Mae's cooking to sustain him."

"Oh dear." Toby's wife's cooking was of the defrost and microwave variety. Whenever Penhallow held a potluck or celebration, she was asked to bring the lemonade.

Griffin dialed another number. "Stella? I need a reservation for Vienna. Yes, Austria. I'll hold." He stood, tapping his foot on the floor.

Rachel, receiver in hand, gaped at him. "Griffin!"

He held up a hand. "Yes…the nine o'clock flight I think…yes…could you book two tickets?" He picked up a pen and wrote on a paper towel. "Got it. Lufthansa #3506, departing Boston, Thursday, July 18 at nine a.m. I'll email you the particulars. Thanks so much, Stella." He hung up and looked at Rachel. "You do have a passport, don't you?"

"I'm going too?"

He picked up his car keys. Without looking at her he mumbled, "Yeah—you know. Kill two birds with one stone. Solve the mystery and tie the knot. I have a friend with a house in the mountains. Might be nice. Er, what do you think?"

Rachel did something very unlike her. She plopped on Griffin's lap and gave him a wet, smacking kiss right on the lips. Before he could react, she jumped off. "I have to pack."

****

In a burst of unprecedented prodigality, Griffin sprang for first class seats, so Rachel barely noticed the bumpy ride across the Alps. As the plane circled closer to the airport, the last rays of a purple sunset glancing off its wings, she watched the lights of Vienna spring up. She'd never been to the city and felt exhilaration and trepidation in equal doses. "Tell me where we're staying again?"

"In the Hotel Opernring. It's a small pension right

on the Ringstrasse. You'll love it."

She shyly touched his hand. "I'm sure I will," she whispered.

He pretended not to hear.

That night, Griffin took Rachel to a local gasthaus for Wiener schnitzel, and introduced her to the local wine made from the Grüner Veltliner grape.

"It's delicious! Lots of citrus and something else…something spicy."

"Some people say it tastes like green pepper. It's produced in vineyards just outside the city. Many of them have restaurants called *Heurige,* and people go out there to eat and taste the wine right from the barrel."

"Oh, it sounds like such fun. Let's do it."

"No time."

Rachel refused to let Griffin spoil her mood. "Fine. On our next visit then."

After dinner they wandered along the Ringstrasse—the beautiful boulevard that encircles the old city of Vienna. Hopping a trolley, they rode down to the Hotel Sacher. In the tiny bar, Griffin ordered cognac and a slice each of Sachertorte.

Rachel took a small bite. "Oh my God, Griffin. This is incredible!"

"Isn't it? Franz Sacher invented it in 1832 for Prince Metternich while only an apprentice chef of sixteen. A thin layer of apricot jam is spread between two layers of rich chocolate cake, then the whole is frosted with a bittersweet ganache."

Rachel had polished off her slice and begun on his before he finished his explanation.

In the following days they explored Vienna, from the Hofburg Imperial Palace to the magnificent

Belvedere, to St. Stephen's Cathedral. Griffin refused to stand in line to watch the Royal Lipizzan horses practice at the Spanish Riding School, but did take Rachel to the Prater, the enormous amusement park in the middle of the city. They rode the Riesenrad—the ferris wheel featured in the classic thriller *The Third Man*—and walked among the bizarre life-sized statues that dotted the little squares. Rachel balked at entering the Imperial Vault, the underground crypt where all the Hapsburgs were buried in huge stone sarcophagi, but agreed to visit St. Peter's Church when she learned the service featured a quartet playing Mozart.

After reading of the tragic murder-suicide of Crown Prince Rudolf and his mistress, they took the train to the beautiful country palace of Schönbrunn. Rachel wandered the luxuriant gardens, imagining Rudolf—heir to the thrones of Austria, Bohemia, and Hungary—walking arm in arm with his mistress, the Baroness Mary Vetsera, despairing of happiness. The night in 1889 when he took her life and then his own had been kept secret for decades. She stood before the palace he had loved and sighed for as long as Griffin would allow, which turned out to be about thirty seconds.

On the fourth day of their trip, Rachel woke to a beautiful sunny day. A tap told her Ursula, the concierge's daughter, stood outside with their breakfast tray. She stretched and called, "*Herein!*" The little girl came in shyly and placed a tray on the table, bowing her way back out. Rachel gave the traditional Viennese greeting. "*Grüss Gott, guten Tag.*"

"*Grüss Gott, guten Tag.*" Ursula smiled and closed the door.

"Griffin, wake up! Breakfast is here."

He groaned. "You'll be the death of me, Rachel. I got no sleep last night. You're insatiable."

She pulled the pillow out from under him. "It's just that you're so good at it. However did you find that spot—what is it?"

"The G spot. It's right where it's always been."

"Anyway, it drives me crazy."

"I *know.* Now shut up and eat your eggs. Give me fifteen more minutes, and I'll be yours for the day."

She shrugged, which he didn't see because he'd dragged the covers over the pillow on his head. Fifteen minutes later, true to his word, he got up, showered, ate the remnants of their breakfast, and remarked, "Shall we seize the day?"

Rachel bounced on the bed. "Where to, oh fearless leader?"

"It's time we got down to business. I propose we visit our lady's shop and ascertain the status of Sheba's map."

"Did George give you her name?"

"Yes." Griffin checked his notebook. "It's a Frau Wechsler."

"And directions as well?"

He nodded. "Poor George. He looked so pathetic sitting there behind bars. As I left, Edna Mae was bringing him lunch."

"Oh dear—adding insult to injury."

They took a taxi to an address on Rechte Wienzeile, near the huge city market, the Naschmarkt. A painted wooden sign hung from a pole. "Wechsler Kunsthandel. This is it."

They walked into a cluttered, dusty, dark hole of a

place. No one came forward. For five minutes they sifted through mismatched pieces of china and silverplate piled willy-nilly on wobbly tables, and peered into tall glass cases peopled with strange and exotic statues and fetishes. One large cabinet opened to reveal stacked clay bowls and figurines obviously looted from pyramids.

A noise at the rear of the store drew their attention. From behind a door sauntered a young woman dressed in tight jeans and a sheer blouse. She gave them a cursory look and spoke in English. "May I help you?"

Rachel didn't stop to wonder how she knew they were Americans—body language, clothes, and facial expressions were always a dead giveaway. "Are you Frau Greta Wechsler?"

The girl frowned. "No, of course not. I'm Fräulein Liesl Wechsler. Frau Wechsler was my mother. She passed away a year ago."

"Oh, I'm so sorry." Rachel waved her hand at the jumbled merchandise. "Did you inherit her shop?"

This time the girl rolled her eyes, intensifying the macabre effect of her violet eye shadow and jet black mascara. "I did. I'm in the process of liquidating most of the inventory. No one wants this old trash."

Griffin spoke. "We're here about a particular item that your mother brought back from Sudan. A stele. Is it still here?"

"What's a stele?"

"It's a standing stone—a carved monument. It had two kinds of writing inscribed on it."

"Oh yeah—that's in the back. Too heavy to move. I'll burn it with the rest of the building for the insurance." She grinned at the joke.

Griffin apparently decided to let that slide. "May we see it?"

"Sure." She led the way to a second room. A columnar stone about eight feet high leaned against a wall. In the dim light Rachel could make out figures and pictures etched deep in its surface.

Griffin took out a magnifying glass. "Do you mind?"

"Knock yourself out."

He sat on his haunches and studied the writing for a long time, checking now and then in a small paperback he'd brought with him. Finally he rose. Fräulein Liesl raised her eyebrows. "Well?"

He asked mildly, "Was your mother an archaeologist?"

"Mother? Not officially, but she dabbled in Middle Eastern artifacts. She was pretty knowledgeable. Did you see those Assyrian pots in the cabinet by the front door? They're supposed to be quite valuable. Couple of years ago a guy from National Geographic came in and photographed them for a magazine article." She pursed her lips. "Can't understand why nobody bought them after all that publicity." She arched her brows and gave Griffin a coquettish smile. "If you're interested, I can make you a good offer."

"We might be." Griffin peered into the shadows. "When Frau Wechsler bought the stele, she mentioned to the dealer in Khartoum that it would help her solve a mystery. Do you have any idea what she meant?"

"Nah. She was always dreaming that she would come across something unique or historic. In her cups, she used to claim she knew where King Solomon's mines were. And where the queen of Sheba is buried."

She sniffed. "Stuff and nonsense. Silly old fool."

Rachel could feel the man beside her tense. He remarked casually, "The queen of Sheba's tomb, huh? Did she say how she discovered it?"

Liesl closed her eyes. "I never paid much attention to her fantasies—she was always prattling on about the pharaohs or some ancient civilization or other. I think…yes…she said something about a mummy."

"A mummy?"

"Yeah. She bought a mummy case on one of her earliest trips. It was after Papa died. I think she found it in Ethiopia or Somalia or some outlandish place like that. Anyway, it sat in a corner for years. When she brought the stele back she kept saying it was the key."

"The key?"

"Yeah. The box had writing all over it, but she hadn't been able to decipher it. She said the stele gave her the way."

"The way to what?"

She fixed Griffin with a what-kind-of-an-idiot-is-this-guy look. "What else? The way to read the writing on the mummy. She spent a whole year translating the words. Finished it just before she got sick." A tear rolled down her cheek and Liesl wiped it away, leaving long black streaks behind. "She died a couple of months later. Pneumonia."

Griffin started to pace, but Rachel caught his elbow, forcing him to stop. He took a deep breath and said calmly, "Do you have her translation?"

"Nah. When she passed away I burned most of her papers. They were just gibberish to me. I didn't think anybody would buy them."

"She never told you what it said?"

"Let me see." Liesl closed her eyes. "That's right. She said it was a map." She snapped her fingers. "A map to the queen of Sheba's palace…or was it her temple? Some kind of building." She giggled. "Too bad she never found a map to the fountain of youth."

The two Americans gazed at each other. Rachel noticed a tiny bit of foam in the corner of Griffin's mouth. In a voice tight with emotion he whispered, "Masri's key."

Rachel kept her voice as steady as she could. "Could we see the mummy case?"

Liesl came down to earth. "Oh gee, sorry. I sold it."

Griffin shouted, "You *sold* it?"

She flushed an unbecoming mauve that clashed with her eye shadow. "It's my store. I can sell stuff if I want to. Got a good price for it too. All that rot about a map was just a bunch of hooey anyway." She shook her head. "Funny, right after I sold it some other mug came in asking for it. Too bad—I could have started a bidding war and made a pretty penny."

Griffin's eyes lit up. "Masri."

Rachel put a soothing hand on Griffin's sleeve and turned to the girl. "You said you've had the store for a year? Do you happen to remember who you sold the mummy case to?"

"Let me check." She went into a tiny office, and came out a minute later with a huge ledger. "One of these days I'm going to get a computer." She blew the dust off and opened to the last page. "Here it is." She looked up. "I've only sold a couple of things—I don't know how Mother made a living at this. I'll be glad when I can close down."

"Did you find the name of the buyer?"

"Yup. An American like you two. She paid to have the box shipped back to the States." She blinked, causing more blobs of mascara to dribble down her face. "Cost her a ton of euros."

Griffin squeaked, "What was her name?"

Liesl pointed a long fingernail at the page. "Mrs. Hannah Sundstrom, 20 Bridge Street, Penhallow, Maine."

****

"But Griffin, what about your friend and the house in the mountains? What about…you know?"

"It'll have to wait. We've got to get back. You say the mummy case was still in Hannah's shop? When did you see it?" He hailed a taxi. "Airport."

"I can't remember. It was a long time ago." She watched the beautiful ornate buildings flash by, her spirits sinking faster than, well, than a body with cement shoes.

They had rushed back to the hotel, Griffin restless and taut. The concierge put them through to Lufthansa, and they were able to get on a flight early the next morning. Now he sat back against the car seat and let his breath out with a loud whoosh. "Try to remember."

"Um. I'd gone by the store and saw Ingrid there. She's planning to renovate. Bill Taylor was giving her a paint estimate."

"Did you go inside?"

"Yes."

"And?"

"She had all the stuff in big piles in corners. I don't remember a mummy. Wait! I do remember a totem pole."

"This is not helpful."

"I'm doing my best, Griffin." She tried to go methodically back through the prior months, but her encounters with Griffin kept interfering with more mundane memories. Finally, one date cropped up. "There was the night of the fourth, remember? When Toby arrested Maude." She giggled. "I'll never forget the guilty look on her face. No way I'll let her live it down."

Griffin glared at her. "You won't forget poor Maude's discomfiture, but you can't remember when you saw a six-foot high mummy case?"

Rachel paid him no attention. "Let's see...no. We didn't go into the store that time. It must have been earlier..." The cab pulled over to the curb and let them off at the terminal entrance. They had checked their bags and reached the departure gate before it came to Rachel. "That's it! Maude. She was taking care of the store for LuAnne. Must have been back in early June— she asked me to go with her. I'd had my eye on this lovely little music box and went along. It has figurines of a man in evening kit and a woman in this lovely sparkly gown, and plays 'Diamonds are a Girl's Best Friend.'" A mischievous smile playing across her features, she said dreamily, "It's my favorite song. So saucy...so true..."

"They're boarding."

Sigh.

When they'd settled into their seats, Griffin said, "And?"

"Champagne, please."

The stewardess handed Rachel a flute and a half bottle of Pol Roger. "And for you, sir?"

"Beer. Keep it coming."

She grinned. "Yes, sir."

When the stewardess returned with a glass and a bottle of Schloss Eggenberg, Griffin picked up the bottle and took a swig. "And?"

"Hannah had left her shop in a mess when she fell ill. LuAnne didn't remove or arrange anything because no one knew what would happen to the place. Everything was dusty and in no particular order—just like Frau Wechsler's store. Estate jewelry, glassware, porcelain figurines, that sort of stuff, all in disordered heaps. I remember Maude had to go in the back for something, and I was wandering around looking for the music box when I noticed this full-size mummy case standing against the wall in a corner. It was all decorated."

"With writing?"

"I guess. I didn't look that closely."

He sat back and slugged his beer. "Ah." It was his last word until they reached Portland.

Rachel was busy with her own thoughts as well. Mainly on the subject of how she was going to wiggle out of this engagement before he did. *He obviously never meant it. I mean diddly squat to him.* She mused sadly on her now defunct dream of floating down a mountainside à la Maria von Trapp in a flowing white gown. She'd have flowers in her hair—edelweiss of course—and step daintily to her waiting groom. Who would be scratching his lederhosen to be sure, and refusing to wear his hat, but *there.* She began to think of her work and home.

"I'll get the car."

She waited on the curb while Griffin brought the

Jeep around. The canvas top was in tatters and black smoke spewed from the tailpipe. "I'll have to get the oil changed when we get home."

She didn't answer.

They stopped at the Muddy Scupper outside Freeport for dinner, then pushed on to Penhallow. He dropped her off at her house. "Get a shower—you need it. I'll meet you at the Trinket Shoppe tomorrow."

"What time?"

He stared at the sky. "I need some sleep. You probably do too. I'll give you a call."

Rachel trudged up the steps, dropped her suitcase on the floor, and collapsed on the sofa. She didn't wake up until the late afternoon sun trickled across her eyes. Leaving the case where it stood, she showered, then made herself some toast. The stillness unnerved her a bit until she remembered that Katie had Spot duty. The phone rang.

"Where the hell are you?"

"What do you mean?"

"I've left you fifteen messages. You are aware that we need to be there ASAP?"

"I'm sorry, Griffin. I overslept." She didn't expect sympathy and didn't receive any.

"Well, get off your ass and come over here. I'm walking up to the store now." *Click.*

When she arrived at the shop, twilight had begun to lick at the edges of the light, making it hard to see in the gloom. Griffin stood outside. "It's locked."

"Oh." Rachel pulled out her phone.

"Who are you calling?"

"Maude. She has a key."

"Why not Ingrid?"

Rachel shrugged. "I don't have her number. She's living in Hannah's Bluff Road house."

"Okay, Maude it is."

Maude was amenable to coming over and opening up the store. When she arrived, darkness had fallen, and she scrabbled around looking for the light switch. "At least the alarm hasn't been set this time," she tittered.

"I'm glad you're taking your recent arrest in stride, Maude."

She grinned. "Turns out it's made me a celebrity. Whole town wants my autograph. I got one of the sisters' parts in *Arsenic and Old Lace* on the strength of my acting ability!"

As the lights flickered on, a taxi pulled up in front and a large figure tumbled out. "I'm here! I'm here!" George puffed up the sidewalk. Rachel eyed Griffin.

"What? I called him. He deserves to be on the spot for the grand finale."

"I thought he was in jail?"

"Toby let him out on bail. The Institut d'archéologie ponied up the money. You know, I think our good sheriff may have some doubts about Hamdani's guilt."

"Must be his impressive powers of persuasion."

George pushed past them into the store and immediately planted himself on an upholstered chair in a corner. Dust rose in little puffs behind him and something black scurried out from under it. "Why did you want to meet here, Tate?"

Griffin looked at Rachel. "Well? Where is it?"

Rachel swept the premises with her eyes. Ingrid had cleared away the tchotchkes and knick-knacks that had littered the counters. Most of the cabinets were empty. Drawers were pulled out and stacked neatly on the floor. Where Bill had been painting swatches she saw a gaping hole in the wall. "Look at that. Ingrid must be considering some really serious renovation."

"Either that or she's looking for hidden treasure." Griffin spoke lightly.

They looked at each other and spoke simultaneously. "Pinkney's money. She knows about it."

"I sure do."

The four turned at the voice. Standing in the back door, a vicious looking pistol pointed at Rachel's chest, was Ingrid. She wore a trench coat and a snarl. "I might ask what you're doing here, but I'm assuming it's for the same reason."

George wheezed, "Actually, no, *madame*. We're here on a different mission. We—"

Without looking at him, Ingrid spat out, "Shut up. And who the hell are you anyway?"

The fat man pursed his lips. "George Hamdani, Institut français d'archéologie. Forgive me for not standing, but the press of the crowd..." He raised his stout arms helplessly.

Ingrid rolled her eyes. "Don't worry your tiny head. You can die sitting down if you like. I'm easy that way."

She must have seen Griffin move, for she swung the pistol in his direction. "All of you, back against the wall next to Chubby Checker there." She took a couple of side steps, her eyes glued to the people now clumped together around George.

Rachel looked to Ingrid's right and nudged Griffin. "The mummy." His eyes swiveled to it, and he tapped

George's shoulder. The big man followed his pointing finger to the case. He half rose from the chair, his mouth hanging open. "The...the..."

Ingrid glanced at it. "Yeah. That's where the rest of the loot from the heist was. You, sit down!"

George resumed his seat but kept his eyes on the mummy case. Rachel spoke to Ingrid. "How did you find out?"

"Hannah told me."

"She knew about the money?" Rachel tried to remember Hannah's last months. *Did she seem any different? Could she have been in on it after all?*

Ingrid chuckled. "Poor chump. She had no clue what John had done. Found the money by accident, get this—*cleaning.* My sister, the freak. She started cleaning when she was five and never stopped. Gawd, I don't know how Ma managed to heave out two such different daughters."

For once Rachel agreed with her.

Griffin prompted, "So Hannah called you when she found the stash?"

"Yeah." Ingrid grimaced. "She was in a tizzy—didn't know what to do with it. She was pretty sure John had hidden it, but didn't know why. When he took off, he only told her he had a job in Belize, and she couldn't come with him. She never knew about the robbery."

Maude piped up. "How did *you* know about it, then?"

"Didn't. But I always figured John wouldn't have lit out of here so quick if he hadn't done somethin' wrong. When Hannah told me about the cash, I put two and two together and figured he'd stolen it from his job." She shook her head. "Not Hannah though. She was so gullible. She thought he'd saved it from his lunch money." An ugly guffaw came from the vicinity of her mouth.

"What about Mary then? How did he explain her going with him?"

"No idea. But John is such a smooth operator. A real salesman. Pa used to say he could talk a virgin into a threesome." Ingrid's face softened and her lip quivered.

That's right. Bert Weems claimed Ingrid was sweet on Pinkney. Rachel wondered if there was a way to exploit that chink in her armor.

"So, she asked for your advice," Griffin prompted.

"I tell you, it was all I could do to keep calm. Told her to put the money somewhere safe until I could come up. She came up with the idea of dumping it in the mummy. *Pah.* I was stuck in Memphis with that lousy salon job through April. Had a contract I couldn't get out of. Pissed me off no end." She waved the gun around while her audience bobbed and weaved, trying to stay out of her sights. "By the time I got to Penhallow, Hannah had died."

"What did you do?" Rachel snuck a peek at Griffin's face and saw fascinated interest plastered on it. *He's stalling for time.*

"I had to hold fire and make it through the damn funeral, pretending I was, like, grief-stricken over Hannah's death." She wrinkled her nose. "Nothing like a small town to drag out any social occasion until you want to strangle every last citizen. When I finally got into the store, I discovered the goddamn bitch had taken the money out of the mummy and hidden it somewhere else." Her lips twisted with anger. "Hannah never did listen to me. Took me a month to go through her house. Nothing. Started on the store a couple of weeks ago. Nada."

"So…the mummy case was empty? Hannah didn't leave any clue as to what she'd done with the stuff?" Griffin strained forward like an eager puppy.

Boy, can he act when the situation calls for it.

"Uh uh. Well, except for this key." She held up a small silver key, its head embellished with elaborate filigree.

The key. Wait, Pinkney found it too. And left it there. "Do you know what it goes to?"

Ingrid fixed Griffin with a suspicious glare. "Hey—wait a minute. I know what you're doing." She stuck the key in her pocket and cocked the pistol. Pointing it at George, she spoke out of the side of her mouth. "Don't think you can keep me talking. I ain't dawdling for no—what's that word for a slam bang finish?"

Maude whispered, "Dénouement?"

"That's it. Day-noo-mon. I ain't stickin' around for that."

Rachel said in a voice that surprised her by its firmness, "That's fine, but you don't have to kill us. We only want the mummy case. Take your key and go."

Ingrid paused, as though thinking Rachel's suggestion over. "Maybe you're right. I've already got a couple counts of murder if I'm caught. A big pile of dead rats such as yourselves just might tip the coppers off to me."

Rachel stared at her. "Murder?"

"Had to clear the decks." She grinned at Rachel.

"What, you didn't think I planned to share the money with all John's floozies, did you? No, sir. How'd I know about them, you ask? I followed him after he skipped. Trailed him to Belize. Found out all about him and that bitch Noreen. Two timing prick."

Does she mean he was two-timing...Ingrid? Or Hannah?

"At least Hannah's death gave me an excuse to be here so I didn't have to sneak around. When I saw John and Mary in town I knew I had to act fast."

"Did you talk to them?"

"Nah, just kept an eye on them. It was nice to see John." A dreamy look passed over her features. "I was even thinking of maybe changing my mind and letting Mary stick around, when the little sheep had to go and fuck things up. I couldn't believe my ears when I heard her tell John she wanted to take the rap for him. She would have ruined everything."

"You killed her."

"It was so easy." The creature smiled reminiscently. "Told her I had a message from her mother that she'd passed to me on her death bed." She giggled. "Stupid kid had no idea that Hannah was gone by the time I got here. Told her the message was for her alone and not to bring her father. Never questioned it. She met me up by the bridge." She paused and rubbed a scab on the back of her hand with her gun. "Who'da thought she'd fight back? Scratched my hands up something awful. Made me mad." She held her palm up. "Waited till she had both hands up. One shove and the puny little chicken went right over. Easy peasy."

Rachel felt Griffin shudder beside her. "What about Noreen? Did you kill her too?"

The woman nodded with satisfaction. "She was horning in. Like she had a right to the money. Not even his wife, for Chrissakes. Betcha didn't know that." She wagged her head. "When I was in Belize looking for John, I ran across the guy who forged her marriage license. Bitch had the gall to want the whole cache for herself—she wasn't even going to share it with John. After being all lovey dovey with him. I don't know how he could stand her." She blinked and Rachel thought she saw a tear well up. "He always was a spineless dick. Went along with any woman who talked dirty to him. I could have taken care of him. I'm the only one who really loved him." She wiped her nose. "May he rot in jail the rest of his life."

Don't hold back, Ingrid.

Griffin continued to pump her with questions. "How did you kill Noreen?"

"Ah, that took some work. She didn't trust me. Just because Hannah was my sister." She gave a derisive snort. "Had to come up with something. Pretended the key went to a closet at the Windmill Motel. She bought it. Went traipsing off to Freeport. Probably planned to force open every door in the place. Dimwit." She tapped the gun barrel on her chin, then whipped it down to point at George's forehead. "I'm watching all of you. Don't try any funny business."

"No, we sure won't." Griffin's face was blank. "So, how'd you kill her?"

Ingrid's eyes narrowed. "No reason not to tell you. You won't be blabbing to anyone else when I'm done with you." She patted her pocket. "I always keep a bottle of potassium chloride handy—in case some schmuck wants to paw at me in a bar. A coupla drops in their beer and they get palpitations. So I tell Noreen to meet me at the Hot Potato. She gets there early, and I find her hanging around some jerk's neck. So, me, I make this big scene and like your typical gutless male, he dumps her and runs."

"Then what?"

"Place erupted—it's a cinch to get those guys into a brawl. No one was paying attention and I followed her to the john with my insulin syringe. Stuck her in the ass." She giggled. "What's that expression? Sumpin' about irony. Anyhoo, injected the whole bottle. It's a wonder she made it back to the motel."

Maude cleared her throat. "Ingrid, why don't you put the gun down? You don't really want to shoot us."

The pistol swung toward the older woman. "Oh yeah?"

"Actually, Maude's right. That would be a really bad idea."

The voice came from behind Ingrid. Cary stepped around her, a miniature pink Beretta leveled at her chest. "Drop the gun."

She dropped it. Cary hesitated. Rachel wondered if he'd even thought beyond the dramatic entrance. "Yeah. So. Stay there." He backed up a step. A siren sounded in the near distance. "Sheriff's on his way."

The tableau remained motionless while they listened to the approaching police car. When Toby came in the door with Jeff, he found them frozen in place—George in his chair, Rachel and Griffin side by side, barely touching, Maude stiff and straight, eyes glued on the pistol. Ingrid stood near the back door. Cary faced her, holding his gun with both hands.

Toby looked at Ingrid. "That new alarm system

you installed worked like a charm. Rang in the station. Here we are. What's up?"

Cary nodded at Ingrid. "Slap her in irons, Sheriff. I set off the alarm when I saw her go in with the gun."

Rachel found her voice. "She killed both Mary and Noreen. For Pinkney's money."

"Which used to be in the mummy case."

To everyone's surprise, George leapt out of his chair and shrieked, "Which is the map!" He took both Rachel's arms and danced a little jig. The entire building shook.

Chapter Sixteen
The Keys

Toby paused a moment to take all this in. Finally, in slow motion, he gestured to Jeff, who unclipped his handcuffs and locked them on Ingrid. Only then did Cary lower his pistol. Rachel noticed his hands were shaking.

"I think maybe we should all head down to the station where we'll be more comfortable. Jeff, call Harry to come secure the crime scene."

George popped up. "But the mummy! We must examine the mummy!"

Toby's gaze swept over the Lebanese. "You. I thought I told you to stay at the hotel."

"But Sir Sheriff! Our discovery! It is of the utmost importance that Professor Tate and I remove it to a safe location where we can study it thoroughly."

Toby gave George a look identical to the one he gave Edna Mae when she insisted he go to a red hat society function. "This building and everything in it is off-limits until further notice. You—Hamdani. You'll come in the squad car with me. The rest of you, meet me at the station in five minutes."

George cast an agonized expression at the mummy case, but followed the sheriff out.

Later, Ingrid having been fingerprinted, read her rights, and relegated to the second jail cell—the first being still occupied by Pinkney—Toby sat at his desk and steepled his fingers. "All right, who's first?"

Cary began to speak but Griffin cut him off. "This whole kerfluffle can be broken down into two issues. The Pinkney robbery and attendant would-be thieves, and the map to the queen of Sheba's tomb."

"I see." Rachel noted the tiny uptick of Toby's lips. "Go on."

Finding himself on the spot apparently flustered Griffin. He hemmed and hawed, then croaked, "Um…er…you tell it, Rachel."

She patted his arm. "All right." She faced Toby. "As you know, John Pinkney robbed the Penhallow Bank and Trust and took his daughter, under duress, to Belize. His wife Hannah was not involved. John met Noreen Fowler in Belize and had an affair with her. Somehow she found out about the robbery and that he still had some of the loot hidden in Penhallow, and ditched him to go look for it. Meanwhile, Hannah found his stash and called Ingrid. Ingrid told her to hide it somewhere safer, and Hannah picked the mummy case."

"Wait, wait." Cary raised a hand. "Didn't Ingrid say the money was gone when she arrived?"

"That's right. Hannah must have decided it wasn't safe there either—"

"Or that she might be implicated in the robbery if the money were found in her store."

Rachel pointed a finger at Griffin. "Correct. So she removed it and stowed it somewhere else, leaving behind a key to the new hiding place."

"Why?" Everyone looked at George. "I mean, why would she put the key in the case? Why not just keep it?"

Toby rubbed his chin. "She must have left it there for someone."

"John?"

"If Hannah did indeed tell Ingrid about the hoard, then it's likely she left it for her sister."

Rachel added, "Because she knew she was dying."

The group nodded sagely in unison, until Cary, ever the spoiler, spoke up. "What about John?"

"What about him?"

"Where does he fit in?"

Toby took the stage. "We know Pinkney arrived after Noreen but before Ingrid."

"That's right," Rachel cried excitedly. "When John heard that Hannah was dying, he decided to sneak back to the States to see her, and while he was at it, retrieve the rest of the money. Noreen arrived around three years ago but hadn't been able to locate the stuff. When John got here Hannah was dead, so he broke into the store, found his stash gone—"

"How did he know to look in the mummy case?"

"He said he searched the store. The box would be an obvious place to check."

"But the mummy was empty, except for the key…"

"Which he left there."

Maude sat up. "Why?"

"Why what?"

"Why did he leave the key there? Why not take it with him?"

Rachel stared at Toby. "Did John explain?"

Toby sifted through some papers on his desk. "He talked about it at his confession, didn't he?…Ah, here it is. Apparently, he figured it was as secure there as anywhere. He didn't know Hannah had told Ingrid, so he didn't expect anyone to be rifling through the shop contents."

"But Ingrid did find it."

George said suddenly, "Ingrid put the key in her pocket. It's most likely to a safe deposit box. Sir Sheriff, did you recover a key among her effects?"

Cary interrupted. "Where is it? I'll be able to tell what it goes to."

Toby said mildly, "Luckily we have professionals for that. I'd like to save your expertise for more complicated investigations, Mr. Marx."

"Oh." That seemed to satisfy Cary.

"Now, where are we?"

"Hannah is dead. All the players have converged on Penhallow."

"Okay, then what?"

Griffin took up the tale. "Ingrid goes to the store after Hannah's funeral, finds the money gone from the mummy case, and takes the key. Since then she has been scouring Hannah's house and the shop, looking for it. She's also been following John and Mary, and overhears Mary say she wants to confess. This would mess up all her plans, so she kills her. Then Noreen gets in her way and is eliminated as well."

Maude said, "You know what, Toby? Ingrid was in love with John all this time. I think she wanted to be with him. The old rumors were true."

Toby stared at her. "So for once Edna Mae was right."

Maude smiled. "Edna Mae is *always* right, Toby."

Cary—evidently starving for attention—suddenly yelled, "She was going to murder all four of these guys if I hadn't stepped in." He brandished the gun. In a lightning quick motion, Toby ripped it from his hand and unloaded it. Cary gaped at him. "You can't take that away from me. I have a permit!"

"Civilians are not allowed to carry loaded guns into police stations. Your...er...ladies' pistol is confiscated until further notice."

When Cary subsided, Toby sat down, thoughtfully tapping a pencil. "Before we move on to Masri's murder, it would be nice to tie up one loose end."

"What's that?"

"Where's the money?"

Rachel had been silently petting herself for doing such a fabulous job of detecting. At Toby's words, the happy bubble ruptured, little pieces of ego drifting to the floor.

When no one responded, the sheriff continued to muse. "I mean, John didn't find it and Ingrid didn't find it. What did Hannah do with it?"

Rachel could almost hear five minds clicking away. *Now if I found a hoard of cash, what would I do with it? Hide it?* "No! I'd spend it!"

Everyone stared at her. "Hannah may not have hidden the money—she may have bought something with it...But what?"

Cary spoke first. "A Porsche?"

"Don't be silly—where would she hide that?"

He pouted and kicked the desk leg until Toby rapped his knuckles with a ruler.

Griffin said slowly, "You're right, Rachel. It must be something small..."

"And valuable..."

"And in plain sight."

"*Hmm.*"

Rachel stood. "Maybe we should go back to the Trinket Shoppe."

"The Trinket Shoppe?" Griffin made a face. "Why? Both John and Ingrid turned it upside down and didn't find anything. What makes you think we'll be successful?"

"Because they were looking for a sack of bills. We're looking for...for..."

Toby stood. "I hereby deputize all of you. Meet me at Hannah's store."

Ten minutes later he pulled the police tape off and unlocked the door. The place smelled of dust and fresh paint. He turned on all the lights. "Go for it."

George went straight to the mummy case. As he reached a hand out to it, Toby spoke in a voice that meant business, "Touch it and you go back to Edna Mae's cooking. That's evidence."

"Yes, Sir Sheriff. Of course." The Lebanese took a step back but continued to gaze hungrily at the box.

Two hours later most of them had given up. Only George—who apparently had made his peace with his frustrated desire and thrown himself into the search—seemed undaunted. "I have unearthed treasures before that others have overlooked. I shall find this one too."

Rachel sat on a stool fashioned from an elephant's foot, chin in hand. "If we only had a clue as to what we were looking for..."

"That would help—at least then we'd know *where* to look."

She clapped her hands. "I've got it. John."

Toby paused. "You mean Pinkney? How could he help?"

"He was married to Hannah—presumably he knew her well. He might have a clue as to what she would buy and where she would put it."

Toby stood and headed to the door. "It's worth a try."

Pinkney sat huddled on the cot in his cell. Ingrid, her hands gripping the bars between their cells, stared at him, unblinking. Toby unlocked the door. "Come with me."

The man stumbled out and held his hands in front of him. "Aren't you going to cuff me?"

"Nah, we just want to ask you a few questions." He led the way to the interrogation room. Everyone filed in after them.

Toby sat across from Pinkney. "John, we need your help." He told his prisoner about their search of the store, and Rachel's theory that Hannah had bought something with it. "Any idea what she might have bought? Or where she would hide it?"

Pinkney almost smiled. "She was a deep one, wasn't she? No, I never did deserve her. Should've taken her with us…"

"John?"

"What? Oh yes. I know exactly what she'd buy. Can't believe I didn't think of this before. Diamonds."

"Diamonds? What would she do with them?" Rachel had trouble seeing the quiet, self-effacing little woman she'd known buying flashy jewelry, let alone wearing it.

Apparently so did Griffin, who raised his eyes to the ceiling. "Hannah Sundstrom? Buy bling?"

"They'd be for Mary. She always said if we won the lottery, she'd buy Mary lots of diamonds, so she'd never have to worry about money again." He gave the semblance of a fond chuckle. "Hannah used to sing to Mary when she was little, but instead of lullabies, she'd croon Cole Porter and Lerner and Lowe. She loved musicals. Her favorite—the one she'd sing last every night, was 'Diamonds Are a Girl's Best Friend.' " He blinked a tear away. "She never did get the lyrics right, but she didn't care—it was the sentiment she liked." The words seemed to remind him of his predicament, for he slumped in his seat, his eyes troubled.

Griffin brooded. "Hannah died before you two made it back, didn't she? So if Hannah did use the cash to buy diamonds, Mary never got them, right?"

"No. I mean, right."

"But wouldn't Hannah have made some effort to inform her daughter of the gift? Left a statement in her will or in a note somewhere? I can't imagine Hannah going to such pains and then not having a plan to make sure Mary got the stones."

Maude spoke. "Hannah didn't have a will."

Silence filled the room. It seemed to Rachel that they would never solve the mystery now. Too many people—all the ones with the answers—were gone. Pinkney raised his head. Wait…"

"What?"

"Maybe…maybe it was in the note."

"Note?"

"The note. Along with the key I found in the mummy case, there was an envelope addressed to Mary."

Toby said. "That's right. You mentioned that in your confession." He scrabbled through his notes. "Here it is. Quote: 'I found a key and an envelope.'

Meaning in the mummy case." He looked up. "She told you it was just a note and put it in her flowered purse."

Rachel leapt up. "The purse! You still have it in the evidence room, don't you, Toby?"

"Sure, but we made a list of the contents." He read again. "Deposit slip, tissues, pen, ten-dollar bill, and comb. No note."

"Maybe we should look again. Purses always have secret compartments—you know, for intimate things. I might be able to find one."

Toby dispatched Jeff to the evidence locker, and five minutes later he reappeared carrying a large purse covered with pink and purple flowers. A few catcalls followed him from the lobby.

He handed it to Rachel. She checked the outer pouches, then systematically went through the inner sections. Unzipping one pocket, she found a second pocket about three inches square. From inside she pulled a small envelope. Toby gently plucked it from her hand and opened it. He took out a note. As he unfolded it, a small key dropped to the floor. Griffin picked it up and turned it over. "This is a different key from the one Ingrid had."

John took it from him, eyebrows raised. "Yes, it is. The one I left in the case was larger, and quite fancy." He handed it to Rachel. "What would a key like this go to?"

Rachel examined it. "It's too small for a door. Maybe a diary? Or a jewelry box?"

Toby glanced at it, then down at the note. He read, "Heart shape or pear shape, they don't lose their shape, diamonds are my Mary's best friend."

Rachel tossed the key in the air, caught it, and

began to hum.

"What's that tune? Reminds me of someone." Griffin stared off into the distance, his eyes vague. "I see a blonde with a bright red mouth. Marilyn Monroe? Come on, Rachel, what's the song?"

She grinned. "It's my favorite."

"And what the hell does that mean?"

"It means I know where the diamonds are."

"So, back to the Trinket Shoppe?"

"Not at all. Home to Amity."

Toby locked Pinkney back in his cell, and they all trooped to Amity. Rachel left her retinue in the living room and went up to her bedroom. She picked up the little music box she'd bought so long ago, wound it with the key, and walked back down the stairs to the living room. The afternoon sun shot through the curtains and glanced off the tiny dancers. The female figurine, a long, white, gauzy dress floating around her, twirled in the male's arms. As she turned, bolts of many-colored lights went spinning off in all directions.

The men watched the couple, mesmerized. Finally, Griffin held out a hand. Rachel gave the music box to him. He grinned and said, "*Bling.*"

****

The next morning, back at the police station, Toby continued to marvel. "So that's why no one could find the diamonds in the shop—they were sitting on Rachel's bureau all this time! Amazing."

George put a hand on Rachel's arm. "Perhaps the key was meant to be the key."

"Huh?"

He looked confused. "I mean…I mean…English fails me I fear."

Griffin spoke up. "He means, I think, that maybe Mary wanted you to find not just the deposit slip, but the key and note as well."

"Then what was the other key? The one in the mummy case?"

Rachel thought back to that day in Hannah's store. "I think I've got it—it went to the cabinet the box was in. Remember, Maude? You had to open the door with a hairpin."

"That's right." Maude ran her fingers through her hair. "Now we know what happened to both keys. I take back my disparaging remarks about Hannah's untidiness. So *that* key was meant to direct Mary to the cabinet and the music box."

"I guess." Rachel thought this over. "Perhaps the deposit slip wasn't the most important clue she left."

"What do you mean?"

"Mary wanted to confess to the robbery and take her lumps, but I think she wanted to do more. She wanted to return the money. The slip was meant to focus our attention on Penhallow Bank and Trust, but then her plan was to have me find her mother's note and follow the clues to the music box. She may not have known it was no longer at the store."

"Or she knew you had bought it, and that's why she came to you."

She heaved a sigh. "So sad."

"What?"

"Poor Hannah. She lost her husband and daughter. When she found the cache, she must have been so happy—at least she could provide for Mary. Her dying wish was thwarted. So sweet and sad."

Griffin started. "Why on earth would you say that?

The woman was just as guilty as her husband—worse, I think."

"Hannah wanted to ensure her daughter's financial security. She knew she couldn't trust John—"

"So she stole his hot money and put it to better use? Ha." He paused. "Wonder what she'd have done if she knew about Eddie the Falcon."

George's eyes popped. "The Mafioso! Indeed." He turned to Toby. "Now that we have recovered this bird man's money, should we return it?"

Rachel would long remember the sound that erupted from the sheriff—a combination of hysterical laughter, incredulity, and terror. When he'd caught his breath he merely said, "Oh shit."

"Why Tobias Pendleton Quimby, you watch your mouth!" Toby's wife filled the doorway, her ample bosom heaving and her nostrils flaring.

Toby sprang up, his face aflame. "Edna Mae, what are you doing here?" The lady in question stepped into the room. Behind her hulked the detective from Augusta, his shoulders hunched as though still warding off Edna Mae's verbal blows. "I want you to arrest this man. He's been snooping, and when I confronted him, he actually, he…he…" She stopped as though the memory were too painful to revisit.

Toby looked at Blanchard. His lip twitched. "Well, what do you have to say for yourself?"

The man tried to retrieve his dignity, but Edna Mae locked a baleful glare on him and shook her umbrella. "He was interrogating…*interrogating*…Audrey Carver about her father. Can you imagine? Harassing the poor thing. I know it's been ten years, but it still hurts that he abandoned her on her wedding day. Mr. Blanchard has no right to dredge that episode up again."

"Audrey Carver?" Toby turned surprised eyes on the detective. "What does she have to do with anything?"

Edna Mae, apparently unused to anyone else actually speaking, raised her voice. "Oh for heaven's sake, Tobias. It's all about the Penhallow Bank and Trust bankruptcy. You remember, Audrey was born a Crocker. This…this *detective*"—she managed to make it sound less respectable than a dogcatcher—"thinks Audrey's father didn't just run out of money—not that that came as a surprise to any of us. The man was an idiot. Of course I'd *never* let on to Audrey what everyone thought of him, but…where was I? Oh, yes. This man"—she waved a dismissive hand at the cowering Blanchard—"has the temerity, nay the audacity, to insinuate that Edward Crocker may have stolen the bank's funds. Why, that would make him a crook!" She stamped her foot, forcing Toby to leap to catch the desk lamp before it fell.

Rachel tore her eyes from Edna Mae and fastened them on Blanchard. "You agree with me, then?"

"That Crocker may have been the mule? It's possible. I've been doing a little background on the man." He rubbed his chin. "It's…possible."

Rachel so wanted to gloat, but restrained herself. "What about John Pinkney then?"

He rolled his eyes. "Ms. Tinker, John Pinkney is still charged with grand larceny." He held up a finger. "Besides, I've come across some other evidence. I think Pinkney may still be able to help us put Eddie away for good."

"What is it?"

"I found some old files at City Hall concerning the bankruptcy. Pinkney was the chief teller at PB&T for two years. He may be able to shed some light on the transactions between Eddie's men and Crocker."

"That's fabulous!"

Toby stood up. "Come on, let's get the transfer paperwork out. You can have Pinkney today."

They passed an astonished Edna Mae, her mouth gaping.

Rachel and Griffin knew the wormhole of escape would last mere seconds and took their shot. When they reached the sidewalk unscathed, Griffin reprised George's little jig. "That's it! Mysteries solved. We can go home."

"And?"

"And what? Oh, you want to stop in Durkee's for a celebratory drink?"

Sigh. "Sure."

Half an hour later, Toby, George, and Cary found them finishing their second beers. "What are you two doing here? We have unfinished business."

Griffin held up his mug. "Yes, half a beer."

Toby pulled a stool out. "Katie, gimme a Geary's."

Rachel moved over to give him room. George pulled two stools together and wheezed down on them. Cary stood behind Rachel, now and then leaning across the bar.

"What's up?"

Toby pointed at Griffin. "You've forgotten. We have one more loose end. The first murder. I believe you said it also has something to do with the mummy case?"

Griffin explained about the Italian explorer, the

stele, and the mummy. "We think the hieroglyphics painted on the cover contain a map."

George chimed in. "A map to the queen of Sheba's tomb."

"I see. While that's all fine and dandy, it still points to Mr. Hamdani here as the person with the most reason to kill Omar Masri."

"*Moi!*" The fat man's eyes grew round. "On the contrary—I saw him killed."

"You did? Why didn't you mention this before?"

George looked suitably chastened. "For the reason you just iterated, Sir Sheriff. May I explain?"

Toby took a long swig of beer. "Go on."

After a cautious glance, George continued. "I had been following Masri on the streets of Penhallow. When he bought a ticket for the train excursion, I became suspicious. I thought to myself, 'George, he is up to no good.' Or I may have said, 'George, he intends to meet someone here.' I don't really remember."

Toby tapped a spoon on the bar. "And?"

"So I purchased a ticket and waited for him. He went to the inside car, and I chose a seat where I could observe him through the window. In case he met someone, you see. Or exchanged words with a stranger. Or…"

"Yes?"

"Ah, well, the cowboys came up to the train on their horses, shooting and yelling. A frightful display. I kept my eye on Masri despite the hullaballoo. He had bent down to check his valise. At the first sound of the shots, he sat bolt upright, but, as I watched, he keeled over. I fear at that point I was distracted by the clamor. The children were completely out of control. It was not amusing at all. Not at all."

"So…he keeled over."

"That's right."

Toby thought about this. "I think I should take a little stroll down to the train, maybe take a ride. Rachel—can you get hold of Stan Holiday? Isn't he the engineer?"

"Stanley may be in mourning. Let me try Richard."

"Whatever." He checked his watch. "I have a date at the shooting range tomorrow morning with Reverend Peavey. Set it up for tomorrow afternoon, will you?"

He didn't seem to notice the general feeling of anticlimax this announcement engendered. Reluctantly, they trudged out.

"What now?"

Rachel started to walk down Main street. "I have to find Richard."

Maude turned the other way. "I have to go feed the cat."

George signaled for a taxi. "I must keep my promise to the good sheriff and go back to the hotel. Luncheon is only served until two."

Griffin and Cary stood facing each other, their faces guarded. Finally, Cary said, "Hungry?"

"Sure."

When Rachel turned around to see where Griffin had gone, she saw the two men drifting toward Darwin's, almost arm in arm.

Rachel didn't get hold of Richard until the next morning. She persuaded him—a little syrup, a little death threat—to come out from Brooks and drive the train.

"I'll be there at three."

"I'm sure that's fine."

"Tell me again why Stan can't do it?"

It didn't seem appropriate to go into detail, so Rachel merely said, "He just broke up with his girlfriend and needs to sober up."

She saw Griffin from a distance once that morning, as he drove by her house with Cary in the Porsche. They appeared to be laughing. She made some lunch and waited for three o'clock. At 2:45 Griffin came by and picked her up.

"Did you have a pleasant day?" She hoped the jealousy didn't seep through her artificial perkiness.

Griffin flashed a big grin. "Great! Had a great day!"

She didn't really want to be grumpy, but she couldn't help it. "I see you and Cary have become bosom buddies."

He gave her a sidelong glance. "He's not so bad once you learn how to handle him."

"Does that go for me as well?" *Shut up, Rachel.*

"You're much harder. He needs kid gloves. You need those ultrathin latex hospital gloves."

She bristled. "You don't have to hang around me, you know. After all, you neglected to marry me when you had the chance. I suppose that's meant as a message."

He stopped the car. "Get out."

Her heart crumbling, the tears brimmed over and trickled down her cheeks. "Griffin—"

He got out, rounded the car, and opened her door. "Get out, Rachel."

"O…okay."

She got out. He didn't budge. She tried to wiggle

around him, but he put an arm on each side of her, imprisoning her between him and the car. He glared at her. "Annabelle Rachel Tinker, I love you more than life itself, but I will not have you badgering me. When the time comes, we'll get married. Right now, we have things to do. Now shut up and kiss me."

She did.

****

As they approached the train tracks, Rachel saw the sheriff standing by the train with two people she didn't recognize. George sat in the open car facing forward. The train moved a couple of feet forward. Richard leaned out of the cab. "That far enough?"

Toby held up a hand. "Stop!"

Griffin clapped his shoulder. "We're here. What's going on?"

Toby turned. "Oh, good. You two know Reverend Peavey and his son Miles?"

"No. How do you do?"

The tall, gaunt man in a preacher's black suit stuck out his hand, but his eyes were on his son, and they were very angry. Rachel suspected those eyes were normally mild, but now they glittered, and the flesh was drawn tightly across his cheekbones. His son, a boy of about fifteen, stared at the ground, his shock of uncombed brown hair witness to the absence of a mother at home.

Toby climbed aboard the train. "Let's go." They all hopped into the open car and the engine picked up speed. Slowly. It eventually almost made it up to twenty miles per hour, and forty minutes later they pulled into the siding at Brooks.

"Everyone come with me." The sheriff led the way

to the small shack that stood there, leaning into the wind. A shutter hung loose from a small, square window on the side. When they had gathered around him, he spoke. "Reverend Peavey and I had a rather interesting morning."

"Oh?"

"Yes. We met up at the Stockton shooting range for a little target practice. Howard here brought along a Colt revolver. He's a collector. How many guns you got, Hal?"

The minister counted on his fingers. "Twenty-two—twelve shotguns, four antique rifles—including an 1875 Winchester repeater—and six pistols."

"And the 1874 Colt .45 single action Army revolver—that's the jewel of your collection, isn't it?"

"Sure is. Picked it up at an auction of firearms from Buffalo Bill Cody's Wild West show. I've got a certificate proving Buffalo Bill himself owned it."

"So you take pretty good care of it and your other guns, right?"

Peavey grimaced. "Thought I did. They may be beautiful antiques, but they're still deadly weapons. So they're kept in a case in my study. A case with double locks. To which I thought only I had the keys."

The boy shifted uncomfortably. "Dad, I—"

"Quiet, Miles. There's nothing you can say to make this better. I just thank God your mother is in Seattle with her sister."

Griffin surveyed the two. "Want to tell us what's going on?"

Toby took over. "Well, we got to talking about the Masri murder and how we'd never found the gun. I noticed Hal's Colt. Reminded me that the bullet we found was a forty-five caliber, just like he was using. And then—this is the part you'll like, Rachel—I remembered what you said about rifling. Funny…" He didn't laugh. "Don't know why I didn't think of it sooner."

"*What?*"

"I had Hal shoot a round, then we took the bullets over to the lab. And surprise, surprise, the rifling matched the bullet that killed Omar Masri."

Everyone looked at Reverend Hal. Except Hal, who bent his eyes to his son. "You want to tell them, Miles?"

In a voice so low Rachel had to stretch to hear it, the boy murmured, "I took Dad's Colt. Matt Blakey found a site on the internet that showed us how to pick a lock. Worked real well. I opened Dad's gun safe after only three tries."

The sound issuing from between the reverend's lips did not bode well for Miles. He gave his father a quick glance and hurried on. "I just took the gun out for a couple of hours. Dad said he'd take me for a lesson, but that would've been too late."

Rachel asked gently, "Why would it have been too late?"

"I wanted to join the cowboys. I wanted to be part of the reenactment. I asked 'em, but Hank and Elmer just laughed at me. I…I had to show 'em I could shoot."

Toby said, "So you snuck out of the house with the revolver and rode your bike all the way to Brooks?"

"No, sir. I took the train—I hid in a storage bin in the caboose and jumped off as the train pulled in to Brooks." A slight element of pride slipped into his speech. "No one saw me. I slipped around behind the shed and waited for Elmer and Hank. Then, when I heard 'em galloping up, I let off a shot."

His father pursed his lips. "One shot?"

"Well, two."

Toby interrupted. "We only found one bullet in the car."

"Yes," said Peavey. "Unfortunately, when he shot the second one, he bumped his elbow on the shutter. It jiggled his arm, and his aim went off. The bullet went through the railroad car window."

Miles went on, his eyes wide with guilt. "I didn't see anyone or anything in the car, so I figured it had just passed through and out the other side. Was gonna surprise the guys and show 'em what I could do, but I waited too long and the train had pulled back out. So I hitched home. I…I never heard about…about the man."

George, who had been uncharacteristically quiet until then, burst out, "Yes! Yes! It's as I told you! I saw Omar bob up, then fall over. He must have raised his head just as the boy shot through the carriage."

Griffin looked at Miles. "So it was an accident."

The good reverend shook his head. "It wasn't an accident that Miles stole the gun. It wasn't an accident that I neglected to check that the Colt hadn't been cleaned. We are dreadfully at fault in this tragic death." Toby stepped between them.

"In the eyes of God, it is a terrible thing you've done, Miles Peavey. In the eyes of the law, it was an accident. I suggest your father is better qualified to decide your punishment."

Hal put a heavy hand on the portly sheriff's shoulder. "Well said, Quimby." He looked at his son.

"Let's go back to Penhallow."

They rode the train back in silence. When they reached the station, the boy spoke under his breath.

His father looked at Miles. "What was that?"

"I did pay for my ticket."

"Ticket?" Rachel stared blankly at the boy. "What ticket?"

"The ticket for the excursion. I didn't stow away. I paid fair and square." A lock of hair fell across his forehead, making him look about five years old.

"Well, thank you." Something nudged the back of her mind. *Ticket. Ticket. That's it!* "You were the seventeenth ticket!"

Toby clapped her on the back. "That's it! The last mystery solved. Well done."

They watched the Peaveys trudge off, Miles's shoulders bowed. Rachel, Griffin, and Hamdani stood with Toby by the tracks.

"So, George didn't kill Omar Masri after all."

The big man sniffed. "Of course not. I disapprove of murder."

Toby muttered, "I knew that already."

All three stared at the sheriff. "How?"

"Angle of the bullet. It could only have come from outside in and straight across above the seats. So I knew Masri was sitting up when he was hit. Mr. Hamdani was outside in the open car. If he'd shot Masri the bullet would've entered at right angles to where it did."

"And that's why you didn't find any shards of glass either inside or outside."

"Yes. Miles's bullet went right through the open windows."

"Why didn't you tell us this before?"

"I had no other suspects." He nodded at George. "I was not convinced he didn't pull it off somehow—maybe he moved while everyone was focused on the cowboys, or had an accomplice."

The Lebanese opened his mouth, but Rachel intervened. "What about John Pinkney?"

"He had no real motive."

Rachel took Griffin's hand. "So…John Pinkney didn't actually kill anyone?"

"That's right."

Griffin tapped his lip. "What must it be like to be suspected of killing three people?"

"Including your beloved daughter?"

Toby said drily, "I suspect he's glad it's over."

They left George at his hotel—"They put on a lovely high tea." As the three headed up the hill to the police station, Toby remarked casually, "So, I understand you didn't take the plunge yet? What's keeping you?"

Griffin stopped in his tracks. "How did you know?"

Toby just looked at him.

"I…er…we were so caught up in the mystery that we…we…"

"Come on in here." He led the way into the building. A big burly cop stood at the counter. "Harry, get me that shotgun, the one we use for aggressive black bears."

Griffin flinched.

When Harry handed Toby the gun, he squinted down the barrel, then pointed it at the ceiling. Without looking at Griffin, he said, "Tell you what—you go find yourselves a preacher. Maybe old Piddlecock is

317

available, since I suspect Reverend Hal is otherwise engaged. Come on back once you're hitched. I'll be here"—he cocked the hammer—"cleaning my gun."

Griffin backed all the way out to the street. Rachel followed him, trying to keep a straight face. When they reached the sidewalk, she cried gaily, "So...do you know where old Piddlecock resides?"

Instead of the glare she expected, he stared over her head, his eyes glazed with tears. She put a tentative hand out. "Griffin? What's the matter?"

For answer, he gently took her elbow and guided her to a bench in front of the Congregational church. When he'd satisfied himself that no one was within earshot, he said, "Before we get married I have to tell you something."

Oh my God. He's already married. No, that can't be it. But it's something to do with a woman. Someone hurt him badly. She longed to take him into her arms and comfort him, but she knew he had to get it off his chest before they could be together.

Griffin put his head in his hands. His voice, muffled by his fingers, cracked. "I was married once before."

Her mind went blank. A grinding sound came from the vicinity of her teeth. The air around her darkened, and she looked up to find the familiar black cloud hovering directly overhead. Beyond it, the sun burned brightly in a soft blue sky. It was as though they'd dropped down a deep well and the rest of the world had immediately forgotten their existence. She was afraid to shout, certain the cry for help would only echo in the emptiness.

"Did you hear me?"

She managed a weak, "Yes." After a minute she whispered, "What happened?"

"She…she died."

"Oh." Rachel felt the heavy shroud on her shoulders lift slightly. "I'm sorry."

"It's not that. She was an awful woman, Rachel. Vindictive. Nasty. Unfaithful. Did I mention mercenary? She went through my professor's salary like sand through a sieve."

"Why didn't you divorce her?"

"I don't believe in divorce. I married Mandy for better or for worse. So I tried to keep it going. I let her take her moods out on me. I let her spend us into bankruptcy. I ignored the parade of men that traipsed through our house. I buried myself in my work."

Rachel kept the thought to herself that he may have carried the anti-divorce thing a little too far. "How long ago was this?"

"Five years."

"And how did it end?"

He stood up and paced before her, his face a mask of pain. "One night she picked up yet another guy— from that biker's bar—you know, by the railroad tracks in Queenstown?"

She nodded.

"Anyway, I came home early from a lecture trip and walked in on them. They were in the kitchen."

Okay.

"The guy had a butcher knife, and he was threatening Mandy."

"Oh, no! Did you call the police?"

"I didn't have time. My cell and briefcase were in the hall. He was attacking her, and she was

319

screaming..." He broke off as though reliving the terrible night. After a minute, he resumed. "I didn't think. I just launched myself at him, tried to knock the knife out of his hands."

Rachel touched the long, white line on the back of his hand. "That's how you got the scar."

"Uh huh. Now, this guy was big, maybe two-fifty, three hundred pounds, six feet tall. He brushed me aside like a mosquito. I must have knocked my head on the counter and blacked out. When I came to, Mandy lay dead on the floor, and the guy was cleaning the knife off. I pretended I was still unconscious, and he finally left."

"Did they catch him?"

"Yes, but first I had to convince the police that he existed. After all, Mandy had only culled him from the pack that night in the bar. No one saw them leave together. They were all set to arrest me, but when I described the murderer, the detective checked the FBI's most wanted list and there he was. Name of Napoleon Hollins." He shook his head. "Christ, what a name to give to a kid. Anyway, he had a rap sheet two miles long with several rapes and at least one attempted murder. Detective Jordan put together a strong case and eventually Hollins confessed."

Rachel swallowed hard. "How long did it take you to...to get over it?"

He gazed at her in sorrow. "I'll never get over the fact that I failed Mandy. I should have been able to save her."

"Sir Walter Raleigh."

"Yes. I tried to be the perfect gentleman. You know, Saint George slaying the dragon. And I bungled it badly. Even Mandy didn't deserve to die."

Anger kindled unexpectedly. "So you decided to stop being a gentleman? To treat women shabbily? How'd that work for you?"

He drew back, eyebrows raised. "Excuse me?"

It was Rachel's turn to pace. "Let me get this straight. Five years ago, you were married to a woman who ran through your money, picked up strange men in bars, and made your life generally a holy hell. No surprise, she gets herself in trouble and you—you try to be a hero, but it turns out you're not Arnold Schwarzenegger. You know what I think? I think you're hanging on to your guilt because you *do* fancy yourself some kind of Galahad instead of just an ordinary man. You didn't divorce her because it would be admitting you weren't up to the challenge, not because of your superior moral stature. You just don't like to fail. It's an ego thing." She stopped, panting.

Griffin gazed at her, his expression wooden. "Are you through?"

"For the nonce."

He stood. "Come on, let's go home."

"But Griffin—"

"I want to finish this at home."

The anger flooded out of her as a petrified voice buzzed in her brain, *Oh my God, he wants to finish this—it's over. What have I done?*

He held her arm tightly as they strode down the street. When they reached his house, he pulled her inside and up the stairs. He set her down on the bed and stood before her, hands on hips. His voice was deadly quiet. "No one has ever, ever, talked to me that way."

Rachel wracked her brains, but all she could come

up with was, "So?"

He crossed his arms. "I'm not sure how I feel about it." She made as if to rise, but he gently pushed her back down. "Give me a minute, will you?"

She settled back, a little surer of her ground now. "Take all the time you need."

He grimaced. "You might want to tone down the *schadenfreude* a bit. The victory dance is quite enough."

The ticking in her chest subsided. "Are you trying to say I'm right?"

He plumped down beside her. "Much as it pains me, yes, I am. I've been living with this for too many years. Since the trial I haven't spoken about it to anyone. I guess I've never been forced to examine my motivation."

She kissed his cheek. "I'm very proud of you. Admitting you're wrong is not your strong suit."

"It's a good thing I have to do it so rarely, then, isn't it?" When she chuckled, he touched her hand lightly. "I sure as hell hope I'm not wrong about us. How would I survive without you?"

Rachel didn't know what to say, but she knew what to do. And she did it.

****

Two days later, Rachel sat on Griffin's deck. As the sun set with great panache over Penobscot Bay, he handed her a cocktail. She sipped it. "So this is married life. I like the quiet."

"Don't get used to it, Annabelle. As soon as George is finished deciphering the mummy's map, we're off to Ethiopia."

"I thought he said he'd found a reference to Chad

in Straniero's diary. Maybe we should go there."

"George can check out Chad if he likes. I want to see Axum and Meroë. It's my turn. Besides, we have to go somewhere for our honeymoon."

"And after that we head for King Solomon's Mines. I get it…And don't call me Annabelle."

"Yes, Annabelle."

A word about the author...

Although she has lived or traveled on every continent except Antarctica and Australia, M. S. Spencer spent the last thirty years mostly in Washington, D.C. as a librarian, Congressional staff assistant, speechwriter, editor, birdwatcher, kayaker, policy wonk, non-profit director, and parent. She has two fabulous grown children, a perfect granddaughter, and currently divides her time between the gulf coast of Florida and a tiny village in Maine.

M. S. Spencer has published ten romantic suspense/mystery novels.

http://msspencertalespinner.blogspot.com
https://www.facebook.com/msspencerromance
www.twitter.com/msspencerauthor

Thank you for purchasing
this publication of The Wild Rose Press, Inc.

If you enjoyed the story, we would appreciate your
letting others know by leaving a review.

For other wonderful stories,
please visit our on-line bookstore at
www.thewildrosepress.com.

For questions or more information
contact us at
info@thewildrosepress.com.

The Wild Rose Press, Inc.
www.thewildrosepress.com

Stay current with The Wild Rose Press, Inc.

Like us on Facebook

https://www.facebook.com/TheWildRosePress

And Follow us on Twitter
https://twitter.com/WildRosePress